WALKING
with HER
DAUGHTER

**Center Point
Large Print**

**This Large Print Book carries the
Seal of Approval of N.A.V.H.**

WALKING
with HER
DAUGHTER

Jessica Barksdale Inclán

Center Point Publishing
Thorndike, Maine

This Center Point Large Print edition
is published in the year 2005 by arrangement with
NAL Accent, an imprint of New American Library, a division of
Penguin Group (USA) Inc.

The text of this Large Print edition is unabridged. In other
aspects, this book may vary from the original edition. Printed in
Thailand. Set in 16-point Times New Roman type.

ISBN 1-58547-608-0

Library of Congress Cataloging-in-Publication Data

Inclán, Jessica Barksdale.
    Walking with her daughter / Jessica Barksdale Inclán.--Center Point large print ed.
    p. cm.
    ISBN 1-58547-608-0 (lib. bdg. : alk. paper)
    1. Women college teachers--Fiction. 2. Middle aged women--Fiction. 3. Children--
Death--Fiction. 4. Loss (Psychology)--Fiction. 5. Divorced women--Fiction. 6. Large
type books. 7. Psychological fiction. lcsh I. Title.

PS3559.N332W35 2005b
813'.6--dc22

2004030666

For Karri Casner

My thanks to the following: my readers, whether they be from library or bookstore.

To my sister, Sarah Barksdale, for medical information; to Tricia Bernius, for Grand Canyon secret details; to Carole Barksdale, for Arizona photos.

To yet again my tribe of readers and fonts of wisdom: Susan Browne, Julie Roemer, Marcia Goodman, Keri DuLaney, Gail Offen-Brown, Joan Kresich, Lisa Wingate. Ye gads, without you all, early doom.

To Ellen Edwards, stalwart editor, and Mel Berger, trusted agent.

To my students, who inspire and challenge in equal measure.

And, of course, to my family, as always.

One

In the first moments of waking, Jenna could feel the soft arms of the mattress around her shoulders, cradling her hips, the fine cotton sheet on her ankles, stomach, cheek. She hung between her dream and the sunrise on the sound of the waves just outside her cabana, the soft touch of the air, the absence of memory.

And she slipped back to her inner eye, floating above the island, seeing the rice terraces of the interior, the mud built up in agricultural temples. Then she moved up and out, past dense foliage, to the tall, drooping green trees she couldn't name, with their large red flowers and long fuzzy stamens, the waving palms, the red canna flowers, the wetness everywhere. Past the Shiva statues and the stone Buddhas, through the warm air, to the white Balinese beaches dotted with yellow and white umbrellas, thin wooden boats floating on calm seas. Away to the horizon, a sunrise flared gold, peach, fanning into blue. Up to the mountains that peaked over the water, green and brilliant against the aqua, and back down to her cabana.

"No," she said, or thought, as the scene began to tear, what had happened a week ago ripping a ragged edge on this peace, this floating, this pure white light. *No,* she thought again, sinking into cotton as if it were a lover. Weren't she and Mark going to come here before, earlier, Jenna walking into the house with brochures, ideas, plans?

"Look," she'd said, pointing to a photo of a cabana nestled in fronds, the aqua sea lapping at its door, palms frozen in perfect sway, people stuck forever in unnatural, happy poses. "There's a glass bottom in the bar. You can watch the fish swim under you. Those manta ray creatures, too."

Her husband, Mark, had adjusted his glasses and nodded. "Someday," he'd said. "Maybe later."

"When, Mark?" she'd asked, leafing through the glossy brochure the woman at the travel agency had given her. "We should make reservations."

"Soon." He waved his hand as if to make her stop talking, and she did, sitting down next to him on the couch as he read another medical article or chart, making notes as he did. "One day."

But one day, someday soon had never come, and then later he'd left her and Sofie for another woman. An older, smarter woman, with whom he would never have children.

Blinking against the filtered morning light, Jenna felt her dash two days ago through the airport to the pay phone, the terrible message she'd left with Mark's service during her one-hour layover in Los Angeles. And then hours and hours of flying, the sky too soft, too smooth, the phone bringing her too soon to the island full of fire.

Turning on her side, pressing her eyes closed, she listened to her skin slip against the linen, the bed made daily by silent workers who were frightened to meet her eye. When would Mark be here? When would he find her? Would he know how to look for her in this place he had never taken her to? Eventually, he would show up, but it might be after it was over, like usual. As he had for Sofie's graduations from eighth grade and high school, for her dance recitals, for her moving-in day at the dorms at Cal. Why didn't he see what Sofie meant to him? Why did he leave them both in the first place since he'd never really left, coming back to her bed after a day trip with Sofie or a back-to-school night or a visit to his sister's house?

So many nights in the past years after tucking in Sofie, he'd knocked on her bedroom door and then come in, sitting on the edge of her bed, slowly moving his hand to her covered shin, knee, thigh.

"Jenna?" he'd whisper, his breath at her neck, his mouth on her cheek, his glasses on the bedside table.

In her laziness, Jenna opened up, pulled him down, let the memory of their marriage take over for a half hour, hour. And then he'd be gone again.

Mark was neither here nor there, but both, like she was now, asleep—her mind filled with the past—and awake, the sun on her arm, the sounds pressing closer, words she could almost hear.

She turned under the sheet, holding her ears. *No. No. Why?* Why all this? What were the reasons? Why did he leave in the first place? Was it space for thought? Peace and quiet? Why did he marry her at all? Why was she here without him? *Oh yes. No. No.* Her body stilled as the daylight through the bamboo shutters shook her, filled her with memory.

"No," she said again, but of course it was too late. She was awake. She was conscious in a world where her daughter no longer existed. Where Sofie was no longer a college girl on a vacation in Bali, having flown here to meet the Australian boyfriend she'd met when he'd come to Cal for a two-week conference on international water rights.

Covering her eyes against the light with both hands, Jenna felt her daughter's absence on her face and chest like death's night dog. Her daughter was dead. She was no longer all the Sofies she'd ever been. No longer a kindergartner with a large orange chrysanthemum pinned behind her ear, insisting that it was beautiful. Sofie was beautiful, even as it began to slide down her hair, which was the same color as the flower.

She was no longer the seventh-grade girl in her baggy jeans and striped T-shirts listening to rap music on her Sony Walkman during dinner. "Why do I have to turn it off?" Sofie had asked. "You're reading a magazine! Just admit you're not paying attention to me, either."

She was no longer a high school girl crashing her car into the trash cans at the bottom of the driveway, laughing so hard that Jenna smiled, laughed, hugged her daughter to her because she was all right. Safe. The only thing damaged was the can pressed up against the retaining wall, spewing forth white Hefty bags and a broken mop handle.

"I'm fine," Sofie said, holding her sides, her pale face

flushed. "I'm going to hecka fail the driving test, though. Unless there's a trash can part. I'll ace that."

And then, finally, there was the last Sofie, the college Sofie, turning away from Jenna and going inside, up the dorm stairs into her new life.

All Jenna's daughters were gone now, all the Sofies Jenna had ever had. Jenna had seen each of them when looking at her daughter, as if Sofie stood in front of a three-way dressing room mirror, each refracting a girl from the year before and before that and even before that. Jenna knew that there would have been more Sofies in the years to come; working Sofie, married Sofie, mother Sofie. Sofie at Christmas and birthdays; Sofie when Jenna was old; Sofie when Jenna wasn't even around anymore, becoming Sofies to other people, her own children and grandchildren. All those Sofies had been murdered, and Jenna knew that again as she lay wide-eyed on her bed in her Bali hotel, remembering why she was here. To find her daughter's body. To take her home.

THEY ALL SAT on a long wooden bench in a long white room facing a long counter. Behind the counter were several people who avoided looking at any of them, these parents and families of the dead bodies packed in ice in the large auditorium, relatives that spilled out on the sidewalk, friends waiting for other bodies, news, information. Anything. Jenna had been here for two days. Each day, she walked by the new bodies that had been dug out of the concrete, steel, and wood. Each day, she examined the jewelry that had been found in the rubble: Bulova watch, dangly silver earring, gold pendant, crystal hair comb, shell barrette, pinky ring, wedding band, nose ring. Jenna had stared at the nose ring, thinking about her students at Contra Loma College in California, so many of them pierced, some of them fiddling with their tongues, eyebrows, that space between lip and chin. What was that called? It had an official title, something Latin sounding. She didn't know or remember, having wondered always, staring at the light shining off the silver or gold studs as her students gave presentations on Raymond Carver or Gail Tsukiyama or Jane Austen.

But as she stared at this nose ring, she wondered how it could now be disengaged from the wearer. Was the bomb powerful enough to separate piercings from the flesh that held them? Where was the nose that wore this? Or the eyebrow? Or belly button? How could the rescuers have found this tiny piece of metal and not the person who picked it out, slipped it in, went dancing, drinking, heard the explosion, felt the whoosh of air and heat, and then died?

Sofie never wanted a piercing, not even when her best friend Rachel begged her to get her nose pierced when she did. The big plan to drive to Telegraph Avenue in Berkeley, get pierced, and then go dancing.

"It's gross," Sofie told Jenna. "What if you get a really bad cold?"

"I suppose you could take out the ring when you were sick," Jenna said, familiar with and almost liking the way a ring looked on a pretty nose. A pretty nose like Sofie's.

"And the rest." Sofie waved her hand just like Mark did. "Places that hurt. Rachel's crazy. And anyway, who's got the time to wait for those things to heal? It takes months."

So there would be no nose ring or nipple stud or eyebrow bar for Jenna to identify, all of that jewelry for the people next to her. Jenna glanced at them, some of whom she'd held against her shirt, some of whom had held her. Their numbers grew and shrank as bodies were found, as new people flew in for remains. But it didn't matter who they were separately. Together, they were the ones who'd lost what was most important. They were the ones—not a political group or social movement or regime—who were attacked. They sat with their bodies touching, hip to hip, not caring about personal space, wanting to be merged together, needing the conduit of grief to run between them. When finally a person behind the desk would look up, lips pressed between teeth, face still, they would all glance up together, waiting.

"There are new victims," the person would say, maybe an Indonesian man or woman, or a British Red Cross supervisor, or an American from the Australian Embassy, flown over to assist. Slowly, they would all stand up, close their eyes, lean against the person next to them. Breathe. Then they would follow the person down the hall to the auditorium, file by the dead. No, no, no. Never Sofie.

At first, Jenna thought that not finding her daughter was a good thing. The fact that she was not one of the terribly burned, almost-melted people meant—what? That she was alive somewhere? That Sofie and her boyfriend, Robert, had left Kuta and taken a side trip to another island, another beach, another country altogether? But as the days passed, no message came from anywhere, no e-mail saying *Hey, Mom! I hope you aren't worried. Robert and I drove to Nusa Dua. They are restricting traffic, so we can't get back to our hotel. But we're fine. I'm sure you are totally freaked out. Mom, I love you. It is* so *totally beautiful here.*

And then all she wanted was to see her daughter's foot under a sheet. A foot would be all right, and she'd recognize it. Sofie's long, slender white toes, the little silver toe ring she wore on her—what did they call it— index toe? Was there such a thing as an index toe? Jenna was an English teacher, so she should have all this body vocabulary. The thing before the chin, the names of toes. Piggies. This little piggy went to market, this little piggy stayed home. The home toe. That was where the ring was. On the home toe.

Jenna would also recognize Sofie's ankles, the pointed tents of bone under thin flesh, the ankles Jenna rubbed after tying tiny shoes. And calves. Calves would be safe. Sofie was slim but strong from running, and Jenna had always appreciated those muscles—that word she knew, *gastrocnemius*. Jenna had carried that term with her since junior year of high school, when Otis Ojakangas taught them the body. Jenna would recognize Sofie's gastrocnemiuses. Gastrocnemi?

But no face. No hands. That would kill Jenna, do her in. They would have to wrap her up like the rest of the bodies and send her home. She didn't need to see her daughter's face to recognize her body.

During her first day of waiting, Jenna stood up each time a worn, tired couple came into the office, thinking that these folks with their creases of sorrow set under dark, bagging eyes had to be Robert's parents. Jenna knew very little about Robert except that he was six-two and blond, loved the natural world just like Sofie, and had hands the size of giant starfish.

"You should see them, Mom," Sofie had said, after he'd already flown back to Sydney. "He can almost pick me up with just one."

"Honey, why didn't you bring him home?"

There was a silence, and Jenna could hear the other story in Sofie's breathing, the one about days and nights in bed, the sad countdown until the plane took him back to Sydney. The promises Sofie and Robert made to each other: "It won't be long. Only a couple of months. Then we'll be together again," and "I'll never meet anyone like you again."

That promise, they'd kept.

But none of the couples turned out to be Robert's parents. Jenna listened as each couple whispered and then cried to the stoic people behind the long desk and never heard them say "Robert, Bobby, Bob Burke." And when Jenna walked the long death walk the first time, past all the bodies in their white-sheet shrouds, there were too many blond beautiful boys, too many name tags that read everything but Robert, Bobby, Bob.

"Ma'am," the person said sharply from behind the counter, and then swallowed down his irritation, as if remembering again that all the people before him were waiting for death news. Jenna looked up, realizing she must have missed his first call.

"Yes?" She stood, the group sliding together to close the void left by her body, all of their eyes to the floor, not wanting to see anything until they had to.

"A girl was brought in matching the description you gave us." He blinked, a vein pulsing under his jaw. He was the age of some of her students at Contra Loma College, so many of them from Indonesia, a couple from Bali. Most were Chinese Indonesian, often schooled in Singapore before they came to the United States. Many had last names that were poems in themselves—Tanuwidjaja, Wirawan, Tandra, Suliawan, Wijaya, Trairatana, Pranajaya, Widjaja—names that made Jenna pause, holding her breath before releasing them off the roll sheet, often incorrectly, into the air. And then, even though she could barely pronounce their names, she would expect perfect English, correct articles before nouns, past perfect, simple past, future verb tenses exactly where they should be in each and every sentence. Where did he learn his English? she wanted to ask. In her class? Yes! This man could have been in one of her classes, and then come home to find himself behind this desk, waiting for a middle-aged woman to follow him to the body of her dead child.

18

"Ma'am?" His lips were pulling down at the corners, his eyes wet.

"Yes. Of course." Jenna tucked her purse under her arm and waited for him to come around the counter before following him, his thin legs in white pants, the *whoosh, whoosh* of fabric, the *tap, tap* of shoe.

Jenna wanted to hollow herself out each time she stepped into the auditorium or onto the sidewalk, not wanting to feel her heart, stomach, throat. She didn't need any organ or body part at all, nothing except her eyes. She needed to see her daughter; and, of course, she needed her hands to fill out the papers that would allow her to take Sofie home. There were her feet. Jenna needed them to walk in and then walk out. But all the other flesh was annoying, like now, as her heart beat into her ears, her throat closed down on the sobs that hung in her chest like a storm. Her stomach churned and roiled, and she wouldn't remember where the bathroom was. She needed to use it now. She had to stop the man in front of her, tell him that it had to wait. "I have to go," she'd say in clear English. He'd understand, see how she was doubled over. That move would translate in any language.

"Here," he said. Jenna saw he was putting on white latex gloves, the kind doctors and garbage collectors use.

"What?"

"This is the new body—this is the one who matches your daughter's description." The man flipped through papers on his clipboard. "Yes, everything matches."

"The toe ring? On her home toe?" Jenna asked.

The man stared at her. "Maybe we should just look," he said, gentle now, his irritation gone, as if he'd finally recognized Jenna as his long-lost teacher, the one who had given him an A even when he deserved a B. She'd given him the grade not because he was a good writer but because he was a good student, turning in all his homework, coming to every class, even the ones that promised to be dull, hours of lecture instead of a movie or group work. He should be nice to her now, take her out of this room, change his mind about this terrible body under the sheet.

"Ma'am?"

Jenna wondered what his grades had been like. She could ask. She could call him by his name, which was Wayan or Made or Nyoman or Ketut, the four primary Balinese names. She could tell him about her classes. Maybe mythology. He'd like that, living on this island, where spirits lurked everywhere, hiding in the dark green bushes, the overhanging palm fronds, the rocks next to the blue water. If he were of Chinese descent, she could tell him the story of Panku and the egg he cracked open to create the world, people made up of the lice on his body. And then Qu'an Yin and her serpent's tail.

He stared at her, and then lifted the sheet. Jenna felt her eyes betray her, moving away from the man's face to the body, starting with the hair, burned and singed to the scalp, but still red, Sofie like a sunrise every day, Scottish to the core despite Mark's Jewish darkness.

Jenna felt the rest of her body betray her—her stomach dropping into her bowels, her intestines on fire—so she closed her eyes, found a bit of air under the storm of tears. It was Sofie. She didn't need to see more. The freckles like constellations on her forehead were enough. "Orion," Jenna used to tease her daughter. "Or maybe we should make up another name. Sofie's Famous Freckle Helix. There's a story there. That's what all the old cultures did to explain the stars."

"Oh, Mom," Sofie would tease. "When I'm old enough, I'm getting them all lasered off. I want to be as white as the driven snow."

"Sweetie!" Jenna would say, knowing the joke. "Do you know how much that hurts?"

Sofie had thrown her arms out to her sides, laughing. "Nothing is too painful for beauty."

Sofie would never have to worry about changing. She'd never be old enough, and she'd died with her constellation still hanging above her eyes.

"Is this your daughter, ma'am? If so, I need you to make a positive identification."

Jenna opened her eyes, forcing herself to look down, but then her knees buckled and she fell next to Sofie, her hand gripping Sofie's arm, cold and hard. Surprised, Jenna breathed in, and there in front of her, burned and hurt, was Sofie. *Oh, Sofie. Oh, my girl,* she thought, remembering the first time Jenna saw her daughter in a sheet, in the delivery room as the midwife wiped off the blood and vernix, Sofie dark headed with fetal hair. But her eyes. Wide-open blue, looking right up at Jenna, Mark's arms around them both.

Sofie's eyes were closed now, but here she was, her clothes taken off or blown off by the blast. All of her was in front of Jenna, her nose and throat and her breasts that bloomed when she was twelve, her nipples reddish, like her hair. The tent of ankle, the long home toe with its tiny silver band.

The man knelt down and reached out to Jenna's shoulder, his eyes searching her, just like they might have in the classroom, waiting for the right answer.

"Yes," she said, breathing in between the stabbing pain under her heart, her ribs squeezing around the organs she didn't need anymore. "You were right. This is my daughter."

BACK AT THE hotel, Jenna sat at a table in the bar, looking out over the water that was the exact cerulean of Sofie's eyes. Should Jenna have opened her daughter's eyes? But before she could think to reach over and touch Sofie's cold face, the man had called his colleagues on a walkie-talkie and people had streamed in, carrying a body bag and papers for Jenna. They led her out into another room, away from the expectant parents and family, where Jenna answered questions and signed forms, some stamped with the United States insignia, something about flying the body home on a government plane.

She hadn't said good-bye to her daughter, and Sofie was probably already gone, her body in a bag, in a coffin, in the cargo hold of a plane, arriving home even

22

before Jenna could, her plane not leaving until tomorrow afternoon. Would it be too late then to hold her daughter's head, lift the lids, look into the eyes Jenna loved best? Or did the body begin to deteriorate, eyes sinking back into nothingness? Only Otis Ojakangas would know the answer to that, and where was her former teacher now? On a beach in Florida? In a retirement community, where he sat on a rocker and waited for death, for what Sofie had already blown into?

"Ma'am?" a young girl asked, holding a drink tray tightly, a gold name tag on her native garb spelling out her name, NYOMAN. "There is someone who wants to talk with you."

Jenna didn't look up but shook her head. "I'm not talking to reporters."

"This man is not a reporter. A friend. He says he is friend to your daughter."

Jenna looked up at the girl's honest face and then past her, toward the bar, where a tall blond man leaned against the smooth wood, blinking. Robert. The tall blond man she had looked for each day on the auditorium floor.

Not a scratch on him.

Jenna wanted to stand up, rush to Robert, push him down, hold his shoulders in her palms and cry out, "Why did you leave her? Why did you drag her here? Why aren't you dead, too?" Her heart beat against the pain in her ribs. Tears she'd held in all day began to pour from her eyes without even a muscle moving them

23

downward, as if she was made only of water, as if that was all that was left.

"I can tell him no. He will go away. I will make him go away." Nyoman pressed the tray closer to her flesh and moved toward Jenna. "I tell him this is not a good time. All right, ma'am? I am so sorry for disturbing you."

Jenna closed her eyes and reached out for the girl. Her arm was warm and soft. Alive. "No. No. Tell him to come over. Please."

The girl hung in indecision. All the Indonesian people Jenna had met this week were so kind, so thoughtful, so ashamed of the violence, of the bad care they'd provided to the island and the people on it. They all knew that this current batch of tourists staying for free at the hotel was grieving, not looking for warm blue water or big, bright fish. Jenna wanted to pat Nyoman on the shoulder, like she patted her students sometimes when they failed essays or midterms, telling them, "It's just a grade. It's not who you are."

But that wasn't true. Who they were *was* what they did. Jenna was what she did, she was Sofie, her reward, her daughter, and that part of her was dead, so she had failed, like they had.

"Okay. I will tell him." Nyoman swallowed and turned away, looking back once, and then talking quickly to Robert. He looked up at Jenna, adjusting the duffel bag on his shoulder. *Why is he carrying a duffel bag?* Jenna wondered, and then she knew, her head tilting back as if it weighed a thousand pounds. The duffel bag, the fluorescent pink tag, the name and address in black Sharpie pen.. SOFIE THOMAS in firm, solid caps. Her Monte Veda address, not her college one. Inside were the bras, underwear, shorts, and swimsuits she'd bought at Nordstrom before the trip, coming to Jenna's office at the college to get the credit card.

"I can't just, like, wear my Speedo, Mom," Sofie had said, putting the card in her wallet. "And you know it's the trip I've always dreamed of. Come with me. Help me choose. Help me pick."

Jenna had lifted up a stack of essays. "I'm too busy, sweetie. I need to read all of these."

Sofie had shrugged, leaned down, and kissed her on the temple. Then she was gone.

Jenna shook away the memory and concentrated. What else was in the bag? Perhaps postcards she'd bought at the airport. A string of shells she'd purchased on the beach from a vendor. A visor. Bottles of sunscreen, 45—no 50. Cover-ups. A pareo. Probably something lacy. A camisole from Victoria's Secret.

Robert was bringing back what remained.

Jenna couldn't move her head, couldn't find her breath, her eyes feeling swollen, something ringing in her ears, a buzz, an echo, like the sound of an explosion five thousand miles away.

"Mrs. Thomas?" He was almost whimpering, a small animal sound caught inside his body.

Jenna motioned to the chair opposite her, her face red from lack of air. He dropped the bag, the chair creaking under him. She was going to faint; she knew it, even though she had never fainted before. Not once. But the world was spinning in gray and white flecks, so she tried breathing through her nose, one long inhale, another, another, breathing as she had when she was in labor with Sofie. "That's it. A deep, cleansing breath," Mark had said, holding one leg as a nurse held the other, both helping her push. "Another. Oh, Jenna. I can see the baby's head."

"I can't do it!" Jenna had screamed. "Just get it out."

"You can do it. Of course you can," Mark said. "One more breath. Then push. But first, one more breath."

One more breath, Jenna thought now, *and I can look up into the live eyes of Sofie's lover.*

"I've been trying to find you," he began, all the words coming out at once. "I called your house in the States. And then I tried Sofie's father, you know? His wife said he's on his way. He got your message. Should be here now, I think." Robert paused, Jenna hearing his breathing, too quick, almost panting. "I brought her things."

"I found *her,*" Jenna said. "I found her body today."

Robert leaned back in his chair. Jenna looked up, pushing air from her lungs. Pain crackled across his face, and then he hunched forward and leaned over the table, pressing himself down, his hands on his neck, his elbows triangled out like wings. Jenna felt his sobs through the wood, but she didn't comfort him. He left her daughter in a bar, her body melting, her hair on fire. Jenna had seen her daughter's blackened hands, the red, raw skin of her forearms, shoulders, neck. Robert should have protected her, should have been a better man.

"I said, 'Run,'" Robert sobbed.

"What?" A wave pushed against the underside of the bar, a dozen twirling fish spinning under the glass bottom to her right.

"I told her," he said, his voice muffled. "I said, 'Run.' I smelled it first, and I knew. But then it was bright and hot, and people were on fire. Their hair!"

Stop, she thought. She wanted to say, "Please leave me alone." Jenna wished she had a newspaper or a bad novel to open, erasing the image of the explosion entirely. But the scene flickered like an old movie at the edges of her imagination: Sofie, the smell of an inciting agent, some kind of acrid chemical, smoke, flame, heat, burning. Jenna's breath was in her head, her lungs empty.

"Please," she whispered, but Robert didn't hear her or he didn't care, needing to tell this final story.

"I grabbed her hand, and she was on fire."

Jenna lifted her hand, still whole, palm flat toward him, and then noticed for the first time that Robert had bandages on both his arms, white gauze on his palms, his fingers wrapped in some kind of netting.

"How did you get out, then?" Jenna felt anchors on her lips, barely able to say the words.

Robert sat up and wiped his eyes, tears on the gauze, his nose running. "There was another explosion, and then she was under some metal. I couldn't see her. I couldn't find her, and everyone was burning."

Jenna looked for Nyoman. It was time for Robert to leave. He needed to be escorted out of the building. What was he trying to tell her? These stories were like the melodrama her students wrote when the prompt was "Write about your most vivid experience." Everything they turned in was full of exaggeration. Surely Robert couldn't expect her to believe he couldn't just grab Sofie and push out of the building together? Where was the proof? The specific examples? Where was the quotation from the texts to back him up? Words like *metal* and *tried* weren't enough. She wanted verbs like *lifted* and *pushed* and *screamed* and *thrust*. Jenna wanted words like *saved* and *survived*. The story should have ended happily. It must have ended happily. It had to have.

Jenna breathed out into the second where the possible new ending hung in the air, Sofie grabbing Robert's hand, slipping from between the metal sheets. Hurt a little. Maybe a smidge burned. But alive, held in Robert's long, strong arms, whisked out of the burning building and put in the arms of a paramedic. There would have been a different phone call, one Jenna would have taken as she sank into the living room couch, asking her daughter, "Are you sure you're all right? What about Robert?"

"It's really sad. All those people killed," the alive Sofie would say. "But we're fine. We weren't even close to the explosion."

The happy, relieved Jenna would ask, "Should I come? Do you need me?"

"Don't worry, Mom," the in-love Sofie would say, wanting more time alone with Robert. "We'll fly out when we can get on a plane."

"Okay, sweetie, call me when you know your flight times. I love you. I am so thankful."

Jenna's lungs were emptied from this fantasy she'd invented on the flight to Bali and had replayed over and over as she'd sat with the people on the bench. Now she had to inhale deeply, bright spots flickering in the corners of her eyes. She rubbed her forehead and looked up, seeing that Robert was doubled over again. Couples near her left their tables. The bar staff lined up, watching them. Nyoman was crying. The bartender was preparing strong drinks, motioning toward Jenna and Robert. Next to their table, two smiling ceramic dragons glittered in the sunlight.

"I've been looking. I stayed on the street all night, the next day. I searched for her."

She wanted to reach out for him, pat him still and silent, and she also wanted to ask him "Why weren't you at the morgue? Why weren't you there, waiting, watching, sitting on the bench with all the other families? With me? Why did you hide in the open air, digging for people that weren't her?" But she didn't. She began to see. He was a boy, outside, pushing past melted steel and burning wood, a mask over his mouth, his face and body streaked with dust and soot, his eyes watering and red. He was working with people who didn't speak his language, but that didn't matter, not when they were searching for bodies, the outcome clear to everyone.

"I shouldn't have seen that. I shouldn't have seen that," he moaned, leaning back, his eyes closed again. "No one should ever have to see that."

And finally Jenna knew this was real. This was the story.

ROBERT HAD TAKEN a cab back to his hotel. His father was there, waiting for him, having allowed his son to come to Jenna by himself, to say what was his alone to tell. And maybe this parent had let Robert come because he was scared to remember the time between the news of the bomb making the airwaves and the moment when the phone rang, Robert's voice in his ear. Alive. All he wanted was to take his child in his arms and fly him home. Damaged, but alive.

Jenna knew she would never see Robert again, only pictures of him when she went back to the Cal dorm to clean out Sofie's things. There would be pictures and letters, words Sofie would never have shown Jenna. She'd said, "Oh, he is such a cutie. He sounds like Heath Ledger. You know, that guy in the Mel Gibson movie?" Sofie began buying stuffed kangaroos whenever she saw them. Wallabies, koala bears. She talked about how eucalyptus trees came from Australia, why they were terrible for the Berkeley hills but wonderful where they originated. Home to animals. Native animals. The last time Jenna had visited her at her dorm, Sofie had hung up a map of the world from the perspective of people living in the Southern Hemisphere.

Every continent was upside down, Australia at the top.

"The other way is so Northern Hemisphere–centric," she'd said. "It's like, that's the only part of the world."

Jenna wished it was the only part of the world. Then there would be no Bali. No explosion. There would be a Sofie.

After Robert left, Jenna had gone back to her room, and now she sat still in a chair on her private patio, the water in the small pool flat and slightly green. Behind the trees, the sea was a constant crashing whirl, a water bird cawing and flickering white against the reddening sky.

She kept blinking, trying to see what was in front of her, but she couldn't focus, the world full of gauze, the kind on Robert's arms and fingers. When her eyes were closed, all she saw was white, the white of the sheet on Sofie. Either way, open or closed, there was nothing in front of her, not the sky, not the sea, and she reached for the drink Nyoman had brought to the room.

"Here, ma'am. This is from us. Call me if you need something," she had said before leaving the room. "Anything."

Jenna sipped whatever liquid it was, bourbon, whiskey, something local. She closed her eyes. Everything behind her lids was white.

"JENNA!"

She turned, looking toward where the door was, something beating against the wood.

"Jenna!"

Where were her legs? She breathed in, pushed up, found a foot, knee, thigh, moved them, walked, the air thick like cotton, white all around her, the thrum of alcohol in her blood. She hadn't eaten in days.

"Jenna!"

Her hand on the doorknob, she turned it, feeling her skin, whole skin, whole white skin, pulling the door open. She wanted to get in her own way, let the door knock her down, hit her hard. She wanted to pass out from pain, another kind of pain. She wanted to throw down the dark glass, pick up a jagged, broken fragment, and rip into the soft flesh of her wrist. She wanted to jump on the glass-bottomed floor panel until it cracked and sent her into the salty ocean, bloody cuts on her feet, legs, waist. She wanted to bleed into the water until a shark came and bit and bit and bit her until . . . until she could see Sofie again.

Mark pushed into the room, his hair a mass of wild curls, his eyes red. He grabbed her, as if he'd never left her alone with a child, forgetting them both for weeks at a time. He took her in his arms and squeezed and cried, his body shaking.

"Why?" he mumbled, running his hands on her back as if looking for an opening, the place where Jenna had concealed the answer he needed.

"Mark."

"Why?" His voice sounded like a foot yanked out of a bog, deep, wet, full of regret. "How could this happen? What happened?"

What happened? What happened was that Mark left

because neither he nor Jenna could figure out how to live together with their daughter. That terrible decision all those years ago had led to this moment. Jenna knew that. Cause and effect. If she and Mark had had a proper divorce, not needing each other's flesh even though it was wrong, Sofie would have—would have what? Found a man who wasn't Robert? Not needed a man like Robert? Gone to another university, one farther from home?

She opened her mouth to say this, but Mark interrupted her.

"Why did this happen to our girl?" he asked.

"Because," she began again, and then stopped, her answer full of blame and anger and guilt and fear, all the truths of Sofie's life, of her and Mark's life together. This was their ancient conversation, the *why*s and the *because*s and the *it's all your fault*s. And none of it mattered now. Not anymore.

Pressing her mouth against his shoulder, she looked out into the room and began to see everything, the silver wiry twists in his hair, the dark, shiny wood of the cabana, the amber fluid in her glass, the aqua water fading to white at the beach. The red, red skin on Sofie's stomach, the purple bruise that had bloomed across half her face. Her hair. Her wonderful sunrise hair.

THEY WERE ON the wooden platform bed, holding each other, her head exactly where it had always rested when they slept together, nestled between arm, armpit, and ribs. Mark smelled the same, tangy, remnants of Old Spice deodorant and salt. His stubble scratched the top of her head, and she felt her hair stick between his whiskers. It pulled when he shifted, loosened when he hugged her tight. She let her hand move up and down his chest, almost forgetting about Renata, his wife, the smarter one, the one with a Ph.D. in English instead of the M.A. Jenna had. A smart, tiny woman who moved easily into rooms of doctors and their perky wives, asked the women proper questions, not the ones Jenna had asked, not, "Don't you want something for *you?* A life? Why should your husband have all the perks?"

But Renata was far away, and she hadn't lost a daughter. Oh. Oh. Jenna closed her eyes.

"Tell me the story."

Jenna pushed away and lay on her back, staring into the creamy swirl of the gauzy canopy. "The bomb. The explosion. The fire."

Mark didn't say anything, didn't sigh, exasperated with the way she couldn't jump ahead, needing to cover everything a step at a time. Back when they were married, he would have put a hand to his forehead, muttered, "I already know *that,* Jenna."

The wind blew the fabric back and forth, fabric so free, so light, so white. Like a sheet in the wind. Like a sheet on a body.

"Robert and she were in the bar. The bomb went off, and she caught on fire. Then there was another explosion, and she was trapped. Robert couldn't get her out."

At first she thought someone was knocking on the

door, but it was the sound of Mark's weeping caught in his throat like a stone he was trying to cough out. Jenna moved to him, wishing he had stopped her from summing up how their daughter died. How their daughter died? God, why had she done that! She told her students that summary was the ugly twin sister to imagery. Images would have worked, the bang of metal, the panic in the heat, smoke pouring everywhere, would have been softer than the facts of the failed escape.

But even as she comforted Mark, whooshing, "Shh, shh," between her lips, even as she stroked his arms and chest, she knew he should cry. She quieted and let him weep against her skin. No matter their old story of *who did what to whom,* Sofie was his daughter. Had been his daughter.

"My girl," he said, his voice muffled by her shoulder.

"Our girl." She pressed him against her shoulder. *Your girl. Our girl. My girl.*

And then Jenna cried, for their daughter, for their marriage, for the fact that his body and breath and smells still felt right to her. She hadn't changed a bit since Mark had left her and Sofie, not until someone blew up part of an island and their daughter and made them come here together.

NYOMAN BROUGHT TWO dinners, crisp fish nestled in rice and sautéed greens, and now Jenna and Mark sat on the patio, the food untouched. Mark sat with a glass of the local Bintang beer on his knee, his fingers tight around it. Jenna's head pounded from the drink she'd had before, so she sipped 7-Up.

"You take care," Nyoman had said as she placed the plates carefully on the outdoor table. "I go home now. I think of you always."

The horizon glimmered in a thin white streak, the sea and sky folding down upon each other, the early light of stars and moon reflecting on the dusky water. It hurt to look out with eyes that would see what Sofie wouldn't, so Jenna stared at her hand, noticed the slight brown spots, the beginning bulge of veins, the scars from ancient activity—the time she tried to fix Mark's and her Volkswagen's carburetor, ripping off flesh instead of bolts. Lately, at night before bed, Jenna rubbed lotion onto the tops of her hands, lotion that promised to restore in eight days what time had done in forty-five years. Nothing had changed, of course, and her hands were beginning to look like her mother's, save for the arthritic joints. In time, that would happen, too, her bones curving into one another, crone joints and limbs replacing her own.

"What are we going to do?" Mark took a sip of his beer.

"Huh?" Jenna looked up, almost dizzy. "I don't know."

He shook his head and then sighed, leaning back against the chair.

She looked at the foot of the bed, Sofie's duffel bag slumped on the floor like a shrunken Labrador. What was in it? A young man had carried it from the bar for her, and she stared at the white athletic company logo on the side. Was there a clue? Something Sofie had left for her? A message? A note that would change how Jenna felt about Sofie's death or life?

Jenna wanted to ask Mark to unzip it and carefully place every item on the bed so Jenna could see, each article of clothing lined up. . . . Like the dead bodies in the auditorium. She put down her glass and leaned her elbows onto her knees, liking the sharp point of bone on each kneecap. "Do about what? The funeral?"

Mark nodded, his eyes closed. "Yes."

"We never talked about that," Jenna said, though she was lying. Once, while on a whale-watching boat near the Farallon Islands, Sofie had tugged on her sleeve and said, "I want this! Just like this. Tossed out to sea. Sprinkled like fish food."

"You know how people are turned into little bits, don't you?"

Sofie rolled her eyes. "Duh! Fire, Mom. Really hot. Cremation."

"So you want your children to scatter you out here in the ocean?"

Holding the rail of the boat, Sofie looked out to the horizon. "Right here in the bay. I don't want to be too far from home."

Jenna had laughed, but later in the *San Francisco Chronicle*, she'd read an ad by the Neptune Society, a service that facilitated just that, a scattering over the waves.

Would Sofie really like that? She'd only been twelve at the time, and she'd never brought it up again. So why had she told Jenna that? Had she known? Had some voice said, "Make arrangements now. You have eight years left." Is that why Sofie had always wanted everything—backpacking trips to Alaska, summer classes at Cal when she was still in high school, every book on Emily Dickinson she could find, foreign movies that played only once a week at the Roxie, a special Portuguese cheese she read about in the *San Francisco Focus*? Maybe Jenna had always known because she gave Sofie everything, and then didn't say a word when Sofie began to get what she wanted for herself. Robert. A trip to Bali.

"Have you talked to your mother?" Mark asked.

"Yes," Jenna said, lying again. She'd called Stan, her mother's husband, because she knew that her mother's voice would hurt her, awaken the little girl under Jenna's skin that still needed to be held and comforted. Not now. She didn't have time for that now. She had to get home. She had to make it home, where it was safe and quiet and the only people she'd have to talk to were her best friend Dee and her students.

"Oh, Jenna, what now?"

"I want you to unpack her duffel bag."

He sucked on his bottom lip and then sighed. "What's inside?"

"Clothes. Plane tickets. Souvenirs. Her things. She touched them."

"I don't want to do it. I can't do it."

"That's what you've always said," Jenna said, standing up. "You've always done what you've wanted

38

to do. You will keep doing that."

"That's not fair," he said. "You can't say that."

"Why not? It's true, isn't it? You're the one who left. It wasn't my decision."

Robert rubbed his eyes and breathed in. "It may as well have been."

"Oh, forget it. I'm sick of it all. Can't you just unpack the damn bag? Why do I have to do everything? Why do I have to be the one to look? It's your turn. It's your turn to see."

"I've been looking. You just didn't notice." He took a huge swallow of his beer, his Adam's apple bobbing as he swallowed.

"How could I notice when you haven't even been there?"

Setting the drink down, he rubbed his eyes and then bent over, his arms folded against his chest. "I've been there. You just never paid attention. You don't know anything about the relationship I had with Sofie. You were too busy pretending to be her only parent."

Words pounded against her teeth and lips but Jenna sucked them down, swallowing before she spoke again. "Of course I know you had a relationship with Sofie. But really, what difference will this make to your day-to-day, Mark?" Jenna said, keeping her back to him, her voice filled with air and sudden power. "Where have you been for the day-to-day for years? You've gone actual weeks without talking to her. All you have to do is go home and pretend that this didn't happen, and your days will be like normal. But not for me. She was

39

everywhere. In everything. All over the house and in every part of my life."

"You're wrong, Jenna! And don't lay all of this on me because you've never had a life. You never gave yourself a chance to have one. You never wanted anything but her. You expected me to be like you. Just a parent. Not a husband—not a husband to anyone. Just a dad. And I was a dad. She and I had our separate life away from you."

She blinked, seeing nothing, her heart a cave in her chest. Of course, Mark was right. Sofie had been Jenna's best-loved, her sweetheart, her love, her *consintida,* the Spanish word for "special favorite" her students had taught her. Nothing, no one, had ever matched the rush of hot, red feeling that swept out of her womb and into her heart when she held Sofie for the first time. No one had ever come close.

"You're right. And that's why you left me. You wanted what I gave her."

She turned to Mark, and he stared at her, silent. Even through his grief and despite all the years, she could still see the premed student he'd been, skinny and pale in the night, his eyes almost blind without his glasses, his lips on her cheeks, throat, body. "I've always wanted this," he'd said, touching her all night. "You are so warm."

Then there'd been the wedding downtown at the courthouse and the series of small apartments, each growing slightly bigger—oh, my God, a closet! A dining room! A gas stove!—through his residencies, her first job at Chabot College teaching ESL students pro-nunciation at night. During the day, she read novels and filled out applications for full-time jobs. She baked. She painted. She wrote terrible poems. She waited for Mark to open the front door and drop his coat and backpack on the floor.

And then Sofie was born.

Mark sighed, his face wet again. "You loved her so—too much."

"She was the only thing I ever wrote," Jenna said, hearing the verb slip out before noticing it was wrong.

"Wrote?"

"I—I mean did. Only thing I ever did."

"No," Mark said, leaning back in his chair, the wicker creaking under his weight. "You *did* me. You *had* me, Jenna. All of me. And you let me go. Like erasing a page. You unwrote everything."

"How can you blame me?" She walked closer to him, looking over him, seeing the tiny bald circle on the top of his head. "You're the one who left. You're the one who came home saying 'There's someone else.' I didn't unwrite anything."

"Jenna, let's stop this. We've done this before. We've done it over and over again. We've memorized this script. And now it doesn't matter. Nothing matters. It's all over. I'm sick of it. I'm not going to look in her bag. I'm going to put it on the plane and wait to unpack when I think I can cope. You don't have to do anything with it."

Jenna turned back to the night, wishing she could slip

41

into the dark sky. She wanted to disappear entirely. Her heart hurt, her lungs ached. And Mark was right. Nothing mattered. All their history together was unimportant because the only thing they'd ever made together was gone, wiped out by their bad marriage. Sofie would never have come to Bali if Mark had stayed. Mark would never have left if Jenna could have loved Sofie less. Right now, Mark would be at Alta Bates Hospital with a patient, Jenna in her office reading essays, and Sofie walking under Sather Gate, headed for Peet's and a double decaf latte.

Laughter hurtled over the flat pools and cool tile paths from the bar. Jenna could hear the *crack crack shake* of ice for a martini echoing toward the cabanas. In a few weeks, maybe months, people would forget the explosion, the bodies, the blood, the grief. This place would bloom back into the tourist island it wanted to be, unwriting its own terrorist history as fast as possible, needing the foreign dollars. Maybe somewhere else, politicians would use it as an excuse to bomb someplace else, but no one would invoke Sofie. No one would say "Her daughter had sunrise hair." No one would plant a sign by the destroyed bar, memorializing those who died while trying to have fun. Robert would go home, return to school, and in a short time, find another woman to love. She and Mark would grow old and die, and any idea of Sofie would fade and float away.

You could unwrite anything you wanted to.

MARK DIDN'T GO back to his hotel. After picking at his

42

cold dinner, he stood up and went into the bathroom, showered, and then climbed into Jenna's bed. After listening for a while longer to the noises echoing from the bar, Jenna did the same, and now she was pressed up against his back, listening to his body, his heart, his blood under her hands, his breath deeper than it used to be, more nasal. An older man's breath. He had white hair on his thinner chest. An older man's body.

He turned and lay on his back. Jenna left her hand on his ribs. "I can't stop seeing it over and over," he said softly. "I want to go in and save her. When I imagine it, I can save her. I can go in and pull her out."

"Robert couldn't save her, Mark. He tried. Robert's a big man. It was too late."

Mark wiped his eyes. "I'm a doctor. If I had been here, it could have been different. I could have saved Sofie."

"Maybe we should have saved each other first."

A breeze blew the gauzy curtain around the bed, and Jenna felt as if they were being lifted off the floor and carried away. But to where? Was there a place where she wouldn't feel Sofie's absence? Where could they go? Maybe this, the desperate need to forget everything, was why people took heroin. Mark was a doctor. He could prescribe something. Valium. Demerol, maybe. She'd had a shot of that when she was in the worst of labor with Sofie. Morphine. What about that pain pill all the movie stars were addicted to? The one that actress took as she shoplifted from Saks? Jenna could get enough to last a year, the time that grief was the worst. That's what she'd read, at least, articles saying that after a death, you shouldn't make any important decisions for a full year. But without Sofie around, what decisions did she have to make?

"Are you seeing anyone?" he asked, turning to her, his hand on her waist. Her thicker waist. An older woman's waist.

"No," she lied, rubbing her face and inching away from him.

"Jenna."

She breathed out. What did it matter if she was almost lying? She wouldn't want to think about Tim Passanante when she returned home. She wouldn't think about his advances, questions, dark brown eyes. His big front teeth, long lean chest, his laugh. He always laughed. She wouldn't consider that he was eleven years younger. And really, since Mark, there had been very few dates, a couple of short-term boyfriends, a few weekends of slightly sad sex, but no one or nothing of importance.

"Really. No one."

"I'll worry about you now."

"And you didn't before? You didn't worry about me when you left?"

"Did I need to?" He pulled her back to him. "You and Sofie were complete."

Should he have worried? Should he have worried when she loved having the king-sized bed to herself, the days when she and Sofie didn't have a real dinner, eating salad and cooked green beans with olive oil, and brownies for dessert? When she didn't put on makeup unless she was going to work? When Sofie and she wore "fancy" dresses (things Jenna would buy at Remy's consignment store—bridesmaids' dresses, old tea gowns) around the house on Saturday afternoons? Were those things to worry about?

Maybe they were. Maybe Mark should have worried about Jenna and her too-focused life. Maybe he should have worried when Sofie grew up and stayed out all night with girlfriends, Jenna falling asleep on the living room couch, not waking until Sofie slipped in at six in the morning. The fights would have worried him. And then the way Sofie began to leave even before college, kissing Jenna on the cheek, saying, "Rachel and I are going to Tahoe for the weekend. Back on Sunday night, okay?"

But no amount of worry would have changed that life, and nothing could change the one that was to come. Not Mark's well-intentioned phone calls, the ones that would be frequent and then fewer and then not at all. Not Tim. Not even Demerol or heroin or morphine.

"No." Jenna moved her hand, pushing her word away, and turned toward the open window, the moon a stripe of white on the flat sea.

FINALLY, THEY SLEPT, and then, like before, like always, even when they both knew they shouldn't, he was inside her, his hips fitting between her thighs exactly, his breath against her neck, the same rough love sounds in her ear, the ones he'd always made. She wasn't surprised, really, Mark having turned to her in the past after he drove Sofie home, staying for a glass of wine, leaning in, touching her shoulder, pushing her hair away from her face. Up in her bedroom, their bedroom, she let him back into her life the way she could, infrequently and with no commitment or promise, only moments of pleasure.

And as in those few times, Jenna was as she had been before Sofie, before she was worried that their noises would wake her, before she was too tired to even bring her hand up and touch his face.

She had no sense of pleasure—no tingling, no burning, no heartbeat, beat, beating—but simply the dense feeling of her body, her insides filling with the blood she'd felt drained of for days. There was her arm, pulling him close, feeling his neck against her chin. How had they made Sofie all those years ago in the king-sized bed they'd bought with Jenna's first teaching paycheck? Had Jenna pushed her fingers through his hair like this? Had he kissed her the same way as now? Slow, then harder, his tongue tasting of alcohol and sadness? Did her legs move in the same way, fanning out beneath him, letting him in, pulling him in, and then forming a triangle over him and pressing him tight?

Holding him deep inside her, she tried to take back what she had lost, imagining the path that Sofie had sailed before conception, sperm shooting through his body and into her egg, the empty ritual Mark and Jenna could still enact with their older bodies. She felt him slide in and out of her, and she held his back, shoulders, neck, and let them both move and pulse in the gauzy breeze of the bedroom, let herself forget that anything else had ever happened but this flesh.

AFTER DROPPING JENNA off at the airport, Mark was going to the U.S. consulate for final information.

"What else do you need to know?" she asked as she packed her bag. "What else matters?"

"I want to know who is responsible for this—this tragedy. I want to know what they're doing about it." Mark put on his glasses and picked up her bag and Sofie's.

"They're still looking for bodies, Mark. What can they do but search?" Jenna thought of her fellow travelers on the bench at the morgue, like passengers crossing the Styx, gold coins on every tongue. Who was still there, waiting, looking up for answers anytime the phone rang or a person spoke? Who had been surprised, perhaps, by a miracle phone call, the kind she'd dreamed about? A child stuck in Sanur, unable to phone out until now. How would such a call feel? Why couldn't she have felt that? Why did it have to be Sofie? For a second, she stopped moving down the thatch-covered wooden pathway and watched Mark walk away, one bag over each shoulder. She was leaving Sofie— no, Sofie was already home by now.

"What?" Mark turned to her, Sofie's duffel bag bumping against his right hip.

"I can't leave her."

He dropped the bags and came back to her. "She's home, Jenna. She's already there."

"But alive Sofie. I'm leaving the alive Sofie. She was in love here, Mark. She was a woman here. This was the last place she touched earth." Jenna closed her eyes and felt the wood under her feet, the shifting aqua water, the air of the island that Sofie had breathed in. The hot air turned to flame that was her last sensation.

"This isn't where she is," Mark said, pressing Jenna against his chest, his hands on either side of her head. "She's in us now. Back where she came from. We can take her anywhere."

Jenna jerked her head up, her chin on his shoulder. He spoke as if he knew what he was saying. Had he learned to carry Sofie—her voice, her face, her laughter, her energy—with him after the divorce? For a second, Jenna remembered watching them sit together in his BMW at the curb in front of the house. Mark had turned toward Sofie and she to him, their hands moving as they spoke. Of course, Jenna had no idea what they were talking about, but as Sofie told him a story about Rachel or math class or maybe even about Jenna, Mark must have been saving up memories, hoarding them for the time when he'd be without her.

But he'd never said anything about that. And why was he so wise now that he wasn't with her anymore? She wanted to push back, shake her head, stamp her foot, but he was right. Maybe he always had been wise—and she hadn't known how to hear him, too busy with the wild life that was Sofie. Against his shoulder, his shirt rubbing against her forehead, she saw Sofie racing across Monte Veda Elementary's front lawn in her white spring dress. Later, there she was with dark black liner under her eyes, a tight maroon T-shirt stretched across her new breasts. There. There. Everywhere in Jenna's mind, her body. And she was in Mark, too, her father. He had memories, too.

Jenna nodded, gently wiping her face on his shirt wondering if she'd have the strength to remember anything. Without this soft air, the same air that had held Sofie in the hours of her best happiness, Jenna thought she wouldn't be able to think of anything but fire.

Two

Before he dropped her off at the airport, Mark shook a few blue pills into his palm. "Sonata," he'd said. "The drug is efficacious for about four hours, but once you are able to fall asleep, you'll most likely stay that way. But, Jenna, don't take any more than you need to."

She nodded and held out her hand. "Okay."

He reached over and slid them into her palm, his forehead creased.

"Don't worry," she said seriously. "I won't take them all at once."

When she sat down in her first-class seat—upgraded by the airline for free—she took the pill with the first offer of water and slept until the plane landed. Groggy, she walked down the gate, ignoring the reporters' questions, letting the airport personnel accompany her to her connecting flight, slipping her onboard even before the men and women with walkers and wheelchairs, before the parents with strollers. Before the babies.

At Sofie's funeral, though, the Sonata didn't work. She'd had the idea she could move, soporific, through the day, awake enough to mumble hellos and nod at the condolences everyone would dole out but numb enough to keep away the pain. But Jenna was awake. She knew that because she kept pinching herself under her sweater. She felt the pain in the wedge of flesh between her fingers, knowing her skin was glowing red, welting under her grasp. She could hear all the cries and sobs and moans, her own mother's muted hysteria, Mark's weeping, Renata's polite, annoying sniffles. Renata. She couldn't even go ahead and cry, probably worrying about her Laura Mercier cosmetics that Sofie had sometimes filched during a visit. "Twenty bucks. For eye shadow!" Sofie had said, holding up a brown plastic square. "Ha!"

And Mark. He could have had Sofie so much more than he did. Weekends and weeks in the summer. He had wasted so much, and now he cried. Like everyone who didn't get enough of Sofie. In row upon row behind Jenna, all she heard was the sorrow in each colleague, friend, relation, student, stranger, even reporter. The room was like a sad ship, heaving and moaning

50

under ugly skies, and the drug wasn't working. Jenna had to hear it all.

"We come here today to mourn the passing of a young woman. . . ." the preacher intoned. Jenna didn't know him, save for the fact that her best friend Dee's mother went to his church. Now he stood in front of the crowd at the Monte Veda community center, his arms held wide. "She was taken from us too young, and when those too young leave us, we don't know what to do, how to act. We say to god, 'Why? Why her? Why now?' We think god is unjust, unkind, unloving, but Sofie's passing is part of his plan, no matter what we here on earth think. No matter how angry we may be at those who did this, thinking of themselves and not god."

The drug must be working somehow, Jenna thought, or she would stand up and cry out, "Bullshit! You tell that mother-fucking god of yours that he's an asshole. Tell him to go fuck himself." She would turn to face the crowd (the television crews at the back who wanted to tape all this sorrow condensed into one funeral) and say, "Look at this guy! He's all dolled up for the cameras. His hair is so perfect, it looks like wax, like it could take off and fly away. He doesn't believe a word he's saying. How can he? How can he believe god was even near Sofie? You didn't see her. I did. I saw what god did." She would tell them what Sofie looked like now, closed away in the wood, her face worse than it had been on the floor of the Kuta auditorium, purple and red and blue and so pale, her Botticelli looks fading to death.

How could god approve of that? Stand by and watch that? Let that happen to Sofie, to anyone, to hundreds of beautiful young people in paradise?

But the drug—or her mother's arm across her shoulders—kept her still and weeping, mentally echoing the preacher's exact questions: *Why? Why her? Why now?*

After the closed coffin was wheeled out, Jenna; her mother, Lois; Stan; Mark; Renata; Jenna's cousin Gary; Mark's sisters, Candace, Jaclyn, and Miranda stood at the front of the church shaking hands, tolerating hugs. "So sorry . . . I don't know what you're feeling. . . . What a tragedy. . . . A waste. . . . A horror . . . you're so strong . . . I will always remember her."

Jenna nodded, hugged back, wiped her eyes, and then Tim was in front of her, gangly in his black suit and thin black tie, shifting from one foot to the other, pushing his hair from his forehead.

"Oh, Jenna," he said, shoving his hands in his pockets.

"Tim."

"I called." He shifted on his feet again, his brown eyes watery and red. "I'm so sorry. But I don't know what to do."

Mark leaned in to Jenna, and Tim glanced at him, biting his lip. "I'm sorry," he said, reaching out, touching her arm, squeezing, moving his hand down to hers. "I'm so sorry."

They hadn't gotten much past this in their relationship, holding hands across a few dinner tables, their shoulders rubbing softly at the movies, her knee against his in the car on dark rides home. She often looked at him, knowing that if he were only a couple of years younger and she'd been a wild, precocious teen, he could be her child, Sofie's much older brother. As they ate and laughed and talked about literature and the theater and music, she had thought of how Tim's chest and stomach must be smooth and firm under his clothes, and how hers were not, the pucker of stretch marks on her belly and breasts, the added flesh on her waist, thighs, her skin having moved down with the years. She wanted to tell him all this, so he wouldn't be surprised. But then the call from Bali came, and she was gone.

Even though Mark was staring at him, Tim watched Jenna, squeezed her hand, his fingers long under her palm, and then he was pushed aside by the grocer, the first-grade teacher, the neighbor, the best friend, the colleague, and on and on and on.

IF ONLY THE students would stop staring, Jenna thought every day on her way home from work, and then she would turn on the tape player and listen to another book. Since the funeral, she'd gone through *Blue Shoe, The Last Girls, Sense and Sensibility,* and half of *Drowning Ruth.* She hadn't been able to listen to that; too sad, too many lives not lived. Too close to home. Today, she'd started *Pride and Prejudice* because she knew the whole story by heart and no one died.

But she couldn't listen to a book when she was in class or at a division meeting or walking across the quad to the bookstore. Perhaps she could do what some of her students did and surreptitiously slip a CD player in a pocket, string headphones under clothes, and face forward. No one would see that instead of listening to people, she was in another world altogether, ignoring the wide-open-eyed looks of her colleagues and students and all the comforting words they wanted to say to her.

Now in the classroom again, she held a copy of *Catch-22* in her hands, listening to Travis talk about the names. "*Dreedle* is like Wheedle. And *Sheisskopf* means 'shithead' in German. You knew that, right? And *Minderbender.* Mind bender, get it? *Peckham*—you know, peck 'em to death. That kind of thing. But what about *Yossarian*? What's that?"

"Armenian."

"What's Armenian?"

Jenna sighed, wishing for the thousandth time that she had a map like the ones her high school teachers had. Junior year in world history, Mr. Meno used to yank it down in exasperation when someone thought Bulgaria was in South America or someone else declared the Caspian Sea was in Mexico. No one knew where anything was anymore or who anyone was; everything boiled down to what you believed in or whom you prayed to or what color your skin was. Sometimes not even that.

"Mrs. Thomas?"

"Yes?"

"Armenian?"

Jenna grabbed the dry-erase pen and drew a squiggly

Turkey, Greece, the Middle East, circling a corner for Armenia, knowing that Armenians would want the circle drawn bigger, taking up all of Turkey, reclaiming the millions of murdered lives that lay in Turkish soil. "Here. Armenia."

"Well," Travis said, folding his arms. "Why an Armenian? He's supposed to be every man, right?"

The two other students—Grace and Borin—who'd done the homework nodded. For the first few days after her return, all of them had tried to pay attention, but now, Steven, who wore a black fedora, stared out the window every single class, and Natalia never said a word though she turned in all her homework. Anthony and Alison chatted in the back of the class, and Ramzi slept, his head against the wall. Dustin simmered darkly in his long leather coat, staring at Christine, who ignored him. Randy combed out his long blond hair as he sat at his desk, wearing pants from 1972, the bottom half of a beige leisure suit, and a top from 1979, flowery and disco, a mixed metaphor. Zu Ren undid his belt, tightened it over his prodigious belly, and smoothed his shirt. He took off his glasses, wiped one lens and then the other with tissues he pulled from his pocket with a flourish. Scarlet opened a box of animal crackers and ate them one by one. The rest of the class sat numbly at their desks, *Catch-22* uncracked, spines straight, covers clean and unbent.

She stared out at them, knowing she couldn't teach them anything that mattered. And what was the point? They didn't care. She didn't care. She had better things to do. Right now on her *Pride and Prejudice* audiotape, Lizzy Bennett was looking at Fitzwilliam Darcy for the first time, so proud, so haughty, so needful of the juice Lizzy could provide him. But he didn't know that. Wouldn't for pages and pages. Jenna loved that scene, the one where at the dance, Lizzy overhears Darcy say that no women in the room would suit him. What did he say? That there wasn't a "woman in the room whom it would not be a punishment to me to stand up with"? Ha! What did he know? Before long, Lizzy would own him body and soul.

"Mrs. Thomas?" Travis said.

Jenna looked up, surprised the room wasn't full of dancers, women in ball gowns, men in silk trousers. "Hmm . . . class dismissed. Read the novel."

"But what about Armenia?" Travis gaped, clutching the book against his chest, his wide blue eyes full of questions.

"What about Armenia?"

Travis sighed. "Why Yossarian?"

"We'll talk about it Wednesday."

BEFORE JENNA HAD come home from Bali, Dee had gotten the spare key from the secretary and reorganized Jenna's office.

When Jenna thought about it later, she knew she would have done the same thing for Dee. Since they were hired together almost twenty years ago, they'd taken care of each other. Through divorces and terrible students and the basic sadness or drudgery or joy in living, they'd been in side-by-side offices, ready to listen to each other.

"Free therapy," Dee once said as she wiped her eyes, sad about a fight she'd had with her husband, Rick. "I'm saving thousands by canceling class and crying in here."

In the office, Dee hadn't taken down pictures or hidden mementos in drawers. Rather, she'd made Sofie less of a focus. Before, it had been as if Jenna was at the apex of a triangle, all points of her body fanning out to something Sofie: the pinecone ornament Sofie had made for Christmas 1986, gold sprinkles and red beads, on the lowest shelf directly in front of *Love in the Time of Cholera*; a photo of Sofie on Snip, the pony in Tilden, the only one she'd ride, framed and sitting right under the lamp; senior-year photo on the file cabinet. Then there was the Mother's Day poem hanging on the wall, the one Sofie had copied out by hand and decorated with two tiny handprints.

> *Sometimes you get discouraged*
> *because I am so small,*
> *And I always leave my fingerprints*
> *on furniture and walls.*
> *But every day I'm growing.*
> *I'll be grown up some day,*
> *And all those tiny handprints*
> *will surely fade away.*
> *So here's a final handprint just so you can recall*
> *exactly how my fingers looked*
> *when I was very small.*

When Jenna came to work a week after the funeral, she noticed the pinecone was now on the top shelf, the photos turned away from her place at the desk, moved out of the lamplight. The poem was on the opposite wall behind another bookcase. At first, she had felt a flush of anger, as if someone was trying to take away something else from her, making Sofie more gone. But then, as she sat there facing her bookshelf, *Love in the Time of Cholera* visible now, she breathed, studying the orange spine of the book. And then in the couple of weeks that followed, she pulled down all her photos— the tea party for Contra Loma College women, all of them in hats; a party to celebrate a colleague's first book reading; three friends on Stinson Beach, wet and covered in sand; and Sofie, every Sofie photo. Then she put away the knickknacks: the Russian nesting doll and the Russian spoon, given to her by a Russian student who was accepted into Haas Business School; the stuffed teddy bear a student had herself stitched together with velvet; a red plastic tulip a reentry student had handed her on the last day of class. Jenna shoved everything into the back of the cabinet and then dusted the shelves with Pledge.

Before the explosion, before Sofie, Jenna and Dee had almost run the English division, heading up assessment and evaluation committees, mentoring new teachers, creating a yearly literature week that brought poets and fiction writers and journalists to campus for workshops and lectures. So Jenna assumed that no one would react when she came back

58

to work after the funeral, as if her presence was needed and expected, despite everything. But as she made Xerox copies or graded essays in the faculty lounge or picked up her mail, Jenna heard the whispers about her. By the coffee dispenser, she heard Marcie Gee saying to Darien Lieberman, "Why is she back? I would be in my bed. I'd sleep for a year. Two! You'd have to come over and keep me from slitting my wrists. She must be in denial. She needs some serious help."

And if people weren't whispering about Jenna, they were watching her, trying to see what, in fact, was holding her together, as if she was a puppet with strings no one could see. If she'd had enough strength, Jenna would have told them that waking up with a place to go, showing up in her classrooms every day was holding her together. For those few blessed moments when she was reading aloud a poem or drawing out Armenia or explaining illogical parallelism, she wasn't thinking about Sofie.

Now, holding *Catch-22*, she sat at her desk dumbly, jumping when Dee knocked and opened the door.

"Hey," she said, sitting down. "How's it going?"

Jenna turned to her. That's what everyone asked, and at first she'd actually answered them. "Sofie's dead," she'd say. "How could it be 'going'?"

But Dee had only nodded when Jenna first said that to her, as if expecting the truth.

"I don't know, Dee. No one's reading the book. It's like *Night of the Living Dead*, half of their brains falling out when they walk in the room. I can't teach them anything."

Dee nodded, tucking her thin legs under her. "I don't know why you're doing this to yourself. Have you thought about taking that leave? You don't have to go through this semester. It's midterms, and all the psychos come out. The excuses roll in like waves. Car accidents. Terrible, debilitating illness. And in no time, it's going to be finals. I mean, for Christ's sake, Dan Miller took disability for depression caused by that fight over protest signs in the quad. A whole year. And then Lani Reed was out for what—five years? Because of her weight? Remember how she rolled around in that wheelchair in preparation for it? You don't have to be here. You, of all people."

Jenna looked for Sofie's smile, but her senior photo was still turned away, the light catching only one loop of red hair, a part of a shoulder, the dark blue background, blue as the deep Bali ocean. "What would I do at home? There's—there's nothing there, Dee. All I'd do is think."

"The tutoring program I told you about!" Dee said. "One day a week at the library. The kids won't be like these. Younger. And it's one-on-one, just you and your student. Easy stuff. Some grammar. Essay ideas."

"Maybe," Jenna said. "But I've got to finish out the semester."

"No, you don't, Jenna. There are no rules for this. You could go upstairs and talk to personnel this very minute."

"No, I can hang on. I can probably do the whole year."

Dee shook her head. "Have you at least called Dr. Kovacic?"

"Yes."

"Okay. So how's it going?"

Jenna let her hands fall into her lap and stared out at the almost bare liquid amber tree, its yellow and red leaves squashed and soggy on the pathway. Talking to Dr. Kovacic had been fine. He was a soft-spoken man who nodded as he listened and didn't look at his notepad when he wrote down notes. But the best part had been the Zoloft, the little oblong pills that he'd prescribed. Along with the dry mouth and some slight jitters, she already felt the dampening of her nerves, the space the chemicals carved in her brain where she could sit quietly, whole moments going by when she didn't think of Sofie.

But her chest hurt, her head ached. She hadn't even reread *Catch-22* because she couldn't get past chapter two. Everyone in the story was either dying stupid deaths or killing someone else for no reason, but that wasn't what bothered her. She just didn't care about anything, real or imagined. She wanted to go home, feel different, and learn not to think. Feel something else. Feel nothing. Think nothing.

"It's terrible."

"Honey, like I said, you can't do this. You shouldn't."

"What else can I do?" Jenna said, knowing the only other thing she could do was be a mother, and she would never have that opportunity again. And anyway, why would she do that? And with whom? She could never replace her daughter. "I can't do anything but this. I am completely unemployable."

Dee brushed her short gray hair up off her forehead and sighed. "Listen, you know you don't have to work. You can go away. You can take yoga classes. You can go to therapy. Ask Mark or your mom to subsidize you for one full year. Mark can afford it for sure."

Jenna put down the book and leaned back, looking up at the bookshelf where there used to be a photo of Mark, just in front of *Tender Is the Night*. He'd called every night since they'd returned from Bali, his voice ragged with tears, wanting her to fix him. "Call me, Jenna. I need to— Just call me." She'd waited to return his call when he was working, not wanting to get near to his familiar skin and hair and breath. It was too dangerous to talk to him or see him, because it would be so easy to let him slide back into her life. It would be unfair to use his body, his memories of Sofie, his familiarity to dampen her pain. Pulling him back into her life wouldn't be fair to either of them, and it certainly wouldn't be fair to Renata, as if their continued sexual relationship ever had been.

She would wait to see him until she'd stopped feeling his body inside of hers, the known rhythm of their being together, the waves she could still ride.

"Maybe I can ask," she said.

"No maybes. You can't be here like this with those little shits. I'm about ready to can my entire developmental reading class. I walked out a half hour early today because no one did the homework. It was like talking to a glass wall."

As Dee commiserated about unwilling, unmotivated students, Jenna wondered what Lizzy Bennett was doing now. She looked past Dee as her friend talked on about discipline and writing strategies, a renegade plan for a seating chart that would stop the girls in the back from giggling all through class.

Back at the ball at Lucas Lodge, Lizzy was staring out across the dance floor, her beautiful sister Jane and Mr. Bingley dancing in the first throes of love. Darcy glowered at her, half in scorn, half appreciatively from across the room, and nothing was available but a perfect future, the one Jenna could fast-forward to whenever she wanted to.

THERE WERE THINGS to do at home. First, because it was cold and dry, the early rains having come in September and then stopped abruptly, she had to water the strip of perennials alongside the driveway, the lamb's ears and salvia sucked dry of juice every four days or so. Then she had to feed Bean and Peanut, her cats, the cats Sofie named when she was ten.

"Mrs. Roemer said legumes are full of nutrients," Sofie had said.

"But do you know how stupid I'm going to sound yelling 'Bean' and 'Peanut' outside? 'Bean, here kitty, kitty.' People will think I'm crazy." Jenna shook her head.

"Mom," Sofie said seriously, "why would anyone care about that?"

"What about the names you picked out last week? Petey and Max."

Sofie crossed her arms and rolled her eyes. "So like boring. I wasn't thinking. Bean and Peanut are cute!"

Sofie, her eyes wide, stared at her mother until Jenna shrugged. "Let's go practice," Jenna said finally. "Let's see if Bean and Peanut come when we call."

Now older and slightly stiff, the cats stayed indoors most of the time, waking up and stretching when Jenna walked in the door, purring and curling around her legs as she dumped kitty kibble into their dishes. When she'd left for Bali, she'd forgotten to get anyone to feed them, and her next-door neighbor Susan had climbed through a bedroom window to check on the cats and ended up not only feeding them but cleaning the entire house as well. All the cobwebs Jenna had let hang like little hammocks in the corners were gone, her floors shone, and the strip of dark green mold in the shower was bleached out.

People couldn't stop helping her. Dee and Susan and the brigade of colleagues and neighbors delivered food and books and flowers. Sofie's former teachers and best girlfriends, dates she'd had to the junior and senior balls, her soccer coach, her Girl Scout leader all called and wrote short, sweet notes. So did her sixth-grade teacher's assistant. The clerk at the Safeway. And Jenna's family. Jenna's mom had camped out in the guest room for a week before Jenna asked her to go home.

64

"But, sweetie, what will you do?"

Jenna shrugged, turning away from her mother's soft brown eyes. "I have no idea. But I've got to figure it out. And you need to go home to Stan, Mom. You have a life, too. I'll manage. I always have."

So her mother flew back to Phoenix, and Jenna went back to work. Every day, she came home, watered the plants, fed the cats, turned on *Oprah* or the local four o'clock news, and wandered from room to room. Despite her best plans to stay busy and active, she ignored the phone, her desk, the papers in her briefcase, the leaves on the back lawn, the dishes in the sink. Dr. Kovacic had urged her to start a journal, but the black-and-white speckled notebook Jenna had bought at Safeway sat uncracked on her desk.

She sat on Sofie's bed and studied the empty walls, the spaces where Sofie had hung posters before rolling them up and moving into the dorm. In that, Jenna had been lucky. Sofie had moved herself out before she died, sparing Jenna that pain. And it had been Mark—not Jenna—who had gone to Cal and packed up Sofie's dorm room. The only things left here were what Sofie hadn't wanted. In one sweep, Jenna had found the tiny pink ballerina from a broken music box. When she'd turned on the closet light, she'd seen the pink tutu, the beige legs, the arms frozen in a permanent plastic arch.

Jenna rushed to pick it up, recognizing the ballerina from the box her mother had given Sofie on her fourth birthday. In one of Sofie's many redecorating fren-zies—bed here, no, here, dresser over there, mirror on the back of the door instead of by the bed, blue, no, green, paint on the far wall—the box had fallen off the dresser, the ballerina catching on an open drawer and cracking off.

Sofie had stood quiet and solemn for about a minute, and then held up the little ballerina. "I guess her dancing days are over."

Then she went back to moving her furniture, the box stuffed on the top closet shelf, forgotten.

Jenna left the ballerina on her nightstand, leaning it against the clock, staring at it as she lay awake in bed all night. When she finally fell asleep, she imagined it spinning as it used to to the song—"Edelweiss"?—on Sofie's dresser top.

Today after the cats were fed, Jenna opened and closed kitchen cupboards. She might have six casseroles in her refrigerator, but what she really wanted was some Triscuits. As she dug through the shelves, all she could find were a half-eaten bag of saltines, a bottle of white-wine vinegar, navy beans she'd bought years ago for a recipe she'd never made, toothpicks, coffee packets from the Embassy Suites in Los Angeles, and three boxes of strawberry Jell-O she'd bought during Sofie's last bout with stomach flu. Years ago. Lives ago.

Jenna closed the cabinet and leaned against it, sliding to the floor, holding a box of Jell-O. When she was a girl on the swim team, she would bring a box of Jell-O to the swim meets. "You need your energy," the coach Larry said, so they all stuck wetted fingers in the boxes, licking the sugar until their mouths and lips were red and orange and yellow. After twelve years on the swim team, she could never eat Jell-O again. Even making it for Sofie when she was ill made Jenna feel fluish, full of a sympathetic nausea.

She closed her eyes, seeing Sofie on the couch, Mark coming over to check her in between patient appointments, his hand on her forehead, side of her neck, wrist. The bucket beside the couch for vomit; the television on all day, cartoon after cartoon. And then, by night, she was whining for food, and Jenna brought her Jell-O, little squiggly bowls of orange or strawberry or cherry or watermelon or lemon. Then saltines. Then 7-UP. And then finally, sleep, Sofie free of fever.

Pressing the Jell-O box against her chest and then bringing it up to her face, Jenna tried to hold back the tears. No more. Sometime it had to stop, all of this grief. What was left inside her? How could there be energy for one more tear?

The cardboard smashed under her palm, Jenna could smell the old smell, the sugar, the chlorine from the pool, the sticky cherry redness deep in her throat, the vomit in the bucket, Sofie's hot acid skin under her hands, Sofie's burned, bruised face. The fire. The smoke. The bodies lined up in white rows. The young man leading her to Sofie, the fetid smell of the auditorium. The way hope left her body like air.

Jenna pushed herself up and ran to the sink, throwing up whatever she'd eaten for lunch. Yogurt? Cheese? She didn't know what she ate anymore, but whatever it had been, she rinsed it down the sink. She dropped the box and then washed her face, drying it on the dish towel that smelled like dust and old milk. She bit down on her lips and swallowed, pushing back what gurgled inside her.

As she wiped off the water and sweat, the phone rang. She watched it, and then reached out, grabbing it, hoping for the first time since Bali that it was Mark. He could come over and cover her with his body. She would forget about Sofie for just a moment, and that would be worth later having to rationalize what they had done, what they had always done.

"Yes?" she said, pressing the phone against her face, liking the hard plastic on her cheekbone.

"Jenna. It's Tim. I can't believe I reached you."

Jenna breathed in, holding the sound of his voice in her chest. She could hang up. She could pretend she was an answering machine. "Yes. You've reached the home of Jenna Thomas. Please leave a message at the beep. *BEEP*." She hadn't done that since grad school, when the student loan collectors kept calling her and Mark.

"Hi. I'm here," she said, not knowing if she really was here. "How are you?"

"I'm fine. How are you?"

There the question was again, but before she could say anything in reply, he said, "Of course. I know. I don't know why I asked."

Jenna leaned against the counter, wishing she could go back to the day she met him at the first English division meeting in August before the fall semester started. Everything had been all right then. Sofie was preparing for her second year at Cal, taking summer-school classes. For the past two or three years, Mark hadn't had a reason to visit the house. After a year of Sofie's bugging them both about needing her freedom, Mark and Jenna had finally agreed to go in on a used Infiniti G20, and since then, Sofie had driven herself to Mark's. So there had been no late-night dropoffs, no reason for Mark to slip his arm around Jenna's shoulder on the couch and pull her close. She'd almost begun to forget the feel of him.

And besides, that day at the division meeting, the late summer light was the exact color she liked—soft and warm, a strip of cool whisking around everything. Her classes were full, the students eager in the flush of their first semester at college. And here was this charming, smart, tall, dark-haired, brand-new colleague speaking to her about Joseph Campbell and the hero cycle as their colleagues filed out of the room. Of course, she'd said yes when he asked her out to coffee to talk about courses. By all means she would share her syllabi and help him brainstorm ideas. Sure, she would meet him for breakfast to go over the evaluation process. And then, yes! She'd agreed to go to dinner. The movies. A concert. *Why not sleep with him?* she'd thought, just before the call came about Sofie.

"I'm terrible," she admitted, sliding down to the floor. "I know."

"No, you don't."

"You're right. I don't. Can I come over?"

She kicked the Jell-O box with her foot. What was she going to do for the rest of the long day and night? Sit on her kitchen floor and kick food around? Talk to the cats like the old lady she was? Watch *Entertainment Tonight* and *Jeopardy!* before drinking a glass of wine and trying to fall asleep? Take the rest of the Sonata and sleep so hard and long she missed class the next morning, the Zoloft and wine interacting with the sleeping pill to put her in a wakeable coma? Call Mark and beg him to come over and sleep with her again? Think about Sofie, Sofie, Sofie?

"Fine. Yes. Come over."

HE WAS AWKWARD at the door, his hands in his pockets, his bottom lip under his teeth. As she stood there holding open the door, Jenna realized her breath probably smelled of vomit. She hadn't thought to brush her teeth or comb her hair or take off her work clothes and put on something casual, comfortable.

"Come in," she said, trying not to expel air. Then she sighed. Who cared? What did it matter? She was the fire-breathing crone, the maidenless mother, a Mrs. Robinson plus some.

Tim smiled and walked in. Looking out into the quiet street and her yard, she closed the door behind him, and they walked to the dark living room. Jenna hadn't opened the curtains since she'd been home, scared that a reporter from *Newsweek* or *Time* or the *Monte Veda Review* would be lurking outside. After the one photo of

70

her appeared on the front page of the *Chronicle*, her hands on her anguished face, Mark's arm across her shoulders, she parked in the garage and closed the door before she even got out of the car, not wanting to make a statement for anyone. Republicans. Democrats. The Green Party. Libertarians. The oil lobby. Terrorists. Antiterrorists. The NRA. Gun-control advocates. Antiwar protestors. The military. She didn't want her old therapist to call her, begging her to return, forcing her into some support group for parents of assassinated children. She didn't want the AP to pick up the photo, a Phoenix newspaper printing it, her mother roaring back up here, staying for weeks and weeks. All she wanted was for everyone to stop staring. She wanted to be left alone. But here was Tim, sitting on her couch, looking at her with the same round eyes of her students.

"You look . . ." Tim searched for a word.

"Old. Tired. I look old and tired. I feel worse," she said, closing her eyes, leaning back on the leather couch, the one she'd kept after the divorce.

"You don't look old. You do look tired."

Jenna opened her eyes and slapped her palms on her knees. "So, how are your classes?"

Tim started. "Oh. Um. They're good."

"You feel settled in at school now?"

He pushed his bangs away from his forehead and looked at her. "I don't want to talk about me."

"Well, I don't want to talk about me, either," Jenna said, standing up, facing the closed curtains. "I don't want to talk about anything."

He crossed his legs, silent. Jenna breathed in and out, the sound of her exhales audible in the room. Outside, the sprinkler system for the front lawn went on, a *hush, swish, hush,* and then water pelted the front window.

"Let's watch TV then. Bad TV. *Judge Judy.* The shopping channel. *The Nanny* reruns, Nickelodeon. A Spanish telenovela—I don't care," she said. "Nothing smart. No news."

"Fine." Tim stood up and grabbed the remote, juggling it in his hand for a second and then turning to her, his still, dark gaze on hers. She swallowed and felt her body relax, just a bit, her shoulders falling from her ears, her knees unlocking.

He walked to her and took her wrist, bringing it up to his face, kissing the pale, thin skin over her veins. And then he led her to the couch and sat her down, keeping hold of her hand. He pressed on the TV, turning through cable channels, settling on QVC, a platinum pendant sparkling across the screen. "There. Here."

She watched the jewels, listened to the women as they displayed glittering strands in their long-nailed hands. Jenna held Tim's hand, felt his long fingers and soft skin.

TIM STOOD AT the stove, scrambling eggs. After watching the shiny, sparkly parade of necklaces and rings and bracelets—zirconium, Austrian crystal, rhinestone held up in front of the camera by perfectly coiffed blond women—she'd pushed up off the couch, excusing herself for a moment. For a shower. To brush her teeth, the ancient feel of Jell-O still on her gums.

Now, her hair wet, her mouth clean, her face soft with Olay retinal lotion, she sat like a child at the kitchen table, waiting for her meal.

"I have a secret ingredient," Tim said, sliding hot, steaming eggs on a plate.

"What is it?"

"I can't tell you or it wouldn't be a secret, would it?" He smiled, putting the eggs and a slice of toast in front of her. "But suffice it to say, you had it in your spice cabinet."

Jenna picked up her fork but waited for him to sit down, sliding his chair up to the table. Even though he'd been through a long teaching day and hours of terrible television with her, he looked so good. So handsome. Still a person that events couldn't affect, death or sorrow or longing not apparent on his face. What had happened to him in his life? Jenna didn't even know. She was eating eggs with someone she barely knew.

"These are good," she said, chewing, tasting the light, lemony lift of tarragon.

"I told you. My specialty."

She was hungry, ravenous, her stomach never so empty as now. She scooped up the eggs fast, the buttery warmth filling her, the crunch of the browned bread soothing as she chewed. She'd lost weight since coming home, her clothes baggy on the rear, hanging off her waist. And her face, haggard and tired and lined. Just last night, she'd dug around for the retinol, putting on more than the tube suggested. Pretty soon, it would be Botox injections or at least a glycolic peel, a whole series of them. She imagined her face like an onion, layer after layer ripped back to expose the smooth white surface. But with whatever treatment, in five years she'd need a face-lift to keep her cheeks from drooping to her shoulders.

"That was so good. Thank you." She put her fork on her plate and sat back.

Tim nodded, chewed, took a sip of orange juice. "I think it's all I ate in college. That and Top Ramen."

"Tuna. We ate lots of tuna, the cheap kind that's packaged like cat food. It said TUNA on the label. Ragú sauce on noodles, whatever was on sale. Generic macaroni and cheese. It's a wonder we haven't grown tumors."

Tim sat back. "You and Mark."

"Yeah."

"He seemed nice," Tim said, pushing back his plate.

"He is. I've known him since I was eighteen. I think I'm stuck with him, in one way or another," she said, but even as the words left her mouth, a pain keened through her chest. She'd been connected to him by Sofie. Now there was nothing, no reason to call him about grades or behavior or summer-camp tuition or a wild boyfriend. It was over. She would lose a person who had known her more than half her life.

"That's good. Divorce can be so . . ."

"It is so everything. I've had to work harder on my relationship with him since we divorced. Worked on not hating and resenting him. Worked on letting him into her—" Jenna stopped, not wanting Sofie to swirl

74

around the room as she always did at night, a pale flame in the corner of her bedroom. "It's not easy."

"I know."

"You know?"

Tim stood up and cleared the dishes to the counter, running the faucet. "Yeah. I was married for about a minute in college. It was stupid. We thought we were made for each other when all it really was was the excitement of actually being able to be with someone. Waking up every day together without a mom or dad bitching about it—putting down rules and strictures. We had our own apartment, bought our own food, did whatever we wanted when we wanted. We felt like adults, and so we drove up to South Lake Tahoe and got married in the Chapel of Love."

"Chapel of Love?" Jenna smiled, imagining the white stucco, artificial flowers, canned wedding march, professional reverends spewing out the same speech couple after couple after couple.

"Totally cheesy, but we thought it was the real thing." Tim stacked the plates in the dishwasher. "Maybe at the time it was."

"What was her name?"

"Karen."

"Where is she now?" Jenna stood up and brought the skillet to the sink, standing next to Tim as he rinsed the silverware.

"In Iowa City. She runs the Writing Center at the University. She's remarried, has a baby."

"Do you miss her?"

Tim took the skillet from her and poured some soap into it, scrubbing at it with a sponge. "She's a good person. We really liked each other, and we had the same interests. What I miss is the connection of being with someone for real. So I suppose it's not Karen I miss, but what I could have with someone."

Jenna breathed in, trying not to react. If she thought about what he wanted and how she couldn't give it to him, she might ask him to leave. So instead she looked out the window. The night stretched across the lawn and shrubs, casting back Jenna's and Tim's reflections against the glass. There they were, Tim rinsing and washing, her owl-eyed at the window. In this view, they looked like a couple, any couple, doing the dishes at night after a long workday. In another world, they would go back into the living room and play with their children, read them stories, tuck them into bed. If she had managed to do anything right, it would be Mark standing next to her, not this young man. But it was Tim, not Mark, and there was no child to tuck in.

Jenna turned off the faucet, put her hand on his, looked into the shiny reflection of the window, both their eyes wide and blinking.

SHE HAD TOO many electrical gadgets in her room—two alarm clocks, the carbon monoxide alarm, the phone, the electric toothbrush in the adjoining bathroom, the computer's surge protector—little buttons and blinks casting a green-red glow against the walls. For a few years, she worried that electrical currents would create tumors or some kind of immune disease; reports always in the papers. After one article, she ran up to Sofie's room and took out everything electrical, ignoring Sofie's upset about the CD player and the television and VCR.

But as with so many of the worries on the news, people seemed to forget about electrically caused brain tumors and cancers, and slowly, all the electrical devices snuck back upstairs and into Sofie's room, and then into Jenna's.

Jenna cared again, though, because in the weird green light, she knew Tim could see her body, his eyes adjusted to the darkness.

So Jenna closed her eyes, liking the feel of his different skin against hers, his long thighbone against her hip, his flat, lean belly, his arm on her back, gently rubbing the skin above her rear. He was so *not* Mark, so someone else, something she'd found for herself. She tried to breathe that idea into the space in her chest, the empty, grainy hole of her heart, and maybe it spilled in, he spilled in, a little. She just wouldn't think. She would feel, and she reached out for him again, pulling herself on top of him, liking his mouth, his kiss, soft lips, no angry, adolescent tongue; a patient tongue, a warm tongue, warm mouth, warm everything.

In the morning, she was sore, as she hadn't been since . . . when? College? The mornings after she and Mark made love all night because they could? Just like Tim said he and his wife, Karen, had done.

Tim pulled himself up on his elbows and looked at the

77

bigger of her two clocks. "I've got a 1-A class in an hour."

Jenna contracted her muscles, feeling where he'd put himself all last night, imagining her vagina red and happily wounded. "I've got myth class, too. Do you want to take a shower?"

"Yeah. The students won't notice I'm in the same clothes as yesterday. Maybe our friends and colleagues will."

She stood up and grabbed her robe, pulling it quickly around herself and then standing up. She walked to the curtain and opened it six inches, enough to illuminate the room with morning light. "I'll get you a towel."

"Jenna," he said, patting the bed. "Come here."

She looked at him, her heart pounding, her stomach full of last night's scrambled eggs. Something like fear and sadness crept up her throat, but she walked to him and sat, let him take her hand.

"I loved last night," he said. "Thank you."

She stared at his eyes, concentrating, knowing that her forehead would crease in five orderly lines. Air filled her mouth, and all she could do was watch him. His hair stuck up on the back of his head, his eyes wide, and she squeezed his hand, wondering when their relationship would end and how. In fire? Or in absence?

Jenna swallowed, finding her voice. "So did I. You're welcome."

She smoothed his hair back, but in that instant, she felt Sofie under her hand, Sofie's morning hair wild with dreams.

"I've got to get in the shower," Jenna said, standing up and quickly walking to the bathroom, needing hot water, the classroom, essays, anything but her own thoughts.

Three

Like, my printer broke. Really. I went up to the computer lab to print it out, and it couldn't read my disk." Dustin held up a CD, waving it in front of her face, just in case she thought the round plastic circle was as much of a mirage as his excuse. "So can I e-mail it to you? Tomorrow?"

"This afternoon by four." Jenna packed up her books and papers.

"I have to work," Dustin began, but Jenna held up a hand and looked at him, waiting, not saying a word. "Fine." He turned and stormed off.

This was her new plan. She said exactly what she meant, and then didn't explain a thing. Students shrank from her like kicked kittens. No one ever asked her if she had Wite-Out, paper clips, or a stapler anymore. No one asked her for extra credit, extensions on their essays, or chances to rewrite already rewritten essays.

As she walked down the corridor to her office, she wondered why her plan hadn't made her feel better inside. The place inside her that was usually roiling with their excuses and demands was empty. But now her stomach felt prickly, as if she'd swallowed an armored sea creature, her ragged, uneven breath stuck somewhere in her throat.

Sure, she wasn't arguing with them, saying things like "Excuse me? What did you say? Do you talk to your mother like that?" or "I'm sorry about your mother and the accident and the funeral in Hong Kong and your grandfather's anxiety, but no, I will not take your essay. No. Really. Sorry. Tonight? Tomorrow? At noon. No later. I mean it."

She had a midgrade depression, she could tell, Sofie like a dark poster in a room she couldn't leave, sadness on her tongue and in her windpipe, with memories that kept her away from sentimental movies and in Dr. Kovacic's office once a week and on Zoloft, the blue pill she chipped in half every morning to take with orange juice. In fact, it had been Dr. Kovacic who'd taught her the new plan.

"Why do you listen?" he said. "It's your class. Your rules. Say what you feel and don't argue." That was on one of the days Jenna hadn't sobbed about Sofie for an hour. A good day.

"And what about that journal, Jenna?" he asked. "Have you started that?"

She shook her head, embarrassed by her writer's block. Every semester, she told her students, "Writer's block is all in your head. How you cure it is to write!"

But the black-and-white notebook still lay untouched on her desk.

"Just start with your feelings," Dr. Kovacic said. "You don't have to say anything mind-blowing. It's not for an audience. And then maybe you'll find yourself writing to someone. Maybe a lot of people. Maybe Sofie."

Jenna bit her lip, turning to look at the landscape photographs on his wall.

"Well, at least work on the plan with your students," Dr. Kovacic said after a moment of silence. "Showing them you have boundaries can change everything."

So for the weeks that funneled into finals, she'd practiced, holding up a flat straight palm, looking Dustin and Susanna and Jovan and Danny in the eyes, telling the truth, the sea urchin of pain pulsing in her stomach.

Despite the plan and the drugs and the doctor and the activity, she thought she should be more depressed, flat on her back or curled in a fetal position or diving off the edge of some cliff. She should be underwater with stones in her pocket, or in the kitchen with her head in the oven, a rolled towel under the door. Or maybe she would take a more masculine approach, like Hemingway, a shotgun bullet to the head. She could drink herself to death like Fitzgerald, or smoke herself into cancer like Cheever. She shouldn't be walking because Sofie wasn't walking; she shouldn't be breathing because Sofie wasn't breathing. Her skin should be bruised and burned and bludgeoned.

The Zoloft or something else inside her kept all her fear and sadness far enough away that she felt suspended in air, two seconds behind the action, catching up to reality after it had softened just a bit, the edges smoothed by the whir of time. She was a walking box of air, letting nothing in, except at night when Tim slipped his arms around her. She could let herself feel him, her heart pound, pound, pounding on her bones, her breath, her muscles, every part alive for those minutes, and then the air settled around her, dead and white.

She slid open Dee's door and slumped in the chair by her friend's desk. Dee hung up the phone and looked at the stack of papers and books in Jenna's arms. "You're carrying your weekend, I see. What are those? Journals?"

Jenna nodded, squeezing the curly wires of the spiral notebooks. Inside were entries most of her students had written the two nights prior to the due date, staying up late with Red Bull and black coffee and cigarettes, reflecting on stories they'd only glanced at. "Yeah. The fruits of their labor."

Dee patted her arm. "It's almost over. One week. Hold on."

"I don't know if I can. I am completely menopausal. I'm all hot and heartbeaty. And my period's really late. It just stopped. My ovaries have gone supernova."

Dee nodded and then shook her head. "You're stressed, honey. You've lost a lot of weight. You're tired. This has been a horrible, horrible time. You need the vacation. More Dr. Kovacic. More Tim?"

Jenna felt like she was going to blush, but then she didn't. Since she'd been taking the Zoloft, her blush response seemed to be turned off, the nerves cut dry, her feelings dampened. Sometimes her face felt slightly tingly and paralyzed, like she imagined Botox would feel.

"More of everything," she said, wondering if she could increase her Zoloft dose on her own, the holidays approaching like a black hole she wanted to fall into. "But I'll be with my mom for a week. Her and Stan. Tim's flying down after Christmas, and we're going to fly home together. But we decided to visit the Grand Canyon first."

"You wild woman."

"Hardly." Outside Dee's window, the last of the liquid amber leaves fell from rain-darkened limbs, the world a swirl of hovering fog and muted light. Jenna was the tree, losing everything.

"What does Mark say about all this? About Tim?"

"He doesn't know."

Dee squinted a little, the way she always did when confused. "How can he not know? Why haven't you told him?"

Jenna pressed the journals tight. "He's—he has Renata, anyway. He doesn't need to know about Tim and me. Not yet."

Dee relaxed. "Well, I say good for you! Tim is a great guy. You deserve some fun."

Jenna nodded, letting Dee think Tim was fun. Maybe that's what she wanted to think herself, that the way she clung to him, needing his skin and mouth and body was for fun, when it was more like survival. How sick was that? How selfish! Using a human like an intelligent life buoy, holding on with a death grip. But maybe that's what she was used to, Mark's visits all those years just about the same thing. It wasn't fun to sleep with your ex-husband, knowing that if your child found out, she would expect her life to be complete, perfect, the way it should be, the fantasy end of the parental divorce. No matter how much Renata irritated her, it wasn't fun to think of her home alone, looking at the bedside alarm clock, wondering *What's taking him so long? That woman must nag him to death.*

Clutching the notebooks, Jenna stood up. "I have to survive my mother and Stan first. The cocktail and bridge parties. My cousins. The canned cranberry sauce. The nightgown-and-slippers presents, neatly wrapped in foil paper and placed under the fake tree. Her tree actually has a music box *in* it. It plays twelve different Christmas songs when it's plugged in. One year it got stuck on 'Silent Night' for an hour."

"God, a tree. Any tree." Dee sighed. "I can't get Rick to go buy one. He keeps saying, 'In the olden days, folks got them on Christmas Eve.' Pisses me off."

"In the olden days," Jenna began, sliding open the door and stepping out into the hall, cold air wrapping around her ankles. She turned back to face Dee. "People did a lot of things."

Dee sighed again, nodded, her eyes wide now, relaxed. "Tell me. There are hundreds of things I did back then. Many of them a lot of fun."

"I'll call you later."

"Bye, sweetie," Dee said, and went back to her papers.

Jenna closed the door all the way, fumbling with her keys. In the olden days, she had a daughter, a tree already up, strung with colored lights and bunches of tinsel Sofie threw on haphazardly, telling Jenna, "Don't be so anal. We don't have to place them on like one by one. I like it kind of clumpy. When the tree lights are on and the room is dark, it's like the tinsel is a mound of shiny snow."

"But when the lights are off and the room is bright . . ." Jenna began.

"Who cares?" Sofie would say, tossing on more tinsel. "It's just us, Mom. Only us."

They would have already been to several parties, a performance at the school, a dance recital, a sing-along at the community center. They would have taken BART to the city and shopped in Union Square, Sofie clutching her arm as they crossed the packed and bustling streets. Jenna would have bought Sofie a new outfit at Macy's or a pair of shoes at the Nike store or two trade paperback novels at Borders. They would have eaten at Kuleto's and then walked down Powell to catch the train home. Later that night, Sofie would have put on her new outfit and gone to a party, bringing a bag of small, wrapped presents, little things especially picked out for her girlfriends. Jenna would have sat at home in the leather chair in the living room, reading one of Sofie's new novels, her live, green tree turned on, the red, yellow, blue, gold lights burning, blinking, twinkling.

In the olden days, Jenna hadn't been old; she'd been

a mother. In the true olden days, Sofie skipped around the living room floor on Christmas morning, waving a new doll, her hair a wild cloud of red, her eyes bright with reflected light.

THREE DAYS AFTER the semester ended, Jenna was packing for her trip to Phoenix, a task that seemed to take forever, her clothes and shoes and the wrapped gifts somehow too heavy to pick up. She was sitting on her bed, holding a sweater, when the doorbell rang. Jenna thought to ignore it. Tim was already on his way to Turlock to visit his grandma Rosa. Susan from next door had already come by for the key, and Dee had phoned to say she was off for New York. The reporters had long ceased to come by, so it must be a solicitor, someone for the Food for the Holidays Fund for Rwanda or Bosnia or Chechnya or Afghanistan. *I've already paid,* she thought as she closed her suitcase. *I gave up Sofie to the world's misery. A twenty-five-dollar donation won't change that.*

There was another ring and then some pounding. "Jenna! Jenna!" It was Mark.

She went to the window and peered down, seeing him standing on the front step. Pulled by her gaze, he looked up and saw her. "Let me in, Jenna," he mouthed. She closed the curtain and stepped back, too late, and then sighed. He'd seen her. She had to let him in, finally. She'd managed to avoid his visits and calls for almost two months, speaking to his nurse and his service and even Renata, leaving short, crisp messages, hiding in the dark kitchen when he rang the bell, telling Tim as they lay in bed, "Don't worry. I'll call him tomorrow."

Jenna walked down the hall and then the stairs, reaching the front door and opening it, avoiding his eyes because she knew they matched hers, full of disbelief, even now.

"Mark. I'm packing." She gestured with her hand to the house, as if that explained why she hadn't wanted to speak with him since the funeral.

"Can I come in please?"

She opened the door wide and stepped back, letting him pass. He brushed by her, his shoulder against her collarbone. Even with his anger and her resistance, his body spoke to her, his touch, his face, his smells so familiar, she could be the Jenna from twenty-five years ago, welcoming her med student husband home. In an instant, the present and the future were gone, the only story Mark and Jenna. Mark and Jenna. Nothing else.

Closing the door softly, she turned on a light, the house getting dark now at three, the sky outside full of mist and cold, the bare limbs of sycamores and maples breaking through the white air like darkened bones.

Mark stood in the kitchen, leaning against the counter. He must have come from work, his hair neat, his silk tie still knotted tight; and he had a new pair of glasses, stylish, small, dark, and rectangular, giving him a hip, studious look. He was going to be a better-looking older man than he'd been as a younger one, his face fuller, his few gray hairs softening the sharp lines of his cheeks and nose, his body fuller and stronger because now he could afford an expensive gym and personal trainer.

"Why haven't you called me?"

Jenna sat at the table, following an imaginary scratch on the wood with her forefinger. "I did call you."

"I mean me, Jenna. Not my nurse. Not Renata. You've called only when I'm not around." Mark shook his head. "I don't understand you."

"Do you want something to drink? I have wine."

"For Christ's sake, Jenna!" Mark yelled, and she looked up. He stared at her, his eyes wide and full of tears. "Stop it. Talk to me."

"I can't talk to you," she blurted, afraid of the rush of feeling in her body. She closed her eyes and pressed a fist to her solar plexus. "It's too painful to talk. I can't go there. I don't want to talk. I don't want to think."

He pushed off the counter and came to the table, pulling out a chair and sitting down. Sitting at Sofie's spot, where there were indentations from her homework assignments, big looping *A*'s and *C*'s and *S*'s pressed into the soft wood.

"Colonial America," Sofie had muttered as she wrote about shipping sloops.

Tribal culture, she had written during fourth grade California history. *Mission history. Spanish sovereignty.*

One night not long after the funeral, Jenna had come downstairs quietly so as not to wake her mother, and sat in Sofie's chair. She brought her fingers to the table, nothing but moonlight guiding her, and found the marks of her daughter's old essays and book reports, algebra, social studies, government assignments. With her eyes closed, she followed the letters, desperate to find meaning, a message, using the table like a sad Ouija board. Then she'd given up and turned on the light, brought a piece of scratch paper and a pencil back to the table, and tried to capture the message by rubbing over it, but she couldn't pick up anything but darker lines in a field of gray. Finally, she'd turned off the light and gone back to bed, nothing deciphered.

Mark put his elbows on the table. "You look pale. Are you all right?"

"All right? All right?"

"You know what I mean."

"How could I be all right? Are you all right? Will either of us ever be all right?"

He ran his hand through his hair, the curls on end. "We'll never be the same, but we've got to talk about it, Jenna. We can't just ignore what happened to our girl."

Jenna thought of her suitcase, almost packed. Shorts. She needed shorts. And flip-flops. It was warm in Phoenix, even at Christmas. So maybe a couple of sun-dresses instead of shorts. More comfortable. "I'll be fine. I'm going to my mom's tomorrow morning. Early."

"Why haven't you called me?" He took off his glasses, the frames clicking on the wood, and watched her through his imperfect corneas. She must look better like that, skin smoother, hair finer, the stray gray hairs with their stiff curl invisible.

"I've been busy. Finals."

"Jenna, I know the academic calendar. I've wanted to talk."

"What more is there to say?" she asked. "We had a daughter, you left us, she died. We loved each other and then we didn't. At least we didn't love each other enough. It's over, Mark. There's nothing left to talk about. There's nothing left to do."

Jenna felt flat and clear, as hard and cold as the air outside. She tried not to see his reaction, his intake of breath, his blinking, one, two, one, two, the way he bit his lower lip, chewed on it, tears at the corners of his eyes. *Enough crying,* she thought. *No more.* That's why she hadn't wanted to talk with him. All he would do was make her sad and tired and angry. He'd keep the Zoloft from working.

He rubbed his hand along the counter, brushing away imaginary crumbs. "I unpacked Sofie's duffel bag. Do you want to know what was inside?"

"What?" Jenna looked up.

"Her duffel bag. What was inside it."

Her chest seemed to want to birth an idea or a feeling, everything contracting, muscles, bones, blood. Hadn't she gone through enough? Didn't she have to live with enough memories? There was Sofie's room. The old clothes, the stuffed bears, the broken ballerina. And what about Jenna's own desk upstairs? The ordered files containing Sofie's report cards, book reports, early drawings. Her acceptance letters from the colleges. Her SAT scores. Valentines. Birthday cards. Every single day, Jenna brushed by the paper remains of her daughter when she went to get a pencil or pen or piece of paper.

And now Mark wanted to give her this, too, dumping it all over her. "No. I don't want to know what's inside the bag. It's over. I told you that."

"It will never be over. It will always be what happened to us. To all three of us. To Sofie and you and me, Jenna. No matter if I did leave you. No matter if we didn't love each other enough. And that was never true, anyway. You know that. I've always loved you."

"I don't know that, Mark. I don't know anything. I don't know why Sofie is dead. No one can explain that, not even Robert, and he was there. I don't know why everything converged to bring her to Bali, to that club, on that night, at that hour, to be blown up and burned." She took a deep breath and forced her eyes to dry. "I will never know why. And neither will you. So why talk about it?" She sat back in her chair and folded her arms, her stomach pulsing under her rib cage, her throat tightening.

"Jenna," he began, speaking slowly, as he used to do when trying to explain their taxes or why the sewer pipe broke or how the circulatory system worked.

"Don't do that. Don't make me feel stupid. I'm just tired. I haven't been feeling great, and I have to pack. I'm trying to live through this Christmas. You've got Renata. I'm going to my mom's. What else is there to say?"

Mark picked up his glasses and leaned back. He stared at the frames and then put them on. For a moment, he did what she used to see him do with patients: look down and gather his thoughts, showing them that he contemplated their problems and personal life thoroughly before speaking. And then he would begin his speech slowly, carefully, words sliding out, newly minted and useful. It worked with them, but Jenna bounced her leg, wishing he would go away. She wished Tim were here. She wished it were tomorrow.

"Okay," he said, and she looked up, surprised. Mark stood without saying another word and walked down the hall and out the front door, closing it carefully behind him. He left, as he always did. He was so good at it.

As the latch clicked in place, she bent to the table and breathed in, as if she could bring forth her girl and her smells of clean skin, flowery shampoo, chewing gum; the smells of homework and laughter and arguments. But as she pressed her cheek against the cool wood, Jenna smelled nothing but toast, wood, Lemon Pledge, exactly and only what was there.

Four

My goodness," her mother said, rubbing her hands together. "It's never been this cold in December. We may as well have stayed put in Monte Veda instead of moving all the way down here to Arizona."

Jenna clenched her teeth, wishing Lois would stop

talking. Her mother had been chattering since breakfast, discussing the lawn, the home owners' association, Jenna's job, a daytime television show—*Desires* or something—the selection of plus-sized clothing at the local Target. Everything but Sofie.

Jenna glanced outside to the thermometer that hung by the pool. "It's sixty-eight, Mom. Almost hot."

Lois bustled by the kitchen table, a poinsettia in her hands. "I suppose. Look how dry this plant is." She put it in the sink and turned on the water, pulling off dead leaves and talking about the history of the plant, how it was really a tropical plant belonging to the spurge family. "It's the leaves that are red. Not the flowers, you know."

Jenna watched her mother, the familiar stance, her large, strong body always in front of a sink or stove or table, rolling out sugar cookies, poking a steaming pot roast, stirring a chocolate cake. When Jenna closed her eyes, she could see her mother's figure, her large, firm rear in polyester pants—not lumpy with cellulite, but round and sturdy—her thick waist, strong shoulders, capable arms bent as she scrubbed or peeled or stirred. Even now that her dark brown hair was gray and starting to thin and she was approaching seventy, Lois still had the same body, the same energy. The same engine burned in her that always had.

"Hmmm," Jenna murmured, taking a sip of her coffee. Jenna was like her father, thin and fair, her limbs long and gangly and slightly muscled. When she'd been a teenager, she'd worn hip huggers and halter tops and walked apart from her mother, whose arms were heavy with flesh, thick and white, exposed when Lois put on her swimsuit. And Lois loved to swim, not caring about stylish string bikinis like the ones Jenna bought for herself at McCaulou's downtown, every May before Park Pool opened. No. Lois pulled on the black swimsuit that was almost solid material from neck to thigh, tucked her hair into the white swim cap with the floppy pink flower on the side and a thick chin strap, and swam for an hour, her arms confident and sleek in the water.

No one ever whispered to Jenna, "God, your mom is huge!" Maybe it was because Lois didn't seem concerned about her size or what people thought. Or because she laughed as she walked along the side of the pool, her hair standing on top of her head, the cap in her hand like a flattened fish. Or maybe everyone wanted what Jenna had when she was upset or scared. Those arms. The soft chest, the tight hug.

On a Saturday morning when she was fifteen, Jenna had walked into her parents' room without knocking, and seen her father, Ted, on top of her mother, moving and moaning, her mother's arms light around him. Jenna had been horrified, and then backed out of the room and leaned against the wall, trying to blink away the gross images: her father's tightened, moving butt, her mother's spread legs twirling in the messy bedsheets, the wide smile on her mother's face. Jenna had pressed her hands against her stomach, willing the fluids inside her to stay put.

But even as Jenna had tried to breathe out the image

and dampen the muffled sounds from behind the softly closed door, she found that under her horror was something else. As she walked slowly away from her parents' room, she tried to figure out what it was. Relief? Amazement? Curiosity? No. None of those feelings. It was comfort. Her father loved Lois despite her large roundness. Maybe love wasn't all about who was sexy and thin—nothing like the pages of *Seventeen* or *Glamour* magazines told her. Sitting alone on the living room couch while upstairs the bedroom door stayed closed, Jenna felt that something inside her would burst. Even though she was tall and slim and everything a girl was supposed to be, according to the experts, she'd wondered if any boy would be able to get past her long, straight nose and freckles, her flat chest, her skinny arms. But love was more, and her father loved her mother, was loving her right now. He wouldn't leave her for some skinny Lauren Hutton type, all tan legs, flat stomach, gapped teeth. And he hadn't, at least not until he died ten years ago, just before his retirement at sixty-one.

"I should have bought another poinsettia while I was at Target," Lois said. "I think this one won't even make it to the new year." She put her hands on her hips and turned to Jenna. "Do you want to go downtown? We need a few things for tomorrow. Paper plates for the pie. I'm not washing another set of dishes."

Jenna put down her coffee cup. Since she'd been in Phoenix, she'd felt better, her stomach calming down, the spines that for weeks had flared inside her gut every time she had thought of food were gone. Before she'd left for the airport, she'd put a call in to Dr. Kovacic.

"I told you one of the side effects of Zoloft was nausea," he had said. Jenna could hear his pencil tapping on his desk. "Lack of appetite. It passes. Other than that, how are you? Are you writing in the journal?"

Those questions again, Jenna thought, but they didn't bother her coming from him, someone who'd listened to it all. But she hadn't told him about Mark's visit or her faraway floaty feeling, saying, "Oh, fine," as if he were the Safeway clerk, and then she said good-bye and hung up. There'd be plenty of time after Christmas to talk.

Now her nausea felt as far away as the Bay Area, and she stood up and brushed toast crumbs off her red T-shirt. "Sure. Let's go to Target."

Lois smiled, worry slipping off her face, the worry Jenna had tried not to notice. "Great. Let me get my purse. And I'd better write a note for Stan, or he'll think I moved out."

"What?" Jenna asked, pushing in her chair as her mother went into the dining room and grabbed her keys and sunglasses.

"For some reason, the man thinks I could get a better deal elsewhere," she said, walking back into the kitchen. "If it were up to him, I'd have a cell phone on at all times. So he can find me. Ha! 'For emergencies,' he says. I've flat out refused."

"He loves you, Mom."

Lois smiled. "I know. Isn't it the damnedest? Come on, let's go."

THERE WAS A message from Tim when they got back. Her mother had bought more than paper plates and a poinsettia—liquid soaps for the three bathrooms; paper hand towels with Santa Claus designs; just-reduced towels with red-and-white stripes; four bags of red and green M&M's; Scotch tape; three poinsettias (one white); five packages of plates in star, evergreen, snowflake, Santa, and reindeer motifs; and a new pillow for the other guest room. "Your cousin Jolie might stay over. Driving back to Pine Flat after some of Stan's eggnog might prove difficult!"

After she'd helped her mother put everything away, Jenna went into the den and sat on the couch, enjoying the quiet room, the feel of the small black phone in her hands, the strange order of numbers as she dialed. Nothing that had happened today would have happened before, back at home. She'd never have gone to Target to shop for Christmas decorations, nor would she have sat in this dark room to make a phone call to her, what? To her Tim? The man she was sleeping with? Her *boyfriend?*

"Hello?" Tim's grandmother answered, her voice as fragile as tissue paper.

"Hi, Mrs. Passanante. This is Jenna, a friend of Tim's."

There was a pause, and Jenna could almost smell the woman's kitchen, giblets simmering for the gravy, a

97

pumpkin pie in the oven, a lasagna on the counter. "Yes, Timmy's told me all about you. Oh, my. I was so very sorry to hear about your daughter. What a tragedy."

Jenna's body fell limp, her arms, shoulders, head, mouth. The day with its flurry of shopping and cleaning and preparation disappeared, her body tired with memory. Lois's current of words and activity couldn't keep one sentence from busting Jenna back into the truth of what was happening—a first Christmas without Sofie.

Closing her eyes, she counted to three, not wanting to hang up on Tim's grandmother, even though she wanted to hang up on him, too. How dare he tell her? Why did he even have to talk about it? It was her business, not some elderly woman's in Turlock!

But of course, he'd told her. He'd been with his grandmother for almost a week, sitting around her table for three planned meals a day. They had to talk about something, and Jenna was his girlfriend, for lack of a better word. Her business had become his. That's what happened. That was one of the trade-offs.

"Dear?"

"Oh yes. Thank you. Is Tim there?"

"Certainly. Let me fetch him."

Fetch, though Jenna, a word from an English novel, a Jane Austen word, action hidden in the very verb. What really happened when one fetched something? Was it ever really got? Did she fetch Sofie's body?

"Jenna," Tim said, breathing hard.

"Hi." She wanted to hang up now, contact made. She

would see him soon enough. Or she could cancel the whole trip, call up the El Tovar Hotel at the Grand Canyon and the Hertz office. He could stay in Turlock with his nosy grandmother.

"What is it? Did my grandmother say something?"

"No." Her lips pinched together at the end of the stark syllable. She could feel the wrinkles around her lips flare like angry punctuation.

"I'm sorry. I mentioned it once, and she hasn't been able to stop talking about it. I was running to get the phone when I heard it ring."

"I wish—" Jenna paused, knowing that wishing was out of the question. If she wished for anything, it could be for only one thing. "Nothing. It's okay. I had just forgotten—" But then she paused again. She hadn't forgotten at all.

"I'm sorry."

And he was. She could feel it when he held her and talked to her as they lay in bed. She could feel the sorrow that he helped her carry, and she knew that without him, the past months would have been unbearable. "How are you? Are you ready for our trip?" she asked.

"I am desperate for it. Many more dinners while watching Dan Rather, and my head will explode. My parents owe me for this one." Tim's parents had gone to Europe for their thirty-fifth anniversary, leaving Tim to take care of Grandma Rosa. "But at least my cousins will be here tomorrow. And then the next day I'll see you."

Sometimes when he spoke to her like that, she wanted to snort, hold up a skinny leg and say, "You want to see this?" When she was standing at the bathroom mirror, she thought to call him in to look at her face, the one she was getting used to even as it continued to change. "Look," she'd say, pointing to the lines by the corners of her mouth. "Check these out. Three years ago, nothing. Three years from now, prune. And then menopause. It's starting already. I haven't had a period since—" But then she wouldn't be able to continue because she'd dried up the moment Sofie died, all her mother genes and hormones knowing it was over. Her body would flush and flash, her vagina dry up, and her hair thin. She'd be like the sad dog she'd seen once in downtown San Francisco, scrawny from neglect. Finally, she'd have to decide if she was going to haul herself over to the city to Dee's Chinese herbalist for menopausal treatments, the scary bags of roots and herbs and leaves that Dee boiled into a thick, stinky potion daily to counteract all the changes in a woman's body.

"Dr. Liang looks at me and says, 'You still have period. Like a girl. No headache. No flashes. Thick hair. Good skin. No dryness. So what, herbs smell bad? What to complain about?'" Dee had laughed when telling Jenna the story, and as she did, Jenna knew that what Dr. Liang said was true. Dee's skin shone, her hair was a mass of silver spikes on her head, her skin soft.

Dr. Liang could temper aging, keep Jenna feeling herself. So her tentativeness about being in a relationship with Tim wasn't about how she would look in comparison. She would be able to love his flesh and him, despite the souvenirs time would leave on her body. Really, it was all the life between them, years when she was a mother, years she was alone, learning how to be alone. Stay alone.

Jenna thought she should sit Tim down, put her hands on his shoulders, and say, "Honestly, sweetie. Look at your life. Where do you imagine this relationship will go? In five years, sweetie, I'm fifty. You'll still be a young man."

When he was asleep next to her, she tried to conjure up her thirty-four-year-old body, but when it arrived, smooth and lean, she'd see that even eleven years ago, she had marks, Sofie having punched out white lines on her belly and hips, breast-feeding having loosened her breasts. Back then, she would have had no room for Tim, her mind full of Sofie.

Soon enough, Tim would see all that she couldn't show him now. He would wake up one morning and startle, finally realizing he was sleeping with a woman who was as gray as his mother. She should hold on to him while she could.

"The trip will be fun," she said lightly. "I can't believe I've never seen the Grand Canyon."

"In the morning—no, in the evening. Sunset. It's the best. You won't believe it."

Jenna nodded into the phone, listening to him talk about the winding trail to the bottom of the canyon, the color of the winter water, the flurries of canyon wrens and pinyon jays, knowing that really, she didn't care about anything. The holidays. The trip. But she would have Christmas, anyway. And then in three days she would leave in a rental car with three unabridged books on tape and a man not related to her past, and drive to the edge of the earth and see if she dared to look down.

"NOW, JENNA HERE," Lois said, pointing a fork at her and smiling, "she knows some big words. In college, one of her dorm mates called her English Major."

Jenna's cousin Jolie laughed and nodded, waiting for Jenna to spell out *cornucopia*. Rubbing her nose, Jenna sighed, tired of these word questions. A discussion about *A Christmas Carol* had led first to the word *Dickensian*; the ghost of Christmas present had led to *saturnalia* and now *cornucopia*. It was like the Christmas version of *Jeopardy!*

Jolie hadn't gone to college and now worked in a stationery store in Pine Flat, where one of the biggest sellers was a pen that had a vista of the Grand Canyon in it. Just this afternoon, Jolie had brought one for each family member, along with her dish of whipped sweet potatoes dotted with browned marshmallows.

"What is a cornucopia?" Stan's daughter, Elvie, asked. "I keep thinking it's a horn. Or something about a pharmacy."

"It's just that basket. You know, pointy at the end, wide at the top with all the fruit in it," Jenna said.

"Horn of plenty," bellowed Stan, slapping the table, Lois's silver tinkling.

"Oh. Of course," said Jolie. "I've seen that in the store. Little napkins with the horn of plenty on it. A real cornucopia."

"That's what this meal is, for sure," added Jolie's brother, Todd. "Damn, Aunt Lois, you sure can whip up a meal."

Everyone chewed in silence for a moment, and Jenna could hear them trying to think of things to say that wouldn't invoke Sofie. All meal long, it had been Ebenezer Scrooge and cornucopia and traffic and drying Christmas trees; eggnog and nativity scenes and the Wal-Mart super sale on the twenty-sixth. Jolie, Todd, Stan, Elvie, Elvie's husband, Dick, Lois, and Jenna all played the game of hide the tragedy. Jenna wanted to stand up and say, "Look, I feel a million miles away. Talk about anything." She thought to tell them about the Zoloft, the way her fingers didn't even seem to touch anything, her torpor in the afternoons, her head filled with cotton, the sheet of sadness that swathed her body and couldn't be ripped off. It didn't matter what they talked about. "Go straight for the war on terror," she wanted to scream. "Talk about Al-Qaida. Iraq. Iran. The Middle East in general. Oil. Nuclear stockpiles. It doesn't matter. I'll never forget Sofie's gone."

Stan picked up the platter of turkey and passed it to Lois, who took a piece and then handed it to Jolie and Todd, who took some, and passed it on around. Jenna stared at the platter, the one she remembered from her childhood, no longer in her parents' Monte Veda dining room with the dark chair rails, wainscoting, and stained hardwood floors. Here it was in the white room in the white house with the whitewashed kitchen cabinets and the tropical plants outside. Her father had touched that platter. So had Sofie. Her own childhood hands had held it, washed it in the deep kitchen sink, carefully drying the ridges of porcelain grape vines and, yes, cornucopia, on the edges. She could remember the dreamy, after-Thanksgiving and -Christmas kitchen, the warm yellow light over the sink, the ambient noise from the dining room punctuated with laughter, the smell of her father's tobacco pipe, the feel of warm ceramic under her fingers. She had been separate and yet part of the celebration, listening but not there, a rush of something swooping through her head, the future, the past, the ideas she had but could tell no one. Ideas about words and stories and the things that would happen to her, things she could almost pull out of the air and stare at in her palm. She would recognize their shapes if she could just see them, knowing that there was something swirling around in the warm air above her, like a movie she'd watch in a dream.

In the kitchen, there, alone, she felt the presence of what would come, maybe Sofie, maybe Mark, maybe the books she would read and the ideas she would think, all unknown but known in those quiet minutes in the kitchen, as she wiped the platter and stared at her own reflection in the window over the sink.

"Turkey?" Dick asked, the platter and slices of dry meat in front of her.

Jenna shook her head and passed the platter back to Stan. "I'm full."

Lois laughed. "I think you ate half the mashed potatoes. You needed some carbohydrates. God's own food, I say."

"There's more where that came from in the refrigerator," added Stan. "Pumpkin pie. Pecan pie. Whipped cream! Christmas cookies. Fudge. Lois here bakes like a star."

Jolie asked about gingerbread recipes, and Jenna poked her fork through the remains of her mashed potatoes. *Think,* she thought, *of anything.* Think of gravy, the tines of forks, a basket of rolls, the stain on the red fabric napkin, tomorrow, the next day with Tim, the books she'd picked out to listen to in the car, *Daisy Miller*, *The Great Gatsby*, *Vanity Fair*, plots she knew by heart, lives she could predict from memory, no surprises.

JOLIE SAT ON the edge of the guest room bed, holding one of the new pillows in her lap. Stan's daughter and son-in-law had already left, as had Todd, who lived up the highway in Carefree. Lois and Stan were downstairs cleaning up, the dishwasher running on the heavy cycle. Jenna leaned against the doorjamb, wearing the new nightgown and slippers she'd unwrapped that morning, absently hitting her palm on her thigh.

"So, you need anything?" Jenna asked. "Mom went out and bought those pillows just for you. They're a bit on the fluffy side. You'll feel like you're floating all night."

Jolie shook her head. "No, everything looks great. Aunt Lois is so nice. I told her I'd drive home, but she insisted." She looked up at Jenna with the smile Jenna recognized, the one that said, *I will use my mouth and teeth to protect you from thinking. I will smile until you forget I know about Sofie. Do it! Smile, too. We'll both feel better.*

But of course, it wasn't true. No one felt better. The smiler wished for Jenna to be gone, and Jenna wished the smiler would let her muscles sag and fall, wished they could both cry themselves into bits. Dee hadn't done that with her. Neither had Tim. Or Susan. The only person who would have cried with her like that was Mark, and she'd kept him away. Maybe, Jenna suspected, she was really a smiler herself. No one knew how she truly felt at all.

She sighed. "I'm glad. Well—"

"I'm so sorry about it, Jenna. I wanted to go to the funeral. I couldn't get the time off," Jolie blurted. "I thought about you and Sofie every day, though. I really did."

Jenna stiffened, her stomach pulsing, her mind breaking through the Zoloft. She swallowed and turned back to Jolie. "Thanks. Mom told me you couldn't make it."

"I loved that little girl. She was a total sweetheart. I can't believe what happened at all." Jolie put the pillow on the bed and stood up, walking to Jenna with open arms. And then her cousin's skinny arms were around her. "Why did they do it?"

Against Jolie's shoulder, Jenna thought, *Why did who do what? Robert and Sofie go on their trip?* "They were in love," she mumbled.

"No." Jolie tightened her grip. "The people. With the bombs. Why did they do it?"

Jenna closed her eyes, breathing in the smells of Christmas dinner on Jolie's blouse, and underneath, lotion or perfume, something lavender and soft.

Why *did* they do it? Jenna had asked that question since the day she arrived in Bali. Of course, everyone knew some of the bigger reasons: ancient tensions from a time before the bible, hatred, xenophobia, religious persecution, religious intolerance, religious righteousness. But the other reasons had played behind her eyelids, especially during the nights before the Zoloft had kicked in. What was the day like for the men who packed the car full of explosives and drove it to the front of the bar? Did they eat breakfast with their families? Did they take showers, use soap, shampoo their heads? How was it to go to the bathroom when you were planning on murdering later in the day? How did it feel to talk with other people on the street, the old lady next door, walking her dog, the little girl playing with friends in the open field? Could you buy rice, milk, bread on a day you had packed a car full of murder? How was it to live with the knowledge of death on your hands?

And then, when the bombs went off and the

screaming began, the bloody and burned people being hauled out of the building, did it feel good? Was there a way to wipe humanness out of your mind and see death as the answer? But of course, there was a way. Jenna had read enough to know the answer was yes. That's what all wars were, the bigger issues taking over the bodies of individuals like nesting aliens or terminal diseases. Once you were infected, that was it.

"I—I," Jenna began and then pressed her lips against Jolie's shoulder, feeling her cousin's bones.

"Whatever the reason, it sucks, Jenna. I swear."

Jenna could feel Jolie's heart beating against her chest, could feel her cousin's tears on her own face. *Suck* was one of her students' favorite words. They used it for everything—homework, a bad day at work, the weather, a sandwich, a war. They pulled it up from their lungs, letting it fall from their lips like an expletive. Jolie was right. *My god, she's right! It sucks. This whole thing sucks. Today sucks and tomorrow will suck. Nothing will ever be right again.*

"Yeah," Jenna mumbled, crying now. "Yeah."

"How can you go on?" Jolie asked, her voice hushed. "I don't know how you do it." She pulled away and held Jenna's shoulders.

"I don't do it."

"Oh yes, you do. Aunt Lois says you've gone back to work."

Jenna wiped her nose on the sleeve of her Christmas nightgown. "I'm on drugs. I've gone into menopause."

"You need air." Jolie nodded, and Jenna looked at her,

blinking. Air? "Yes," Jolie continued. "Like where I live, Pine Flat. Out of Flagstaff a bit. Lots of air and space. I like the Bay Area and all, but it's crowded with memories. There's nothing here but space. Nothing pressing you in, reminding you all the time about what you've done or not done or where you've been. It kind of holds you. I know I sound like I should be living in Taos or Sedona with all the New Agers, but it's true. And I've needed to forget a few things, trust me."

Jenna nodded, but she knew nothing about Jolie. She'd never been interested, glazing over when Lois talked about her sister's children, Jolie and Todd, relatives with so-so, plotless lives. They grew up and went to work, always remembering Lois, though. Calling and visiting and writing thank-you letters when Lois cared for their mother, Ava, in her final days. Lois went to surprise birthday parties and Saturday-night dinners, e-mailing Jenna facts she forgot even as she read the words. Jenna was a snob. She sucked.

"I'm sorry," she mumbled. "I don't know what happened to you."

"No one does, but it doesn't matter now. All the space cured me. Visiting my mom here made me fall in love with Arizona. I never went back home to Walnut Creek. There wasn't any point to it."

They sat on the bed together, their hipbones touching through fabric. Jolie had opened her window, and Jenna could hear the hum of an insect against the screen. Street light shone against the metal window frame, the air soft and dry. At home in Monte Veda, everything would be wet, the drains clogged with pine needles and sycamore leaves.

"Your work?" Jenna asked. "You like it?"

Jolie shrugged and put an arm around Jenna. "It's nothing I'd want to tell my mother about, should she come back for a ghostly visitation. But it gives me time to paint."

"You paint?" Jenna wished she could take back her question, its amazing spike of surprise at the end. She swallowed. "What are your subjects?"

"Nature. The sun. The desert. Mountains. Phoenix here is amazing for those. I have a painting partner, and we go out on weekend camping trips to paint. I had a show in the summer in Flagstaff."

Jenna nodded, the sharp keen of Sofie loss, Sofie pain lessened with the landscape conversation, the Zoloft reaffirming its hold, her body still and full of calm white air again. She closed her eyes, wiped her face with the back of her hand.

"That's great. I'd love to see your work."

"Well, come over tomorrow with your boyfriend."

"Oh," Jenna said, pausing. She hadn't considered visiting Jolie, never even made the connection that her vacation and cousin were in the same vicinity. "Yeah. Okay. We will. That sounds great."

Jolie smiled and pulled Jenna close. Jenna had a flash of recall, a memory of a Christmas of long ago, the tall Douglas fir glowing with colored lights, her cousin and her opening presents, receiving the same doll, blond hair, blue eyes that closed when tilted back.

Together, the girls sat on the hearth of her parents' Monte Veda home and dressed and undressed the dolls, trading the small gingham dresses (one pink, one blue) and white aprons, deciding the dolls were parted identical twins who had no parents. They had no one but each other. Jenna couldn't remember any other present from that year, only Jolie and the dolls, the sound of the dolls' plastic feet on the tile hearth, the feel of the warm flannel nightgown on her back, her cousin's laugh, high and true.

They didn't say much more, Jolie kissing Jenna on the cheek as Jenna stood up to leave. "Good night," Jenna said, closing the door behind her, the white walls and wood floors of the Arizona house illuminated by a porcelain fan nightlight. This house was nothing like the Monte Veda house Jenna had grown up in. In that house, the hallways to the bedrooms had been narrow, with quick left and then right turns, full of steps and small, awkward windows, quirky enough that one of Lois's friends had said, "I swear. It's the Winchester Mystery house."

Jenna hadn't been sure what Lois's friend meant until the time Sofie was invited to a Halloween party at the Winchester House in San Jose. Jenna accompanied her, driving a carload of girls dressed as witches and ghosts and devils.

Sarah Winchester—sure that she was cursed because of all the deaths caused by the gun her family had invented—kept carpenters building her house, hammers pounding twenty-four hours a day for thirty-eight years, certain that adding on was the only way to coun-teract the curse. As the tour guide led the group around the house, ghoulish music playing in the background, Jenna saw stairs that led to a ceiling, windows built into the floor, and doors that opened to blank walls. She passed through two ballrooms, went through several of the 467 doorways, and walked into four of the six kitchens.

The girls screamed at every twisty turn, Sofie clutching Jenna's arm and whispering into her ear, "Building all these rooms must have worked, Mom. She was, like, eighty-something when she died!"

Now as Jenna walked to her room, she knew that Sarah Winchester hadn't done anything but live as long as she was supposed to. No amount of work or inven-tiveness, no kind of control, could change that. Maybe what Sarah really liked was walking into a new space, a new room, the memories of the past staying behind her in the older parts of the house, at least for a while.

Jenna was glad she wasn't back at her parents' old house or even her own, hoped that this new space would help *her* forget. But that night in Jenna's dream, Sofie stood in her mother's bedroom, back for one last visit to the house she grew up in. As Sofie walked around the room, touching picture frames and clothing and piles of ungraded essays, Jenna noticed that her daughter was connected to all sorts of vines, umbilical and rooty, green and wet and alive. The vines twirled and tumbled from Sofie's back and trailed out the front door and into the street. Jenna didn't think about what these huge, alive, knotty vines really were, but she sat up in bed and said to her daughter, "If you are going to stay here, you're really going to have to get rid of those things. There's no room for them. No room at all."

The next thing in the dream, Sofie was free of the long, dragging roots, just as slim and long of body as she had always been. Sofie turned to Jenna, looking at her mother clear through, and then smiled.

"You know there's no room no matter what I do, Mom," Sofie said. "You've filled it up. You've put something else there in my place."

As Jenna tried to pull herself through the dense, thick air of the dream, needing to touch Sofie, the dream began to break up. The room and furniture and taste of home evaporated until all she could see was Sofie's blue gaze on her. Jenna's eyes felt stuck and slow, and she tried to yank herself back into the dream so she could tell Sofie that it wasn't true. She had room! She hadn't replaced her at all! But as Sofie and all the images faded away, Jenna knew that Sofie was right. There was no room for her among the living. Emptiness had grown and taken up her space. Sofie couldn't stay with Jenna because she didn't have roots anymore.

Five

Your mom is great," Tim said, punching off the tape player, *Daisy Miller* stopped in narrative lurch. Jenna looked over at him, blinking.

"Your mom," he said again, pushing his hair away from his forehead.

"She is." Jenna sat up and smoothed the invisible wrinkles in her pants with her palms. At her feet, she kicked at the journal she'd put up front at the last minute, having dug in her suitcase to find it. But instead of taking a pen from her purse and pulling the journal up to her lap, she turned to look out the window, the rented Taurus sedan pushing past the land along I-17. They seemed to be moving into another terrain, a burst of green on either side of the traffic, ridges jutting up, merging into a series of mountains. Every sign said something about a state park or a recreational facility; nothing left of the flat, dry expanse and toothy mountain ridges of Phoenix, the city grid far behind them.

"So, Christmas? It was okay?"

"It was fine. I got to talking with my cousin Jolie."

Tim turned to her. "I didn't know you had a cousin Jolie."

"Well, I do. She lives in a town called Pine Flat. Works at some kind of stationery-cum-tourist-trap store. I told her we'd stop by."

He looked at her silently, and then turned back to the road. He held the steering wheel tightly, like her father used to, all long fingers and firm grip. She knew they would make it safely all the way to the El Tovar Hotel, but she wanted to open the door and fly out, roll on the shoulder gravel and trimmed sedge. The only thing that had kept her breathing since they pulled away from her mother's house was *Daisy Miller*, and now he'd turned that off. Jenna closed her eyes and willed the drug to come back and hug her tight, keep her from feeling this terrible mistake. Why had she agreed to this trip? Had it been Tim's wonderful description of the rocks and mountains and views? Had she imagined that she was really in love with him? Now, after more than a week away from him, she didn't know what she'd been thinking.

"You look good," he said finally. "I think you must be eating again."

"You mean I'm fattened up like the Christmas goose?" Jenna looked at her thighs. They were still thin, but she'd barely been able to button her jeans, breathing in deeply before forcing the button in the hole. She wasn't a goose; she was a Butterball turkey.

"I'd hardly call you fat." Tim smiled and reached out a hand, rubbing her thigh.

"Lois made every dessert known to holiday feasting. It was disgusting, but I tasted every sweet morsel," she said.

"Sweets for the sweet," he said. She wanted to turn back to the window, ignore his platitudes, his attempts at conversation, his earnest driving. She put a hand on his, more to stop him than to acknowledge his gesture, but he didn't notice that. His skin was warm beneath hers. She wished they hadn't had to jump in the car and drive away. Maybe they should have rented a hotel room in Phoenix, stayed a night before heading upstate. She knew him best with his clothes off. This Tim in the car with her was new, husband-like, Mark-like in the way he took control. She wanted him flat on the bed, under her, moving enough so that she could close her eyes with the motion and imagine nothing.

But that way, sex would have been a diversion from the expanse of time they'd travel on the long highway from Phoenix to the Grand Canyon. All she had been doing since the fall was diverting herself, watching television or listening to books on tape or to music, or reading books she already knew the plot of. Adjusting herself on the seat, she flexed her thigh, and Tim took the hint, putting his hand back on the steering wheel.

Jenna leaned down to pick up the journal and grab a pen from her purse. The journal's spine cracked in thick clicks as she opened it. There were nothing but white pages, lots of them, pages of nothing.

Clicking the pen, she scribbled a bit on the top of the page until the ink flowed, and then she sat silent, listening to the noises inside the car: the *tick, tick* of the turn signal, Tim's quiet breathing, the hush of air coming in through the vents, the whir of tires, slick and fast on the road.

What had Dr. Kovacic said? He told her that she needed to write down her thoughts. She needed to write letters, maybe even to Sofie. Letters to Sofie.

Jenna shook her head, ignoring the sideways glance Tim gave her. When Jenna was a girl, Lois made sure that the day after every major holiday involving gifts, Jenna was sitting at the dining room table with a pencil and a stack of thank-you notes, the address book, and a roll of stamps.

"Get it done," Lois said. "You'll feel better when you do."

And though Jenna resented writing cards to Aunt Frona and Uncle Herb and all the faraway people she'd never even met, she did feel better. Like a burden was lifted. More than that. Like she'd given something back.

She could do that. She could write a thank-you note. So whom did she need to thank?

Closing her eyes, she saw Lois at the sink, turning back to smile at her, a wilted poinsettia in her hands. Lois after the funeral, making tea and sitting down with Jenna at a late-night table, listening. Lois pulling the turkey out of the oven, sweat ringing her underarms. Lois in bed with Jenna's father, loving. Loving. What Lois did best. What Jenna knew she needed to learn how to do herself. She hadn't yet, not even after all those years with Sofie. She'd never loved like her mother did.

Jenna wrote, tapping the pen on the paper:

Dear Mom,

If you hadn't been there for me at the funeral and later, I would have killed myself. You were right not to leave me alone, to stay for a week until the drugs kicked in. When we came home from the church, I was looking for objects to hurt myself with. I coveted the hose in the backyard, knowing that carbon monoxide would be easy, a long dream until death. But it didn't have to be easy. I knew I deserved worse, deserved the pain Sofie felt. Lye or acid or pills or scissors or a fall from the second floor to the entryway would have been fine. But I couldn't reach for anything because you were there, guiding me through all that pain.

I don't say it enough, or maybe I haven't said it for years. I don't know why the words hurt me so much, as if "I love you" is a knife coming out of my throat. I feel the love, though, for you and for Sofie and for Mark and for Dee and for Tim. I feel it inside, but I can't grow it. I can't make it come out the way I want to.

So, this letter, Mom, and all of my best feelings are for you. Without you, I'd be dead, in every sense that a person can be dead. Deader than Sofie is because she could say it, Mom. She was like you, your baby more than I am. She was born saying "I love you" to the world.

Jenna slammed the cover shut and turned to the window, unable to keep the tears away. Dr. Kovacic was wrong. Writing didn't help. It hurt. It would kill her faster than lye.

Her breath grew shallow, sweat formed on her forehead, and she bit down on her lower lip to keep it from shaking. And then, there it was, the drug finally rising up and covering her whole, pressing her softly into the car seat, helping her unclench her muscles. She tucked a strand of hair behind her ear. Sitting up straight, she turned and set the journal in the backseat, putting the pen back in her purse. Plucking *Daisy Miller* out of the tape player, she fitted it back into its plastic box and put it in the backseat next to her journal. She could make it to Jolie's store. Then she would make it to the El Tovar Hotel. She would make it to the Grand Canyon after all.

"The Grand Canyon is worth all this driving, Jenna. It's amazing. Wait until you see it," Tim said, putting his hand back on her thigh, rubbing gently.

She nodded, agreeing. She would wait for everything until she saw it.

"HERE. THAT'S IT," Jenna said, pointing at the storefront, the name LEHMBERG'S STATIONERY AND SUNDRIES written in gold script on the front glass. After checking in his rearview mirror, Tim stopped the car, and they both looked out Jenna's window to stare at the store. Taped next to the door were a number of flyers—for a Christmas and cactus sing-along, a New Year's Eve meditation at the South Rim, a ritual at the Navajo Reservation, a Christian peace festival, and a long-past autumn bake sale for the Pine Flat Junior High soccer team. Below these was a NOW HIRING sign, with a printed SEE WITHIN written below the block letters. As she stared, Jenna became aware of their reflection, the big white car, their dark heads, the glare of the buildings behind them.

Tim pulled into a parking spot in front of the store and turned off the motor. "Her name is Jolie. Right?" He undid his seat belt.

"That's right." Jenna unlocked her door and opened

it, stepping out into the dry air. Blinking, she looked up and down the street, seeing other businesses like this one, the kind that depended on tourists. There was an antiques store with hutches and highboys and bright potted plants neatly arranged on the sidewalk. Next door, the bells on a candy store tinkled as two kids ran out clutching caramel apples. Hung outside the flag store across the street were half-priced Christmas flags and brand-new Valentine's banners.

"Let's go," Tim said.

Through the window, Jenna saw Jolie talking with an older couple, both wearing tidy straw hats that tied under their chins.

She and Tim stepped up on the sidewalk and Tim pulled open the door for Jenna, a blast of cool air whooshing past. A bell *ding-dong*ed metallically as they passed through, a polite warning for whoever was behind the counter.

Jolie looked up and smiled, raising a finger. "That'll be twenty seventy-nine," she said to the couple. The man made a joke about prices, passed Jolie the money in exact change, and then he and his wife left with their purchases clutched to their bodies, his wrinkled, spotted hand careful on her upper back.

"You're here!" Jolie moved from behind the counter, her arms held as wide as they had been on Christmas Eve. She and Jenna hugged, pulled apart, and then turned to Tim.

"Tim, this is my cousin Jolie Ventre. Jolie, Tim Passanante. We teach together."

Jolie's left eyebrow rose a tiny bit, but she didn't smile or say "I bet you do more than teach together." Jenna wondered why she'd invoked *teach* rather than *went out* or the boring but still true *good friends* phrases.

Her cousin let the second pass, holding out her hand to Tim. "It's nice to meet you."

"Jenna told me you paint."

Jolie nodded. "I'm really excited to show you my work."

As Jolie spoke, Jenna remembered Sofie, so pleased as she showed Jenna her Crayola drawings, her weepy watercolors, her glued macaroni-and-red-bean mosaics. For her third-grade yarn-and-fabric self-portrait, she drew in a face with a wide smile and blue eyes, the hair red and wild and three-dimensional. Like Sofie, Jolie hadn't developed a sense of shame or fear of judgment about her own work. Not like Jenna, who had hidden the poems and short stories she wrote in college, and now journaled only when she knew she could tuck the black-and-white-marbled folders away, just as she'd done in the car, hiding what she'd written even from herself.

"That's great. I don't do much that's creative," Tim said. He shifted on his feet, moving closer to Jenna.

Jolie began to speak, but just then the door opened, the bell *ding-dong*ed, and a large man carrying a bag of cleaning supplies walked in. He gave a little wave. "Got a load here." He walked to the counter and set the bag down, smoothing back the few long strands on his head with a thick hand. Tucking in his shirt and adjusting his name tag, he turned to them and held out a hand. "Ralph Lehmberg. You must be Jolie's cousin. Good to meet you."

Ralph's handshake was strong, and Jenna realized that Jolie must have been truly excited about their visit. Waiting for it. Talking it up with Ralph. And Jenna had almost forgotten to show up, the Pine Flat exit off I-17 surprising her. She'd grabbed Tim's thigh, said, "Here. This one," just before they'd passed it by.

"That's right. Jenna Thomas. Nice to meet you. And this is my—Tim Passanante."

Tim ignored her second gaffe, shaking Ralph's hand. "Nice place you have here."

"Naw, just a tourist stop. People on their way to the canyon or the peaks. But it'll do." Ralph waved his hand at the door. "Take 'em to see your stuff, Jolie. It's one hell of a show. I'll hold down the fort."

Jolie went behind the counter to grab her purse, came back around, and motioned for Tim and Jenna to follow her. Saying good-bye to Ralph, they left the store. Jenna looked around for a car, but Jolie kept walking up the sidewalk.

"It's a small town, and this way, I have no commute," she said, turning back to Jenna and Tim. "My place is just up the street."

Tim took Jenna's hand, and they followed Jolie, who began giving them the tour. "This isn't Walnut Creek or anything. No Macy's. Really, Pine Flat's known for the bikers. And Route 66. Forests. Also, there's the Navajo

Depot. Something the government opened during WWII. They wanted the Navajo to work there, so they made hogans for them so they'd feel at home. Ha! It's closed up now. Some people say there's hazardous waste there."

Jenna looked at Tim, who grimaced.

"Why did you pick Pine Flat?" Jenna asked.

"I didn't," Jolie said, stopping so they could catch up, and they all walked three abreast down the empty sidewalk. "My car broke down here. I was trying to make it back to Flagstaff. Ralph ended up giving me a lift, and, well, here I am."

Jolie turned down another street and then stopped in front of a house that was dwarfed by two brick buildings. "Wow," said Tim. "Someone must have fought to keep this from getting torn down."

Pulling her keys out of her purse, Jolie nodded. "Ralph's mom, Sylvie, lived here for fifty years. From the time she was married to the day she died. In my room, no less. Natural causes. Ralph was just getting ready to rent the place out when my car broke down." She unlocked the door and opened it, letting Jenna and Tim enter. "It was like it wasn't an accident. Meant to be."

As Jolie put her purse down and turned on lights, Jenna looked around the small living room. Though it was dark from the forced shade of the two taller buildings on either side, a gash of light swooped in from the front and back windows. On the walls were oil paintings she assumed were her cousin's work, landscapes of red earth, green trees, cities emerging from the background like enormous ships, lights and steel protruding from the skyline. Over the mantel hung a painting of the Grand Canyon, envisioned exactly the way Jenna had always imagined it, the way it should be, layers of red earth stacked up over the deepening crevasse.

"Beautiful," Tim said. "This is a wonderful rendering. It's like I'm there."

Jolie blushed and smiled, trying to hide her embarrassment with talk. "I did the one of the canyon over a couple of days. I was staying at this really terrible lodge about a mile and a half from the rim, so I was desperate to get out each morning. I just sat there and painted."

Walking around the room and staring at Jolie's work, Jenna wondered what it might be like to focus on the thing that made you feel, well, alive. What would it feel like to spend two days simply painting? Homing in on one thing, giving it form and feeling. Making something out of nothing. But she knew what that was like. She'd done that exact thing with Sofie. Jenna had given Sofie life and then spent years intent on her daughter, watching and worrying and nurturing. Jenna kept track of play dates and homework assignments and soccer matches. When Sofie went to Cal, Jenna realized she just had to pretend her child was all right, on schedule, doing well, safe. There was no way she could have possibly kept track of Sofie's every move. So grown up, Sofie would have withheld, avoided telling her mother about frat parties and sex with boys who might not have been around more than one night. She would never have told Jenna about sudden trips in rickety cars to Santa Cruz or Big Sur, sleeping illegally on the beach in thin sleeping bags.

Once, Jenna knew Sofie's every single act, but when she went away, there were days and then months when Jenna was powerless to change anything, as she had been in the end.

She could not save her own daughter, and now she knew that Sofie was never hers alone, never what she should have put all her energy into. Sofie was her own creation. No matter what Jenna had done for or given her, Sofie crafted her own life. Fallen in love. Bought a ticket to Bali. Died all by herself.

"Wonderful," Jenna whispered.

Tim put his hand on Jenna's back. "Really great, Jolie."

Jenna could feel both of them looking at her, and she swallowed. "I'm so impressed."

"I have a whole studio in the back. It used to be a garage—one of those small one-car things. Ralph said I could paint it, and he helped me string up lights so I could work. Do you want to see?"

A womb, Jenna thought, a place where things were born, a dark place where people thought up what they wanted to see, what they wanted to become.

"Sure." Tim led Jenna down the hall. "You've got, what? Three bedrooms here?"

"Small ones, but yeah. Ralph cut me a deal, I'll tell you that."

Outside, the air seemed even hotter than when they'd

walked up the street, so light and dry Jenna thought she could catch it and crack it in her palm. Someone— probably Ralph—had paved the small yard in flat, whitish concrete, only a small circle of cactus and palm tree–type plants in the middle, the dirt hard and sandy. Under a large scraggly oak was a wooden garage. It reminded Jenna of the house Little Red Riding Hood's grandmother would have lived in; door in front, small, square window on the side, a pointed roof, two wooden steps leading to a rickety stoop. Jolie opened the door and turned on a light and then a fan, closing the door behind Jenna and Tim. The room was cool from the tree's shade, the fan pushing the cooler air around the rectangle of space. All along the finished walls paint- ings were hung, the reds, oranges, purples startling against the white Sheetrock. Crimson rock against a yellow sky, lavender wands of sage against earth tones, yellow clouds against the coming night. Jenna felt her breath stick hard in her throat, a fork in her voice box. She hadn't seen color like that since Bali.

She let out a sound, a *whewww,* and Tim nodded, agreeing with what he thought was a compliment.

"You're on to something here," he said. "These are different from the ones inside. Louder."

Jolie laughed, walking to the one where the sky looped in vermilion circles, the rocks brown and onyx in the background. "That's it. I've been needing a name. I'll call it my 'loud' sequence." She laughed again, but she was pleased. Jenna wanted to race out the door, salty despair on her tongue.

Tim looked at her, and as she had been doing with her students since the funeral, she faked it. By not breathing for a moment, she pushed color back into her cheeks. Her eyes glistened with a sheen of tears, making her look, she knew, sparkly. She searched in her throat for her happy teacher voice, the one she used when they wouldn't move their desks into groups or open their novels to the right page or answer a question about theme. "Oh, come on!" she'd goad. "What's going on?"

To give herself more time, she bit her lip and walked closer to the nearest painting. The oil paint was thick and ridged. Jenna wondered what the canvas would feel like between her lips, teeth, on her tongue.

"I never knew," she said to Jolie, and turned to her cousin. And she meant it. Who would have known by looking at the two girls on the hearth playing with dolls that one of them would re-create the world in more color than the eye could bear? Who would have known the other would want to take the pictures from the wall, smash them into parts, let her cousin feel what it was like to lose what she had made. Jenna wanted everyone to know. To feel it. To suffer.

But that wasn't true. What Jenna really wanted was the *lap lap* of water under a Balinese cabana in the moments before awakening, the clear white space where nothing has happened, not yet, just like at the beginning of a novel before the words stream down the page and the plot takes the characters in sentence arms and squeezes them tight.

127

• • •

SHE AND TIM walked back to Ralph's store with Jolie, saying their goodbyes on the sidewalk, and then got back in the Taurus and headed up I-40 to the 64 turnoff. After a few miles, they left the forest behind, Humphreys Peak just a tiny triangle on the horizon. The landscape was empty, arid, the road an asphalt line in sand and stone. Jenna glanced at Tim, who clutched the steering wheel as before and concentrated on the road. He smiled, but didn't say much beyond reading aloud highway signs or asking her for a bottle of water, and she imagined that he was full of Jolie's colors, amazed by the way she could swirl the imagination into substance. Jenna bit her lip and then punched on the cassette player, *Daisy Miller* carrying them along until there was more forest and then the signs for the South Rim, the El Tovar Hotel.

As they pulled up in front of the hotel, she was reminded of all her Girl Scout camping days, the lodge dark with wood and held, it seemed, to the base of the canyon with a solid river-rock foundation. They parked the car and entered the lobby, Tim going to the desk to talk with the clerk. He leaned against the counter, clicking his credit card on the wooden desk. The lobby was vast and wide, and Jenna could almost hear the echoes from around a campfire. She thought of all her Girl Scout friends, sitting in a circle, wearing the Indian vests they'd made out of brown felt and beads and black vinyl strips. Feathers stuck up straight from their headbands, which had begun to slip down their foreheads. They sang,

Just a boy and girl in a little canoe,
with the moon shining all around.
They paddled and paddled so,
you couldn't even hear a sound.

With each line, there was an accompanying move-ment, the arms paddling; a palm in the air, circling to invoke the moon; a hand cupped at the ear to listen for nothing. Eventually, the boy tries to kiss the girl, and she jumps out of the canoe to swim home, the girls all arcing their arms in a sustained freestyle stroke. Did they sing that song because it was about the outdoors or because it was a good morality tale? The troop leaders, Mrs. Kessler and Mrs. Connelly, nodded in approval as the girl stayed chaste time after time.

"Okay. Let's go." Tim jangled a key—not a card key but an old-fashioned metal one on a tiny Thunderbird key ring. "Our room is ready."

He walked ahead of her, excited, looking back over his shoulder. Jenna glanced over at the young woman behind the desk, who followed Tim with her eyes. *I bet she thinks I'm his mother,* Jenna thought, falling farther behind like a mother would, anxious for her strong son to lift the bags and haul them into the room. She and Dee had always made fun of the men in her department who ended up with students—Rich Macher and his young Korean wife, old Ron Meehan and his svelte Dutch girlfriend. Once, Ramón Fuego showed up at a party with the former student-body president on his arm, a girl who'd just been accepted to USC. If any of the women faculty had done something like that, it would be hidden, pushed underground. But as Dee said, "What besides their bodies would I want with the male students? They don't even read their homework."

But Tim was older, read his homework, obviously, and was hired tenure-track. He wasn't a student slouching in the back row with his baseball cap pulled over his eyes. He was a man. He actually understood *Catch-22*. He knew why Yossarian was Armenian.

Jenna sped up, straightening her back and ignoring the whispers she imagined coming from behind the counter, and followed Tim to the Taurus.

"WE HAVE THE hike tomorrow. They'll pick us up at eight." Tim unpacked his suitcase, putting his shirts and underwear in the bottom drawer, leaving the top one for her. When Mark had unpacked, he'd always taken the best hangers, the ones with clips for pants, claimed the top drawer of every bureau, and spread out his shaving stuff on the bathroom countertop. He'd also found the side of the bed in the best position for the television and the lamp, Jenna having to reach over him to turn everything off when he'd fallen into snoring sleep.

Tim zipped up his bag and stowed it in the closet. "Aren't you going to unpack?"

Jenna stood up and grabbed her bag. She heaved it onto the bed, and then saw for the first time the name tag she'd filled out and put on the handle of her bag for her trip to Bali. Why hadn't she noticed it before? Why hadn't she slashed it off with kitchen scissors the minute she came home to Monte Veda? Or at her mother's house? But there it was, blue as the ocean, next to her Southern Airlines tag from her flight to Phoenix. Closing her eyes, she felt the drumbeat pulse in her stomach, or maybe it was her bowels, liver. Something important going bad, turning on her, pushing out cells that would only hurt her, harm her. But would that be so awful? If her stomach became cancerous, liquid, useless, then she wouldn't have to be here anymore, in this place where Sofie wasn't. If her bowels blackened and died or her liver tore apart, peppered with holes, she could check out legally, officially, with no shame. She thought of the meditations cancer patients did, seeing their T cells attacking the cancer cells, envisioning the chemotherapy as tiny bombs that exploded the disease. Could she do the reverse? Could she imagine the cancer being born, thriving, taking over everything? Could she will herself to die?

"Jenna," Tim said, reaching for her, pulling her close.

She stood straight, her eyes still shut, holding herself tight and still. She wanted to shake off his arms, but she didn't want to move or breathe into the moment where this great idea would pass, her stomach, bowels, liver, even uterus, ovaries, spleen on the cusp of malfunction.

"Jenna," he said, more softly, unclenching her hands from her suitcase pull, shifting her onto his lap. "It's okay. I'm here."

His hands on her arms, neck, back, she let the air out

131

of her lungs, feeling how every part of her was fine, whole, intact. Only a fullness in her center, which could be what? Sorrow? Relief? Both? As she leaned into Tim, she knew she wasn't bruised and burned or diseased. As of this second, her body worked, the blood moving in its red sluice stream, the perfect combination of red and white cells. Her heartbeat, *one, two, one, two,* in a perfect sinus rhythm. For this moment, her skin was elastic, giving, the nerves and sweat glands functioning under the dermis. And look! After a few moments of his strong, solid embrace, even her brain picked up the smooth glide of Tim's hand under her shirt, her skin tingling with tiny bumps of pleasure, her nipples hardening, her vagina slick. So for this second, she let herself forget that she wanted it all to stop and lay against Tim, falling with him to the bed, letting her body have what it wanted.

THE WHITE VAN was packed—Tim and Jenna, plus three couples from Kansas City, all of whom were part of the church group here for the peace festival on the thirty-first.

"You should come," one woman said, adjusting her long black seat belt. "We're praying for peace in the Middle East."

Tim looked at her, his left eyebrow raised, but he didn't say anything, busying himself with the map their tour guide, Len, had handed out.

"Diane. My name's Diane." Diane held out her hand. "This is Will."

Jenna took the woman's soft, plump hand. "I'm Jenna, and this is Tim." She finally managed to avoid using *my* followed by any noun, knowing she hadn't a clue what would make sense.

"Where is it?" Jenna asked.

"It's just down a bit, still on the South Rim. We'd had it all to ourselves, but I guess there's some kind of meditation on New Year's Eve, as well. But share and share alike. It's all for the good."

Good of what? Jenna wanted to say. Would it bring back her daughter? What use was peace when it was too late for those who'd already been exploded into bits? But Diane was so earnest, her round white face with her dollops of red cheeks so concerned lest peace escape anyone.

"That's true," Jenna mumbled. She smiled but opened her map, trying to follow the red line of the East Canyon Drive, the twenty-six-mile drive that they would take today. But nothing seemed to make sense at all, the canyon opening down into a darker green, nothing like the wide brownish-red to the left of the van, a true canyon, cavern, crevasse. She could imagine herself tumbling down the bumps and slides and turns, hitting until she didn't feel anything, her skin as raw as the dirt she'd smack down on.

"It's just that people don't understand how important it is." Diane had continued talking, and Jenna looked up and blinked.

"What?"

"Peace."

"We don't understand how important peace is?" Jenna asked, angry now, the seat belt riding under her neck, making it uncomfortable to breathe. "Why do you think you have the right—" But then Tim's hand was on her arm.

"Look, this is where we can stay next time. Phantom Ranch." He pointed to a dot in the middle of the dark green. Jenna's heart beat to the pain caused by the seat belt. She wanted to tell this Diane a thing or two about peace. In fact, she'd like to pummel Diane's face until more than her cheeks were red, but that, she knew, would defeat the purpose.

"Okay, folks. We're off to our first stop, Yaki Point, and an amazing view of the inner canyons. Let's take off!" Len sat down in the wide driver's seat, closed the van door, and started the engine. Diane was quieted by the hum of the motor, smiling at her friends, as well as Jenna and Tim, the potential converts. But converts to what? Why was it that a Jehovah's Witness or the white-haired televangelist on Channel 52 or a persistent propagator of any kind of "peace" made Jenna want to rise up and scream? She'd always felt this way, long before Sofie's murder. Once, while watching Sofie slide down a structure at Montclair Park, a woman had sat down next to Jenna, smiling.

"Do you believe in coincidences?" the woman had asked, tucking her long print skirt around her legs.

Sofie waved to Jenna from the ladder, and Jenna waved back as she thought. But she thought too long, letting Sofie, the squealing children, and the woman's face fade away. Some days, everything seemed preordained, plotted out, contrived by a crazy god. The next, she felt everything was random, a wild accident in the swirling universe, people butting up against situations like tiny toys in a child's game. *Why am I at this park at this instant?* she was thinking as the woman pulled out a flyer. *Why am I here for this specific conversation?*

The woman handed her the flyer. "We pull to us what we need. Like I was broke a couple of weeks ago, really desperate. And I meditated on it, and the next day, I got a check in the mail. That's what we talk about in our group. You can have whatever you want."

Jenna had stared at the flyer and then the woman, shaking her head. Had she wanted Mark to leave her? Had she asked for that? Had she purposefully focused on Sofie until he couldn't stand being alone in his own family? What else? She'd wanted her job, but she'd worked hard for that; no asking there. Did the one egg and one sperm that had made Sofie come forth because Jenna had asked for her? Wasn't that just luck? And who was this woman, anyway, walking around a park, making promises to strangers, telling them they could have what they wanted?

Unclenching her jaw, Jenna stared with the look she'd developed for people like this woman, who wanted one idea to explain the world. "Please leave me alone."

"But all I wanted—"

"Leave me alone."

"But—"

Stopping her mad scrabble up the climbing structure, Sofie turned to Jenna, her hands gripping rope, her feet perfectly aligned on a beam. Afternoon sun glinted through Monterey pines, Sofie's face shaded, luminous, waiting.

Jenna looked at the woman, wordless, and watched as she took back the flyer Jenna held out, stood up, and walked away. Anger made it all happen, made Jenna's words sharp, her hand rigid as she held the flyer. And then Sofie's face made her stop, hold back hateful words, judgment, accusations. None of this was a fluke, chance, a whim. No coincidence at all.

"THIS IS THE Grandview Point." Len swept his arm along the vista. "We've barely gotten this tour started, and this is the best overlook of the whole canyon. But I promise, at Lipan Point you'll get to see the entire geologic sequence of the canyon. Something to look forward to!" Len began pointing to various spots, moving off with Diane and her group.

"What do you think?" Tim squeezed her waist.

Jenna searched for words, but the answer she needed to give Tim was that she wasn't thinking. Opening up before her, through the scrubby Ponderosa and pinyon pines and Gambel oaks, the canyon below flung itself wide like her heart, red and raw and whole, and sucked all her voice away. She felt as though she were in the middle, floating between gaping lips, knowing that within an instant she would fall. But the air here was light, dry, buoyant. If she didn't breathe out, she might float forever, held between rock and sky, the water far below.

"Can you imagine god's plan when he made this?" Diane pushed up behind them, having broken away from Len and his discussion of the Anasazi, the tribe that disappeared from the face of the earth. Jenna closed her eyes.

"More like geology. Plate tectonics. Floods," Tim said, tightening his arm around Jenna. "More like a lot of time."

"But time is his plan, too," said Diane. "He knew in his infinite wisdom that the rain and floods and sun would create this masterpiece."

Jenna pulled away from Tim and turned to Diane. "So then all war is part of god's plan. Why bother with your peace festival? This very minute is god's plan, if we follow your logic."

Diane stepped back, her pink cheeks paling. "Oh."

Tim turned and grabbed Jenna's hand. "Well—"

But Jenna wasn't through, hating Diane and her god with his fancy plan. If Diane was right, then Sofie was blown up on purpose, the events orchestrated by a sick-tempered deity with nothing better to do. "And my daughter? She died, Diane. She was blown up in Bali. So god had his hand in that? He planned that?" She swung her arm as Len had done earlier, as if she were leading a tour on destruction. "What do you say about that?"

Diane's eyes filled, a hand at her mouth. Tim squeezed Jenna's fingers, pulling her closer, but Jenna felt her heart was on fire, the canyon living inside her now, everything burned to the edges and empty.

Hearing Jenna's tense, clipped words, Diane's husband, Will, turned from the edge and walked to his wife. "Hon?" When Diane didn't say anything, he turned to Jenna and Tim, cocking his head.

"Tell your wife," Jenna began, ignoring Tim's grip. "Tell your wife—to leave me alone."

Because of the way Will understood, taking his wife's arm and pulling her toward Len, Jenna could see this kind of thing must have happened before, at parties and in the pasta aisle at Safeway and at PTA meetings near the coffee urn. Diane wanted to save them all, make it better by making it worse, by giving god all the answers to the questions that had no answers. Why were we human? Why did we fight? Why did we kill each other every single day?

Jenna closed her eyes and leaned against Tim's side, but even behind her lids, she could see the chasm below them, the thick crumbling lines of red soil, the dark strip of water at the bottom.

AFTER DINNER IN the El Tovar's dark, vast restaurant and a walk along the Rim Trail that hung on the very edge of the canyon—the night a sheen of gray hovering over the canyon, arcing blue into a black haze with pinpoints of a million stars—Jenna lay awake in bed. On his side and turned toward her, Tim was asleep, his breath a narrative of sound, deep inhales and exhales, pauses, a dream laugh, a light snore, and then the deep inhales again. After trying to talk with her about what had happened with Diane, he'd fallen asleep like a child, talking one minute, unconscious the next.

Jenna had finally fallen asleep, too, but she'd jolted awake from a dream, one where she was in a dorm room, her college dorm room, waiting for the first day of school. She seemed to have many roommates, all of them excited and clamoring, all young and expectant, their suitcases unpacked on their laps. As they sat, Jenna could feel the knowledge she would get—the lectures, the ideas, the words, the stories—pressing against her chest, as if knowledge were something she could hold.

But no one moved from her bed, sitting for what seemed like hours, and, irritated, Jenna stood up and walked the space between the bunk beds, asking, "Aren't you going to unpack? Don't you want to get ready?"

None of the girls paid any attention, swinging their hair, laughing. Finally, Jenna stopped at the door, turned back once to look at her dorm mates, and then moved out into the lush green canopy of the campus quad, closing her eyes, smiling into the idea she would find any second. In a moment. Right now.

"Do you have that pack of postcards?" Tim asked as he dug through his almost-packed suitcase. "The ones from Slide Rock?"

Jenna stood at the mirror, brushing out her hair, which seemed somehow more lush in Arizona, thicker, darker, her hair browning with the winter. She needed a cut and, most likely, a dye job. The darkening strands were probably some shade of gray she couldn't see because her eyes were failing. Two veins pulsed down near her groin, and she pressed her palm against her round belly.

"Jenna?"

"What?"

He stood up and rubbed his forehead with his finger-tips. She could imagine him doing that in a class when a student asked for the billionth time when a due date was or if he had a stapler or a paper clip or even glue. She was tiring him as she had tired Mark, not responding soon enough, figuring it all out too late. But then Tim looked up, smiled, his skin red where he had rubbed.

"The postcards."

"Oh," she said, putting down her brush and walking to her purse. "Here."

He took the bag and slid the cards out halfway to his hand. They'd seen it all: the North Rim, Bright Angel Canyon, Columbus Point, Horseshoe Mesa, Slide Rock State Park, Mormon Lake, Little Colorado River Gorge. After their tour of the canyon with Len and the Kansas City Christians, they'd spent two days touring the country, listening to Jenna's books, buying post-cards, eating meals at little roadside diners. The weather had been wonderful, so different from the solid gray skies of the Bay Area, the air here crisp, cool, clear, and light, the clouds full and hanging in an immense blue sky. The land was dry and pared close to the topsoil, everything that grew a miracle. No over-abundance of life, no excess, no waste. And for a few minutes at a time, Jenna had forgotten the rich foliage of Bali. Or forgotten to remember.

Tim put the cards back and put the bag on top of his packed clothes. "We'd better get going. Checkout is at twelve."

Jenna nodded and went to her suitcase. From here, they would drive to Phoenix and then catch a plane to Oakland. In less than two weeks, she would be in a classroom listening to another set of students say the exact same things that this semester's bunch had; she and Dee would sit together at countless meetings. But Tim would be with her, too, and for him she'd pretend to be interested in the agenda. He was still excited. He still cared. It would rain and rain all of January and February and half of March, and by then all she would be able to do is wait for summer vacation.

But why? Why would summer vacation matter? Sofie wouldn't come home, even for long weekends, pushing the front door wide and using her Jack Nicholson voice: "I'm baaack!"

Jenna wouldn't plan a vacation for just the two of them. Mark wouldn't come over to see Sofie, the three of them sitting around the patio table, drinking iced tea and laughing about the way Sofie's environmental biology teacher slammed his books on the table when someone walked into class late. None of that would happen, and then it would be fall semester again, and she would be with yet another batch of students asking her the exact same things for which she didn't have the answers.

"Do you think the lodge would hold our bags?" she began.

"What do you mean?" Tim zipped up his suitcase and stood straight.

"Our plane doesn't leave until, what? Almost twelve tonight?"

"Yeah. We're going to check out Flagstaff and Phoenix today." From his back pocket Tim pulled a map—the same one he'd been using all week—and Jenna thought of her father, wearing his blue fishing hat, smoking his pipe, sitting in the driver's seat of the Buick Sportwagon as they drove across Utah, the salt flat on either side. How he loved to pull over and consult the map, finally tapping the bottom of his pipe bowl on their destination and saying, "Here we go!" and then pulling back on the almost-empty highway.

"But what if we stayed here? For that meditation thing."

Tim lowered the map and stared at her for a second. "You want to go to the meditation thing? Isn't that where that woman will be? That Diane? You don't want to run into her again, do you?"

She shook her head and sat down on the edge of the bed. "No. She's going to the peace festival. I just thought—if we left at seven, seven thirty, we could still make it. It's really only three-plus hours to Phoenix, and the plane doesn't leave until midnight. There's enough time for the security checkpoints and lines."

"What is the meditation for, anyway?" He pushed his hair away from his smooth forehead.

On one of her trips down to the lobby, Jenna had found the same flyer that had been taped to the window of Lehmberg's stationery store, where Jolie worked. This time, she'd read it closely, taking the sheet and sitting down in one of the chairs close to the entryway. It read:

The world is in need of careful contemplation. Our energies need to be focused to engender harmonious change. Come to a group meditation at the rim of one of most beautiful natural wonders, and let's focus together.

Jenna had put it down, blinking against the bright light fanning in from the large front door. It was the same thing as Diane's festival, but quieter, with no real message. Just energy. Good energy. The kind that could make people think. The kind that would keep people from turning themselves or cars into bombs.

She put her hands on her hips. "It's just a good way to bring in the New Year. Hope. That kind of thing."

Tim snorted. "We'd have to really haul ass down there. There's the car rental place, too. And what are we supposed to do for six hours?"

Jenna looked at him, his long legs in black jeans, his white shirt untucked and unbuttoned, his smooth, pale skin, his brown nipples like petite dimes on his chest. What hadn't his body given her these past months? The forgetting as he held her, the way she'd been able to ignore the past. With Tim, her body was a system that worked, her head letting her alone, allowing her to feel the pulses and breaths and urges inside them both. She was able to forget who she was and what she wanted and needed and had to have, all of her desires funneling into one urge in a place that almost seemed not connected to her. In bed with him, Jenna was able to forget her outer self, the lines and marks, the very things she focused on when she stood in front of the mirror, plucking gray hair. She became only what was going on inside, Tim her partner on this amazing ride.

She could stay here for six more hours, six good hours with Tim. And then she would walk to the rim and close her eyes.

"Call up to the front desk."

"What?"

Standing, she walked to him and slid her hand up his chest, still young-man hairless, still untouched, nothing hurting him yet, exploding at him, ripping into him. She leaned her cheek against his heart, listening to the pound of muscle and blood. "Call up to the desk," she said into his warm skin. "See what their extended-stay rate is. Tell them we only need six hours."

"SO EVERYONE CLOSE your eyes. Relax. Get comfortable. It's really crowded, but try to get into your own personal space." The leader of the meditation, a New Age cowboy, wore a white button-down shirt, well-worn jeans, and boots. He stood on a platform feet away from the rim. Jenna knew that in years, a decade or a little more, the ground beneath it would crumble away, the platform falling plank by plank into the canyon below. Where she and Tim sat now might be gone, too, no evidence that any of them had been there at all.

She looked at Tim, but he already had his eyes closed. He sat cross-legged, his hands resting on his knees, his back straight. Before she closed her eyes, she turned to her left and noticed that about 250 yards away, another leader now stood against the pale black sky to lead the peace festival. Somewhere, Diane sat with her husband, Will, desperate to give peace a chance.

"Come on, now," the meditation leader intoned softly. "Close your eyes. There is a lot going on here tonight, but we can get past that. Close your eyes, breathe. Find yourself in your body."

Jenna smiled and hit her knee against Tim's. He nudged her back, and she sneaked one last look at him, loving the way his lips were turned up in a smile even as he tried to center himself and find the rhythm of his breath. All she'd been in for the past six hours was her body, feeling as if she were in his body, his excitement, too. The only thing she could feel right now was her own skin, the soft flesh of her vagina, the smooth tip of his penis, his arms, his tongue.

Turning to look at the people next to her, Jenna saw that they'd all finally closed their eyes, their bodies grown still. But not their minds. She knew that. Inside them were swirls of memory and judgment and fear and hope and joy and future plans. And control. A need to keep things the way they could be. Should be. Had to be. Probably half of them weren't really at the Grand Canyon at all. Instead, they'd flown themselves home or were driving down I-17. Maybe some were already home, fighting with their teenagers about the parties they'd had while the house was parentless. Maybe they were thinking about past Christmases, fights over the ham that fell on the kitchen linoleum. Or they'd gone back to work, imagining the piles of quarterly reports or messages on their desks.

Some of them, like her, were thinking about all they had lost—time, love, children.

"Close your eyes. Breathe," the leader said. "Imagine your breath as a white light, something you pull from your stomach to your mouth with each inhale. With each exhale, slide it back to your stomach. Close your eyes." The leader seemed to be looking at Jenna, and she wanted to shake Tim out of his reverie and tell him she'd made a ridiculous mistake. This wasn't what she wanted at all. She wanted to see Flagstaff and downtown Phoenix, after all. From the other group, the words *peace* and *god* and *hope* and *faith* were flung up like baseballs and batted over the meditators. How ridiculous! How she now just wanted to be in the car.

But it was too late for that. They were boxed in by zombies sitting cross-legged on the cool red earth, listening to some Bozo on a platform. Under her legs, she felt the pebbles and grass she'd missed when she'd swept the ground with her foot. Her heart thrummed;

her tailbone pulsed uncomfortably, which always happened when she sat for too long or on something hard—always, ever since she'd had Sofie.

"Let it go. Let it all go. Feel yourself become full of white light that you pull up slowly with each breath."

Jenna gripped her knees and then closed her eyes, opening them right away, and then closing them again. It almost hurt to press her lids together, and she could still see the leader, his arms held up before them. What had she been thinking? Why had she wanted to sit here, the crazy peace celebrants too close, all these quiet, resting, focused people next to her? She wasn't used to this. She was used to classes full of unfocused, irritable, bored students, their eyes shifting, their feet tapping. So impatient. So desperate to get out of college and into their own lives. Well, they had no idea. Life could be over in a flash, a burst of fire, and all they'd have was that terrible time in her classroom.

"Starting with your stomach, pull the white light up. Up into your solar plexus. You feel it there, just under your ribs. Breathe it in. . . . Yes. And then with your next breath, breathe the white light up to your chest. Feel it there. . . . Right. Breathe."

Her eyeballs burned under her closed lids, the white light in her chest throbbing against her bones. She licked her lips and then closed her mouth, trying to pull air through her nose. Even at night, the air was dry, filled with red dust she could taste at the back of her throat. Water. She needed water.

"The light is in your chest, and now, breathe it to your

throat. Do you feel it there, so light, so bright? Yes. Breathe."

How had it been, she wondered, as the light flooded everywhere in her body, for Sofie in all that light and fire? Had she been able to breathe? To move? Did she try to crawl her way out to Robert? Did she cover her nose and mouth and take in shallow breaths?

"From your throat, move the light into your face and head—let it fill it all up. Behind your cheeks, forehead, all around to the base of your neck. Breathe."

The white light was inside Jenna, pulsing, luminous, grainy with brilliance. She knew this must be the light people saw at the end of the tunnel, the one that pulled people toward death, friends, family, Jesus, Mohammed, god at the other end, beckoning, calling. Who was there for Sofie? Mark and she and Lois were still alive, so it must have been Jenna's father, his arms folded across his skinny chest, tapping his foot as he had on Saturday mornings, wanting Lois and Jenna to hurry up so the weekend excursion to Tilden or Mount Diablo or Santa Cruz could begin. Did he wave? Did he recognize Sofie after all these dead years? He had to, that hair something no one, even in death, could forget. How he must have hugged her tight, pulling her still-beautiful, untouched, unburned soul to his own. *Thank you,* she thought. *Thanks, Dad.*

"Now you are filled with light. I want you to see your body awash in it, the pure light of love. With every inhale, you feel a wave rush up, and with every exhale, you see a wave rush down, like the tide. Ever flowing, everlasting, the love that is in all of us, always. The love that is in the world if we could all find it. In and out, breathe the love that is everywhere."

With her next exhale, Jenna found herself next to Sofie and her father in the light, watched as they embraced, Sofie's red hair the same shade as his own. Over her father's shoulder, Jenna saw Sofie's crooked, wide-toothed smile. They stood apart from Jenna, not noticing her, together in something she couldn't imagine or intrude on, not yet.

"And now, while you breathe, the light flowing and filling you, I want you to go to a place that needs this light, that needs love. It could be a city, a town, a country, or the whole world. Find that place in your mind, and let your light wash over it with every inhale and every exhale."

For a second, Jenna pulled out of the scene with her father and Sofie, confused, the light shutting down in her panic. Where should she go? Bali? Afghanistan? Iraq? Bosnia? Rwanda? West Oakland? But no. Yes. There. It was there in that circle of light in the place where her dead loved ones were, her best people. But it wasn't they who needed the love. It was she, standing apart, clenching her hands, so scared, unable to answer Sofie's smile with her own. After all, look at what had happened to Sofie, blown up while on vacation. And her father, heart attack just when his life of ease was to begin, he and Lois ready for innumerable excursions, every day, not just Saturday.

So she let the light flow from the top of her head to

herself in her vision, let the Jenna in her mind relax, unclench her hands, stop yearning for the people who embraced before her. The light in her mind growing brighter, Jenna smiled back at Sofie, who waved, tilted her head back in a laugh. Jenna's father lit his pipe, sucking in large smoke rings. Together they watched one sail up so high it disappeared into the bright white.

Breathing in and out, Jenna then looked at herself, saw that she was all right. She was—she was whole and beautiful, even though she'd lost her most important part, her child, the person Jenna thought made her alive. In this translucent, lovely light, she could feel she wasn't dying, not yet. Everything inside her worked, functioned, moved, divided, coursed, pumped, pulsed. She was just as alive as she had been all those years ago when this lovely girl, this tall, freckled girl in front of her, was born. Jenna almost laughed along with Sofie. Not even her wrinkles were that bad. Nor her hair or stomach or breasts. Not at all. Had she been focused so much on herself because of Tim's age? Who cared about how old he was? She was strong. Look!

Jenna took in a huge breath, feeling nothing but the pulse of love in her head. She watched herself, looked at her own body, still smooth and useful and . . . productive. In the circle of light, Jenna could see her own pulse, her blood, her heart under the skin. And deep inside herself, the love all around her, she understood what had been making her feel tired, sick, ill, dying. It wasn't only Sofie's death. It wasn't only the weight of grief. It wasn't menopause. No, Sofie was right beside her, holding on to her grandfather. Both turned to face Jenna now, their eyes alight. They knew. They saw. And so did she. All this feeling, all this wealth of symptoms, was pregnancy. A baby. The baby inside her. The baby that had been making her nauseous since . . . since she'd come home from Bali. Mark's baby. The baby she had conceived even as Sofie lay dead. The Bali baby, made over water and in sadness. It was Sofie's true sibling, all this time later.

Jenna jolted, the light wavering, but she clung on, needing her father and daughter for this last minute, even as she heard the leader begin to speak again. She wanted to ask them what to do, how to go on with this wonderful, horrible news, but she had no words that the light could hold. It was love, pure love. Her questions were fear. And as they looked at her one last time, she could feel their love for her, their encouragement, even as they turned, pulling the light with them, until all Jenna could see was a pinprick of light, the sunset of their souls on the horizon.

Six

They were in the car, speeding down Highway 180, the meditation having broken up, the peace festival just ended. Jenna couldn't think, could barely walk, Tim glancing at her sharply as he drove, his knuckles white ridges on the wheel.

What had she done? Sonata, Zoloft, wine, aspirin,

Tylenol, caffeine. So much sex. The baby she was carrying was probably twisted back into prior evolution, a reptile child with flippers. All her fault. All her fault. This is not how she was as a pregnant mother. Oh, no. With Sofie, she'd been so careful, eating exactly the right amount of vegetables and protein and fiber. She took an all-natural multivitamin, gave up coffee and alcohol and sugar. Every day, she walked half a mile, slowly, enjoying the sunshine, the slight lift in her pulse. And every night, she slept deeply, eight hours for her child.

As Tim drove, Jenna turned to the dark night outside the car and wished for the floaty calm of the meditation to come back to her. The enlightenment. The sense of knowing and understanding. The compassion for her own body. The epiphany of Sofie and her father. But all she had now was a rip of anxiety in her chest. How could she possibly have a baby? She who couldn't even keep one child alive. How was she supposed to go home with this news? How could she teach? Deal with her students? Deal with Mark? Mark! Was she supposed to tell him before or after she had an abortion? An abortion? She believed in them, every woman free to make her own decision, but she didn't want the scrape of metal taking something out of her. Something? A child. Yes, a child, even now. A child who could be like Sofie. Maybe was Sofie, come back to another life as quickly as she had gone out of it. And what about Tim? Could she expect him to take on not only her low self-esteem and her ever present grief, but another man's child, her ex-husband's child, her dead daughter's sibling? She'd end up pushing another man away for a child. None of it fit or made sense, and would certainly make less sense if she kept the baby and went off the Zoloft, her world turning sharp and ugly and real again.

She pressed her head against the glass, watching the desert night take over, creatures she couldn't see all around her burrowing and hunting and nursing young. Green exit signs flashed by, the bright white of numbers and names making her blink. Flagstaff, Pine Flat, Oak Creek Canyon.

"Take the exit!"

"What?" Tim turned to her, confused. "This is the way."

"I have to— Take the exit!"

Tim turned, taking the exit that connected them to I-40. "What are you doing, Jenna? We have to get to the airport. We don't have time for this."

Swallowing, Jenna tried to find the words. "I want you to drop me off at Jolie's."

Taking his foot off the accelerator for a moment and then pressing down hard, the car jolting and rumbling forward, Tim shook his head. "I don't understand."

"I can't go home. I just can't."

Tim took one hand off the wheel and pushed his hair back, his eyes fixed straight ahead on the highway. Jenna stared at him, looking for anger, but his face was slack, confused. He rubbed his forehead and then held the wheel tight again. His Adam's apple bobbed in his throat.

She closed her eyes, hoping to see what she had at the meditation—the white circle of light, her father, Sofie, love. She wanted that inspiration to come into the car and hold her through the next fifteen minutes, the minutes when she would be parked in front of Jolie's house, pulling her bags out, ringing the bell. Saying good-bye to Tim.

But there was nothing but darkness and the random flashes of color from lights outside her lids. She pressed her hand against her belly and knew she had to tell the truth, finally, to someone.

"I'm pregnant."

Again, he took his foot off the accelerator for a moment and then pressed hard, the car lurching toward Pine Flat.

"You're what?"

She took in a quick, harsh breath when she saw him begin to smile. "It's not yours."

"What?" He turned to her, his eyes black in the dim light of the car. "Whose is it?"

Then there was the air of Bali, the white gauzy curtain riffling over the bed, the water lap-splashing on the beach outside her cabana. In downtown Kuta, as rescuers dug through chunks of concrete and metal, pulling bodies out from underneath the wreckage, Mark lay on top of her, his hands on her body, just as they had always been.

"Mark's. In Bali. Before us."

Tim's shoulders relaxed for a second and then lifted. "Oh. Oh. When, Jenna?"

"It was grief, the past. It didn't happen again. We hadn't slept together for a long time before that—that part of our relationship was finally over."

He flicked a look at her, his mouth moving at a question he couldn't ask.

"Our divorce was confusing sometimes. Or we were lazy. It took Sofie growing up and becoming a woman for us to finally realize it was over. I don't know, Tim. But I promise you, we didn't sleep together while you and I were together."

She saw his chest heave under his shirt, his knuckles white. "I can see how that could happen, Jenna. That you and he— It kind of makes sense, I guess. But why Jolie's? Why can't you go home? I don't care about whose baby it is. I—I love you, Jenna."

"Oh, Tim. Why?" She shook her head. How could he love her? There wasn't enough of her around to love. Since Sofie had died, she'd felt like a flicker of smoke, easy to ignore, ready to dissolve into the air at the hint of wind.

He pushed his hair back, his mouth tight. After a few seconds of silence, he turned to her briefly, his eyes full. "I can't believe you can ask me that."

"It's just that you're younger. And I haven't really been able—"

Tim raised a hand and shook his head. "Just stop. Don't talk to me like that. Like I'm a kid. Jesus."

"I didn't say—"

"You don't have to say anything." He slapped a palm on his thigh. "I can tell what you think. 'He doesn't

155

know what he's doing going out with me. I'm so old. He's living out some Mrs. Robinson fantasy.' Don't you think I've read enough to understand romance? We connected during that first division meeting, and it was still there after—after Sofie. And love? I've been married. I know what I'm doing, Jenna. And I know how I feel about you."

When she was thirty-four, Jenna knew what she was doing. Or so she thought. She knew that putting all her energy into Sofie and teaching was right and true. She knew that grading papers until 1:00 A.M. and then waking up at 5:00 to finish them was smart. She knew that being available for Sofie in the morning before and in the afternoon after school was the only thing she could do. She was sure that the occasional trysts with Mark were okay, reasonable, rational—or, at least, not detrimental unless anyone found out. The moon and sun revolved around everything outside her, and in her bones, Jenna had been certain that what she did was exactly the way it should be. She'd ignored the late, lonely nights with nothing but papers for company, the long weekends when Sofie was at Mark's. When she stopped to think about it, she knew she had Sofie and her job and Dee and her mother and father. There were her students in a pinch. All of that had to be enough.

So what would Tim think, eleven years from now, about this moment, especially if Jenna told him to get back on the interstate? Like her, he'd probably say, "What a mistake I made. I wish I'd done it differently." But she couldn't make that decision for him—nor could she make her decision because of him and her guilt and her fear, the darkness that floated around the circle of white light she'd seen during her meditation.

Leaning toward him, placing a hand on his shoulder, she searched for words that would make leaving him easy. There weren't any, of course. So she closed her eyes, feeling his muscles tense under his cotton shirt. "I can't go back to work," she said finally. "I shouldn't have gone back after the funeral. I should have done something else. Dee tried to get me to start tutoring. Maybe I should have done that, or I should have gone away. Come here to stay with my mom. Gone to a mental hospital. Been put into a drug coma. I—I didn't know how to not go back and just try to live again. Except for when I was with you, I felt angry. I hate my students. All of them. They're ignorant and lazy, and I hate them because they are alive. I can't do it next semester. I don't know. Maybe I can't do it anymore, ever. But I can't face them or my house. I can't go back into Sofie's room every single day like I've been doing—"

"You can stay with me," Tim said. He glanced at her and then in his rearview mirror at the empty road behind them. In the distance ahead, the Pine Flat exit hung over the highway.

"I can't do that either. It's not like things will be normal now. I've got to figure out what to do. For me."

"So what I want doesn't matter here."

Sighing, she pulled away from him, leaning against the door and staring at his profile. In two weeks, he'd be into his semester, full of adrenaline from the newness of his classes. He'd wear a tie those first couple of weeks, showing his students he meant business, and they'd nod and do their homework and come prepared. He'd start rereading his textbooks, maybe *Catch-22* again or selected poems of Emily Dickinson or Sharon Olds or Wordsworth. He'd go to a bar in downtown Walnut Creek after work and there she'd be, a twenty-four-year-old graduate student. A lit student from Berkeley, who'd just broken up with her boyfriend, a musician. They'd get to talking, and for a moment, he'd think of Jenna in Pine Flat, her belly pushing against all of her clothes, her small breasts becoming full. But then he'd lean into this woman—Gabriela or Katie or Courtney—and ask her to dinner. Some months later, they'd move in together. He'd forget his ex-wife, Karen, and Jenna, how he'd needed them, and his real life would begin, just like that.

Tim looked at her, waiting for an answer, and then turned off at the Pine Flat exit, letting the car slow, stopping at the stop sign. "I don't matter. You're only thinking of yourself."

Looking behind them to the empty freeway, nothing coming toward them for miles, Jenna pulled up on the emergency brake and turned him to her, leaning close. He smelled like toothpaste and the red-brown soil of the canyon. By morning, he'd need a good shave. She could see him in his apartment bathroom, the mirror foggy, leaning down to follow the line of his beard with his razor.

"Of course you matter. God, Tim." She took one of his arms, rubbing it, pulling it over her shoulder. Outside, rain began to fall, drops tinging the car roof and windows. "But all of this—all that has been inside of me since Sofie died—started so long ago, before you. This is really about me and Sofie and Mark. How I was as a mother. A wife. This is about how I can't do it. I can't do what I've been doing. It was too hard. And you—you were like a pond I encountered in"—she held out a hand to the landscape outside, the muted shaggy forms of Ponderosas outside the window—"the middle of nothing. But I have to figure out the nothing part. I've got to find a way to live in the nothing."

He sighed, shaking his head, beating out a slow, sad rhythm on his thigh with a palm. "It's not nothing, Jenna. You've just forgotten how to see it."

"Yeah. I know."

They were silent, the rain swirling down the windshield, the clouds already breaking up, patches of stars in jagged shapes above them. Downtown Pine Flat gleamed dimly before them.

"So, you're going to stay with Jolie."

"I hope so." She squeezed his shoulder and sat back. "I just decided this. It's not like she's had a chance to blow me off, which I certainly wouldn't blame her for doing. But I can't stay with my mom and Stan. I don't even know what my mom would say about me being . . . the preg—. . . the baby."

"You'll keep it?" Tim wiped his eyes and then released the emergency brake.

"Depends. It's not like I was with—with Sofie. I was so perfectly pregnant. Not doing a thing wrong. You know what I've been on. What I've taken. And I really am too old for this. I'll have to go to a doctor soon."

"And Mark?"

Jenna sat straight in her seat, leaning her head against the rest, looking at the buildings as they drove past. "It's so confusing. I just figured it out myself, Tim."

"How did you know? Why just now? You must be two and a half months or so, right?"

With Sofie, Jenna had known the night of conception, the way Mark's semen seemed to be sucked up into her, nothing dripping down her thighs later. Somehow, she'd been able to feel the microscopic activity inside her, the sperm derby, the egg hanging regally in her fallopian tube—the left one, she even knew that—waiting for the victor to plunge inside her. All night, she'd lain awake, her hand on her belly, knowing that her whole life was changing, even if no one but she could tell. Nothing from that moment of cellular struggle would be the same. But this time? Jenna couldn't really remember the act or her own body. Just the gauze curtain above her, Mark's face at her shoulder. And then, later, the haze of the semester, her grief, the lull of drugs, the brief, beautiful sparks from Tim.

"Yeah," Jenna said. "I thought I was going into menopause. But tonight, I knew. It all came together." She didn't mention the light, Sofie and her father, together. Even Tim might think that was too weird, that

160

she was too far gone to be left in Pine Flat with Jolie. Or maybe she was underestimating him again, unaware of his empathy and understanding. But no, she knew about his caring, his arms around her when she awoke in a panic, sure that she could save Sofie, lift the metal sheet, pull her to safety, tamp her burning flesh. How he'd almost sung to her, whispering that it was only a dream, even though it wasn't. If she told him about the light in her meditation, he would think for a moment and nod, picturing it all, almost as clearly as she had herself.

Tim was right. She did treat him like a child.

He stopped at a light and then swung right, pulling up in front of Jolie's house, which sat like a lit pumpkin between the two dark buildings. "I think I knew."

Her mouth opened and she sat back. "You knew?"

"Yeah. Sort of. Once when you were sleeping, I had the thought that you were full. Self-contained. Like a boat. Whatever was inside could float."

A last lash of rain swept over the car and then it was silent, puddles reflecting the light from Jolie's house.

"Oh."

"So you're staying here." His hands were clasped in his lap.

"If she'll let me. For a while. I'll call Dee tomorrow. And then I'll call administration to see how to arrange a leave."

"I could do that, you know."

She swallowed and nodded quickly. "I know you could. But I should do it. If I tell them that's what I want, I'll be making a change. I'll be making a decision."

Tim sighed and then opened his door. "I'll call you when I get home. I have Jolie's card. For her art."

Jenna stepped out of the car into the brisk air, the warmth already circling up from the pavement. Already, all signs of the peace festival and meditation would be washed away, no footsteps or ass-shaped rounds of smooth dirt where people had sat. No evidence left of Sofie or Jenna's father.

Wheeling her bag to the curb, Tim leaned it straight and then shoved his hands in his pockets, putting weight on one foot, the other, and then pushing his hair off his forehead. Like it always did, the hair flopped back as soon as he took his hand away.

"I think I'll go. She's home. See?" He pointed to the living room window, where Jolie stood, a phone pressed against her ear, even as she peered out to the street. "I don't want to have to explain. It's not about me. You're not letting it be."

Jenna brought a hand to her cheek, feeling it as if she'd been slapped. It wasn't about him because it couldn't be about him now. It couldn't be about Jenna and Tim. For the first time since Bali, Jenna knew that she had to face what she didn't want to see, the stories she'd been hiding from. But only one story at a time. Jenna and Sofie. Jenna and this baby. And then, if she could, Jenna and Mark.

She wished it were otherwise, but Tim was telling the truth.

"Okay," she said quietly. "You better go. You've got to make the plane."

As she watched him, all she wanted to do was move toward him and lean against his shoulder, rocking against his body so softly, smoothly, that she would almost moan, their afternoon of sex still skimming the top of her skin, her nerves wanting nothing more than his skin on hers, all of it. She wanted to hold him tight, breathe in, and then push away gently, looking at him in the darkness.

But Tim stood in front of her, his hands still jammed in his pockets. He cocked his head, opened his mouth, but then didn't say anything. Finally, he took a hand out of his pocket and looked at his watch. He was a man ready to leave.

"Thank you," Jenna said.

"There's nothing to thank me for."

"Yes, there is."

Walking back around the car, he shook his head. "I'll call you. Happy New Year."

She began to reply, but the air was stuck at the back of her mouth. A new year. A brand-new year, one Sofie would never know. Pressing her hands against her sides as if trying to force out sound, she said, "You, too. Tim, I'm sorry. Happy—"

Behind her, Jenna heard Jolie open the front door, a swath of yellow light fanning out over the Taurus as Tim got in the car, made a U-turn, waving as he accelerated. She waved back, and then brought her hand to her mouth, holding in her cry. *Stay,* she

163

thought, *don't leave me here.*

But Tim's words came back to her, and for a second, she saw herself as a boat, seaworthy, strong, floating in an empty sea, everything she needed right inside her.

"WHAT HAPPENED?" Jolie grabbed Jenna's suitcase and pulled it through the front entry.

"It's a short, stupid story," Jenna said, realizing that to someone other than Tim or her, the story was strange and ridiculous, based on visions and feelings.

"Oh." Jolie looked at her, her eyebrows raised.

"Well, it's not really a short story."

"Did you have a fight?"

Jenna followed her cousin, blinked against the light of the room and pulsing red and orange and yellow from the oil paintings. So much color. So much life. "No, not really. But I decided to stay."

"Here? I mean, with me?"

Jenna swallowed, her throat dry. "I know I shouldn't ask, but I was hoping I could stay here with you. For a little while. If that's all right."

Setting the suitcase straight, Jolie turned to Jenna, tucking her long blond hair behind her ears. "Of course you can stay. I do have plenty of space. But—but what about your job? Your students?"

"I'm not going to teach this semester," she said. Two and a half months, plus six and a half more to go. July. The baby would be born sometime in July. If she had the baby. If she could bear to have another one. If the baby wasn't wrecked already by her carelessness, her inattention. The poison that was in her blood right now, half of the blue pill active in her blood. She'd call Dr. Kovacic tomorrow morning, first thing. And then she'd look in the Pine Flat Yellow Pages for an OB-GYN. She'd missed her annual this year, not caring about any cancer that might be growing in her cervix or in her uterus or ovaries. *Come get me,* she'd thought in October, when Dr. Zahri's appointment reminder came in the mail. *Please.*

"No summer school either. Maybe—maybe not again."

Jolie blinked. "I don't get it. Is it—is it about Sofie?"

Jenna sat down on the couch, pulling her knees up to her chest. "I'm pregnant."

Instead of the surprise or disbelief or even horror Jenna expected to see on her cousin's face, Jolie was smiling, her hands on her hips. "No kidding?"

"I thought I was in menopause."

Jolie made a *psst* sound in her mouth and then laughed. "Quite the opposite, I'd say." She sat next to Jenna and stroked her hand, taking it in her own. "This is wonderful."

"It is?"

"Of course! Your mom is going to be so happy. Everyone will be."

"They will?"

"Jenna, it's life. It's a miracle. It's the most amazing thing a human can do. Nothing adds up to it in the final analysis. Nothing is as important."

Was that true? Was a child more important than a

novel people still read three hundred years later, or a painting millions flocked to see each summer, the crowds pushing for a perfect view? How could life be that important if people went and blew it up? Spreading bombs over the land like confetti, blowing up bars full of young people, starving whole nations into submission, hacking off feet and arms and ears? How could people be that important if they couldn't get the most essential things, like food and clean water and medical care? Not to mention realistic school and library and college budgets. Jolie was wrong, but Jenna tried to smile.

"Well, it's happening, no matter what I think. I have to find a doctor. Tomorrow. I have to find out if the baby is okay. I've taken a lot of medications."

"It'll be fine. I can feel it."

Jenna snorted and turned to Jolie, but her cousin was serious, as if she was the one who'd had a vision, a perfect child in a field of white.

"It's Tim's baby, right?" Jolie asked. "Or . . ."

"No. It's not Tim's. It's Mark's."

Jolie looked at Jenna, biting her lip. Then she breathed out. "Does he know about it?"

"The baby's mine. My baby. My problem. I'm not going to tell Mark right now. It's too early. And, Jolie, I don't want to tell my mom, either. Not yet. It would be too much for her if the baby were—well, you know."

"Nothing's too much for Lois. She can handle it. She'd know what to do this very minute. And I think Mark could handle it, too."

Jenna pulled her hand away and leaned back into the pillows, resting her head against the soft fabric. Jolie was right about Lois, who would jump in the car if she knew. On the way, she'd stop at the closest Barnes & Noble for any book about expectant older mothers. Jenna could see the titles now: *What to Expect Now That You're Almost Dead: How to Nurse When Your Breasts Hit the Floor*. And then came the old song she used to sing with friends—probably with Jolie, too—when they were little:

> *Do your ears hang low?*
> *Do they wobble to and fro?*

And then how they would change it:

> *Do your boobs hang low?*
> *Do they wobble to and fro?*
> *Can you tie them in a knot?*
> *Can you tie them in a bow?*
> *Can you throw them over your shoulder*
> *like a Continental Soldier?*
> *Do your boobs hang low?*

She knew Lois wouldn't bring up anything that would make her feel worse; in fact, the books would take a positive spin on age and birth defects and child care. Lois would cook huge meals and find the perfect doctor and drive her to her appointments. Jenna wished she could fold herself into her mother's arms and chest.

But Jenna knew she'd been using everyone since Sofie died. Mark at the hotel, Dee at school, Tim in the bedroom. Now she'd moved on to Jolie, ready to use her up, too.

"I know. Mom would do it all. But I want to figure this out for myself. Before I tell anyone. I really don't know what's going to happen yet. If the baby is okay."

Jolie smiled, her face full of a joy Jenna wished she could feel. "The baby will be fine."

"Maybe," Jenna replied, taking her cousin's hand again. Both of them sat still, looking out the large window, the wind picking up pine needles and other tiny flying objects, sending them cartwheeling into the glass, *ting, ting, ting ting,* the pattern of the heartbeats inside her, both of them.

JENNA SAT ON the examination table, dressed only in the cotton gown the nurse had handed to her after taking her blood pressure and temperature and asking her all the important questions: date of the last menstrual cycle (who knew? sometime in September?); prior pregnancies (one only); medications (Zoloft, Sonata, aspirin); alcohol (yes); caffeine (yes); entopic pregnancies; rape; cancer; hospitalizations. None, none, none, none, save for her brief hours in the hospital with Sofie, Mark insisting that he could care well for both of them at home, since he was a doctor, after all.

Now she sat alone in the hot room, the heater on so high that she realized she'd never been this comfortable in a doctor's office. Unlike at Dr. Zahri's office back home, where her feet turned blue and she pressed her thighs together for warmth, Jenna almost found herself wanting to lie down, curl up on the table, fall into a long hibernation. When she awoke, she'd feel the last long pulls of labor, and then she'd push and push and the doctor would pull the baby out in one sleek, wet move. The doctor. Dr. Velázquez. A woman. That was the only criterion she'd stipulated as she and Jolie looked through the phone book. Finally, Jolie had called Ralph at the store, who called a customer he knew well who'd had a baby in September.

Ralph called back and talked with Jenna. " 'You can't find someone here,' my customer told me. 'Go to Flagstaff,' she said. 'Dr. Velázquez. She has all the new bells and whistles. You'll love her—I mean, not you, Ralph. The lady.' I laughed at that, Jenna. Like I was having a baby myself. That would get me into the *Guinness Book*, don't you think?"

After a quick knock, the door opened slightly, and Dr. Velázquez peeked in and then pushed the door open all the way and stepped into the room. "Mrs. Thomas? I'm Dr. Velázquez." She held out her hand, and Jenna took it, the skin thin over the fine bones. How did Dr. Velázquez catch a baby with those tiny hands, Jenna wondered, letting the doctor's hand go after a quick shake. She was no bigger than a child.

"Hi." Jenna felt her smile pull down, and she breathed in and tucked her gown unconsciously around her thighs. What must she look like here? She should be in here for a perimenopausal workup. Not a baby.

"You took the test when you came in, and you were right. One hundred percent pregnant."

Jenna's body heard the words before her ears did, a rush of blood and adrenaline fanning out through all her veins and nerve endings, her body tingling. She wanted to cry. Where was Mark? Tim? Her mother? Why had she told Jolie to stay in the waiting room?

"Okay." She sighed.

Dr. Velázquez turned from her chart and took off her glasses. Her eyes were dark brown, her eyelashes so black she probably never needed to use mascara. "So we have quite a bit to talk about, I think. Let's start at the beginning, okay?"

"My daughter died," Jenna said, the beginning of the sentence out of her mouth before she could revise or edit it. "She died in a bomb in Bali. My ex-husband came to the island, and we slept together, and this is our second child, twenty years later. But—but she won't be healthy. I'm on drugs. For depression. I took sleeping pills. And drank alcohol. And I don't know if I should be allowed to have another child. I already lost one."

Dr. Velázquez rolled smoothly over on her wheeled stool and took Jenna's hands again, pressing them both between hers, listening, her brown eyes wide and waiting.

"I don't know what to do. I saw Sofie in a vision, and she was happy. Maybe this baby is really Sofie come back. So—so I want to try to have it. I think." Jenna stopped, unable to speak, the white vision of Sofie and her father before her again, the pain in her chest like a heart attack, like lightning, like an explosion. She slumped, leaning down on the table, crying, crying as she hadn't before, not even in Dr. Kovacic's office, the tears coming up from her feet into her bones, through veins and nerves and organs and then lungs, the pain a fire in her throat. "Oh," she mumbled, her mouth full of tears. "Oh, oh."

"Yes," Dr. Velázquez whispered. "That's right." And then she was silent again, pressing Jenna's hands, not leaving her to do this alone, throwing a line to Jenna's boat, saving her from the deepest waters.

"SO?" JOLIE ASKED, taking the paper bag full of prenatal vitamins from Jenna's hand, as Jenna put on her sweater. The Flagstaff sky was a swirl of water and clouds over them. A light wind blew Jenna's hair back from her face.

"I'm going to have some tests. Something called a CVS and a level-two ultrasound. She's also scheduled a three-D ultrasound. And at fifteen weeks, an AFP test. For spina bifida."

"Level-two ultrasound." Jolie pulled her keys from her purse and unlocked the Jeep's passenger door. "Three-D! I've only had a basic one."

Jenna blinked, focusing on the sidewalk, flat, gray rounds of ancient gum underfoot. "Dr. Velázquez says it's almost like a photo, you can see that much." Sofie's ultrasound flashed into her head, pasted as it was in her baby book, a blur of white in a grainy black background, fetal Sofie holding out her arms, as if she

171

couldn't wait to be born. So short a time. Perhaps she'd known even then.

They both got into the car and sat down. Compared to Pine Flat, Flagstaff was like Manhattan, cars and people everywhere, the sidewalks and roads full. Even with this slight weather system passing over them, Jenna could feel the summer heat in the cement and asphalt. By June, visits to Dr. Velázquez would be unbearable. If she made it that long. If the baby was healthy.

Jolie started the car and pulled into traffic, heading for the 40 West on ramp. "Did she say—did she talk about how the baby would . . . ?"

Nodding, Jenna sighed. "The odds aren't good. By the time we hit thirty-five, thirty-six, our eggs really start to go to hell. The chances of Down's syndrome and every other kind of problem are just, well, huge. For a mother my age, the chance that the baby has Down's is one in fifty. Part of me doesn't even want to wait for an answer."

Jolie was silent, gripping the wheel just like Tim did, that careful ten and two position, as if both of them felt every outing was potentially fatal. And it was, wasn't it? Right at this very minute, they could be struck by lightning, another car, an eighteen-wheeler. They could flip over the side of the highway and be crushed to death. A suicide bomber could crash into them. A plane could drop out of the sky. Why go on? Why do any-thing?

"You can't give up."

"I—"

"You're so lucky."

Her skin flicking with angry goose bumps, she turned to her cousin, her tongue stiff with words. Lucky? She was lucky? A dead daughter and a potentially damaged fetus were lucky? "What are you talking about?"

Jolie's jaw was tight and she didn't look at Jenna, her eyes fixed on the road. "You have this chance. Again."

"But—"

"I could never have a child. I tried for a long time because I really wanted that experience of pregnancy, of carrying a child, of feeling that amazing life inside me. But I can't. Couldn't. I know all the odds about age and older eggs. And it's a miracle that you've gotten pregnant. When I was forty-three, my doctor told me to let it go. It wasn't going to happen."

"Your doctor? Why didn't we go to her?"

"Him. He's in Phoenix. A fertility specialist. Different group of patients. They don't want a slew of pregnant women walking into the waiting room, taunting those of us who can't. Who never will."

Jenna felt the stab of tears in her eyes. She didn't know anything about her cousin. Jolie had been trying to get pregnant, and all Jenna did was send her a Christmas card every December, signing it only *Love, Jenna*. Lois didn't know or surely she would have told Jenna, encouraging her to call Jolie and say some nice words or send her a happy thought in a Hallmark card. Not that there were those kinds of cards on the drug-

store wall—HOPE YOU ARE INSEMINATED SOON! HAPPY
FERTILITY TREATMENT! or worse, a jingle:

We know you want this baby.
We surely know you do.
We wish you lots of hormones
and happy implantation, too.

"I'm sorry, Jolie. I didn't know."

"I didn't even tell Todd. Everyone always knew I
wanted a baby, but none of my boyfriends seemed to
stick. Finally, I just thought, I'm going to have a baby
on my own. I started when I was thirty-six, so I know
all about eggs dying. I did it all. Every kind of treatment. I used the money my mom left me. Your mom
was so supportive through it all, promising not to tell
anyone, not even you. I felt there would be too much
pressure on me if other people were waiting for news.
But now the money's all gone and no baby. Thank god
for Ralph and the store and his house."

"And your art," Jenna said.

"Yeah. Art."

Jolie stepped on the accelerator, looking in her
rearview mirror as the traffic faded behind them. Jenna
grabbed Jolie's arm, pressing tight, feeling for the
second time that day the way bones lay against skin and
muscle. Dr. Velázquez and Jolie felt so different, but
both were women, human, the mechanism for their
spirits. Since seeing Sofie on the floor of the auditorium, Jenna had been desperate to believe her

daughter's soul had flung itself clear of the damaged body. But not until her vision at the meditation had she really been able to see her daughter as whole and, at the same time, disconnected from her flesh. A live soul even with a dead body.

Jenna shook her head, rubbed Jolie's smooth skin, and then sat back. "Listen, your art is important. It shows what you are inside—"

"A baby is important," Jolie interrupted. "A baby shows what is inside. What your insides were able to do, and then what you were able to do afterward with that baby. Sofie was—she was amazing. So smart. Remember that time when she was what, two? She held up tortilla chips one by one and started telling us what continent they looked like. 'Asia,' she said. 'Africa.' 'South America.'"

Jenna closed her eyes, thinking of the little tin globe that Lois had given Sofie that year and how Sofie had held it between her pudgy palms. She had even held up a thin, broken chip and said, "Madagascar."

"I remember," Jenna said quietly.

"She was all of you, plus what you taught her, what you helped her learn. She was all of that combined."

"I had nothing to do with it." Jenna sat back, letting go of Jolie's arm. The road was a blur of cars and asphalt, the sun bright even in the chill air. "She came out who she was. From day one. Even without me, she would have known how to recognize the world."

"Maybe so. But do you think that without you, she could have been the type of girl who would go to Bali?

175

She fell in love and left everything to be with Robert, even if it was only for a vacation. She could fly. This sounds corny, but you gave her wings."

Wings. That's what Sofie needed to fly so she could meet her grandfather, hover with him in the light, stay there for Jenna when she needed them both. Sofie was in that light when this baby's soul flew to earth, ready to be born, ready to live again.

Jenna shook her head and snorted. Her thoughts sounded as bad as that woman who had accosted her at Montclair Park all those years ago. What had she said? "We pull to us what we need"? Had Jenna needed the baby, or had the baby needed her? Or was it Sofie arranging everything, doing as she had done all her life, making things happen?

Or was it just biology, the random coming together of egg and sperm, the happenstance of Mark's finding her hotel, the fact that she'd come back to the room early because she'd found Sofie's body in the auditorium. Active man, fertile woman, connection, implantation. That's it. Nothing more.

Out the window, the sun broke through onto a planted grove of cottonwoods, the light shimmering on wet trunks. Jenna rubbed her forehead. "Sofie was who she was. I just watched, Jolie. Parents don't have all that much to do in the deal. We pretend we do. We wish we did. I lived in that pretend country of denial, thinking I could control her life, make it perfect. But now I wish—I wish I could have changed so much. I wish I could have clipped her wings and made her stay with me. If I had, she'd be here right now. I'd learn how to say no, no, no. I would have held back. I would have my Sofie here now, not this other baby. Oh, god!"

Keeping her eyes on the road, Jolie reached out a hand. "I'm sorry. I shouldn't have told you all about me now. It wasn't right. But I had to let you know. You'd figure out my feelings sooner or later, even if you don't stay very long."

Jenna blew her nose into a Togo's napkin she'd found in the door pocket and nodded. "I appreciate you letting me stay. Showing up like I did, all 'Here I am! Aren't you glad to see me?'"

"I am glad to see you. I always was."

It was true. All those childhood years, Jolie was always waiting at Aunt Ava's door, eager to drag Jenna into her room to show off her newest game—Operation, Mystery Date, Risk, Life—troll, doll, or plastic horse. Later, she and Jenna listened to music with Todd, who pretended to be bored and then later really was bored, leaving them to go get stoned in the garage and listen to the Doors. Thanksgivings and Christmases and family reunions, one after the other, Jolie had been waiting. And what had Jenna done? Ignored Jolie in the way that was possible with people you never saw and barely cared about, except during a crisis or forced event. And even then, you knew it would be over soon, like the stomach flu or a canker sore. Painful and annoying but soon forgotten.

"Thank you, Jolie. You've been great. Better to me than I deserve."

Jolie waved one hand. "You'd do the same for me."

Maybe now, thought Jenna. *But not when I had every-thing I needed. Not when Sofie was alive. Not when I lived in my little cocoon.* Selfishness flamed red in her chest, and she bit her lip.

"You wouldn't have changed your whole life in the middle of a meditation," Jenna said finally. "Now that I've made this big change, I've just got to figure out what I'm doing. I've got to talk to Tim. I'm going to have to call my mom. And Mark. Eventually."

"You will. Hey, I've got to stop by the store to do the payroll. It's just checks for me and Ryan, the stockboy. But I need to get paid. Do you want me to drive you home first?"

When she thought of Jolie's house, the only thing she could envision was the phone in the living room. Going to the store would stop her from thinking about the calls she dreaded making, keep her from having to say the words that would jolt everyone, especially Mark. *Pregnant. Not coming home. Quit work.*

"I'll come with you. I'll help out while you work on the books. There's got to be something I can do at the store."

Seven

Jenna bent over the case, trying to keep the imported Italian charms in some order. Two sisters from California wanted to look at almost all of them, cupping the small squares in their palms and oohing at each. Jolie had said that when the charm craze hit the States, Ralph had made sure to stock hundreds of smiley face, clover leaf, peace sign, and Barbie doll charms and the bracelets to go with them.

The charms' metal backing *click, click, click*ed on top of the glass counter, and Jenna jumped at each slightly scratchy sound, her nerves alive, awake, responding.

"You must go off slowly, Jenna. Not all at once," the doctor had said.

"But the baby."

"You don't want the symptoms of withdrawal—"

"These aren't addictive, are they? I didn't think they were," Jenna said.

There was a pause, and Jenna could see Dr. Kovacic behind his big black desk. "Not addictive in the traditional sense. But your body has gotten used to the chemicals. If you went off all at once, you might feel sensations that some of my patients call zaps. And there can be nausea, just like when you started taking the medication. And, Jenna, though we don't know the risks of the drugs on the fetus, going off too quickly could affect you both."

So instead of throwing all the pills into the toilet and flushing like she wanted to, Jenna weaned herself from the Zoloft, from 50 to 25 milligrams, from 25 to 12.5, slowly, slowly, over a month. And though she had no zaps or nausea, her ears were full of unwanted noise, the irritations from people and cars and prepubescent girls, needing, wanting, having to have a cheap charm that Ralph sold at a 100 percent markup. As Jenna took one charm after the other out of the case, she longed for them to hurry up, pick one, and then go back to their parents, who were waiting outside in a parked Dodge Caravan.

"That one. No, no, no. That one. The red one," one of the girls said, leaning into her sister's thin shoulder. Despite the cool weather, they both wore tank tops with teeny satin straps and matching shorts. The oldest had a mole on her neck that Jenna knew would make her self-conscious later, like Sofie's freckles had bothered her. The mother waiting outside would be dragged to dermatology appointments to have it removed, and then the youngest would want acne medication, even though she'd only have one or two red bumps on her chin. Leaving the father and younger brother at home, all three of them would go shopping, eating at mall restaurants, full shopping bags by their feet under the table. "I can't have a milk shake," the girls would cry, ordering two, anyway. The mother would smile and then take spoonfuls from her girls' ice cream.

Jenna closed her eyes, her heart pounding in her head, all the shopping trips and milk shakes and doctor appointments with Sofie in her memory at once. Her stomach pulsed.

"This one. This one is sooo cute!" the younger sister said.

Jenna opened her eyes and carefully plucked the charm from the case and set it on the counter. She was working alone in the store, and there was a storm outside, the parked Caravan's windshield wipers going at full speed. Ralph had just fixed the heater that hung from the ceiling, and it huffed air into the room. Dimly, the canned pop music whirled in the space between the gusts of hot air.

The girls were probably only a year apart, the older one sprouting breasts, the younger one still a girl, her stomach round, her legs stick thin. Their long hair dangled in front of their faces and spread across the counter. Both of them needed a good shampoo, bits of canyon dust in their so-white parts. They had such fair skin, Jenna could see the excited pulse beating on their throats. She smelled the candy they'd bought across the street at Rite Aid, and the fruit cologne Ralph stocked in the small cosmetics section in the back. The younger sister had used the tester lip gloss, purple shine on her lips and an accidental dab on her chin.

"So do you have a favorite?" Jenna leaned over the counter, looking up at the older sister's eyes.

"My mom says I've spent way too much of my allowance on this trip. But—"

"Like, they're only five dollars," said the younger. "I don't think Mom's going to go ape sh— She won't be mad about five dollars."

The older sister looked at her sibling and rolled her eyes. "She goes crazy all the time."

"So just buy one fast. You better, or she'll be in the store in, like, a second." The younger girl stomped her foot and tossed her hair behind her shoulder. In a year, Jenna knew, she'd have her own breasts and would rebel in her own way, not needing her sister to be her front man.

"Fine. I want this one. The purple flower. And the bracelet. No one has that kind at home." The girl pointed to a particular bracelet and Jenna pulled it from the case, wrapping it and the charm in tissue paper.

"Is that it?" She looked toward the younger sister, who had now wrapped her arm around her sister's waist, going along for the ride without ever having to do anything.

The older sister nodded. Jenna rung up the purchase, took the cash, and handed the bag to the older sister, but the younger grabbed it and ran to the door.

"Missy!" the older sister said, running to catch up. "I'll tell Mom."

The door *ding-dong*ed as they left, and Jenna stood behind the counter, the heater whine and crackly music swirling around her. Rain slapped against the large front window, the gutter on the side of the store gurgling. For a few minutes, Jenna stared out at the empty parking space the Caravan had pulled away from, and then she sat down in the chair behind the register. Underneath the counter was some mismatched stationery, bits and pieces that no one had bought or sheets that had become separated from a set. She should write to Mark. She'd talked with Tim on the phone a week ago, when he called to tell her which part-time instructors had taken over her classes.

"I miss you," he'd said. "Come home."

"Come home," Dee had said when Jenna called her

the first time. "Stop the madness, for God's sake."

But Jenna hadn't been able to pick up the phone and dial Mark's number. What would she say? And how would she say it? Which particulars would keep him from coming down here or casting her aside altogether? What right words in what right order would make him care about what was happening, but not need to be here in Pine Flat?

She pulled out a purple sheet that a tourist from Oregon had spilled Pepsi on. She could write a rough draft, the beginning of what she needed to say to Mark. Jenna took the pencil from on top of the register and wrote,

Mark.

She stared at his name, the name a word, a symbol, a thing. Leaving a mark. On your mark. Mark the spot. He'd marked his spot on her, in her, twice. She erased his name and started again.

Dear Mark,
I'm sorry I haven't called you. My mom has told me that you've been calling. But here's the deal. I'm pregnant, and it's your baby, the one we made in Bali. The thing is—I don't know if the baby is going to be healthy, so I've been waiting to talk with you until after the tests are in. Maybe I'm just scared to even have you in the same room with me now. I can't look at your eyes. I can't think about what's

going to happen next. Are we going to get back together because of the baby? Will you think this means we can go back to the way it never really was? We weren't happy the first time. We haven't been happy with each other ever, really. And after the two years of not being with you that way, I don't want to start the physical stuff again, Mark, no matter what happened in Bali. I finally learned to not want your body. I finally grew out of my old lust for you, let go of the girl who wanted you so badly she gave up

Jenna shook her head and crumpled the paper into a tight, fist-shaped ball and threw it into the trash can under the counter. That's not what she wanted to say. She wanted to say, "Mark, I'm pregnant. You can be in this baby's life, but it will be different. I am in love with someone else, though I think he'll get over me soon enough. But it means I don't love you."

But how to say that without sounding unkind, selfish, confused? Maybe she should write to her mother, write more than she had in her journal, which was still in her suitcase at Jolie's. Jenna had called Lois from Pine Flat, pretending to be home in Monte Veda, the semester about to begin. She hadn't really said she was home, but didn't say she wasn't. Certainly, she hadn't said, "Mom, I'm up here in Pine Flat with Jolie. And by the way, I'm pregnant."

Who could she write to that would understand? Who would really want to hear what she had inside her? Dr.

Kovacic said to express her feelings, her emotions, but Jenna knew that a good letter, one that deserved to be sent, should not be full of stream-of-consciousness, day-to-day minutiae. Jenna would moan over an essay like that, give herself a failing grade.

She reached for another piece of paper, pulling out a cream-colored, 25-weight piece of typing paper. Setting it on the counter, she put the pencil back on the register and dug for a pen in a drawer, and came up with one of the Grand Canyon pens Jolie had brought to Lois's house at Christmas. She stared at the paper for a moment, the watermark next to her palm. Closing her eyes, she thought of all the words she had in her, the ones that would explain and clear up everything for everyone, except herself, of course. With a couple of sentences, she could give her family hope. A reason to be joyful. Or was it a reason to be worried? Jenna hadn't gone in for the test yet, and she was still full of Zoloft, but the rest of her worked well enough. She'd barely had morning sickness, and none of the hormonal headaches she'd had with Sofie. In fact, when she really evaluated how her body felt, Jenna almost thought she'd never been better. Her breasts were fuller, her hair thicker. She was eating more than she had since Sofie died.

Leaning her elbows on the glass case, she thought of all the words she could use, words she'd taught her students, ways of stringing together sentences for the best effect. Compare/contrast, cause and effect, order of importance, narrative, process analysis. On a thousand blackboards, she'd organized a thousand essays, under-lining thesis statements and topic sentences and con-cluding arguments. But this letter? What to say, and to whom?

One of the last letters she'd written was to Sofie, a long letter folded and tucked into an envelope that Jenna had handed her as she left Sofie in the dorms. Jenna could still remember the first line,

My darling girl, my grown girl, the dear girl of my heart.

Jenna sucked in air, feeling how those words were still true.

Out on the wet street, a Suburban pulled up, all four doors opening at once, disgorging bedraggled day hikers splotched with water and red dirt. Jenna looked at the piece of paper and wrote the word *Hello,* and then shoved it under the cash register and stood up, knowing that the tourists would need her.

AT 6 P.M., SHE LOCKED up the store and began walking up the street toward Jolie's. After the Suburban family had left, a string of folks who'd been rained out of planned activities—day hikes, camping trips, park tours—had streamed down the highway and into the store. She'd sold three more charms, five Grand Canyon pens, Arizona coffee mugs, dream catchers, postcards, and key chains. A toddler from Prescott had messed up the stuffed animals, throwing them in the aisles while his parents looked at road maps, and a sullen teenaged girl had almost stolen a lip gloss, looking at Jenna every so often and then finally sighing and giving up, walking outside to smoke a cigarette. No one Jenna had met in the last week knew a thing about her—none had seen her face on the cover of the *San Francisco Chronicle* or had read about Sofie in *People* magazine. She'd taught none of them anything. Not one person she rang up at Ralph's store knew about the baby or Mark or Tim. As she walked toward Jolie's, she felt something in the air that she swung her arms through. Not the slowly drying Arizona sky, not the evening slipping its skin across the town. Her mouth felt full of a whistle she couldn't yet blow into sound. Her heart felt smaller and clearer than it had since the second before the phone rang and she'd learned about the explosion.

The windows of Jolie's house were clotted with steam, and as Jenna walked in, she smelled boiling vegetables. In the kitchen, Jolie stood over the sink, draining something into a colander.

"Spinach," Jolie said. "Folic acid."

Jenna put down her purse on the kitchen table and took off her sweater. "Folic acid?"

"You know. Dr. Velázquez told you. It prevents neural-tube defects." Jolie dumped the drained spinach into a pan on the range, stirring it into caramelized onions. "When I was doing all my fertility treatments, my doctor had me taking it before I was implanted. In fact, a woman trying to get pregnant should be taking it months before she even starts trying to conceive."

Here was something else to worry about, Jenna thought, sitting down at the table and looking at a pile of junk mail Jolie had neatly stacked. Neural-tube defects. Tiny squid babies without legs. Babies without brains, the skull an empty hat. She supposed folic acid was an ingredient in the whopping orange vitamin Dr. Velázquez had prescribed her, but it was probably already too late. Like everything else. The good feeling she'd had on the street began to evaporate into the spinach steam.

Jolie turned from the range. "But don't worry. It's rare. And they can find the problems in sonograms. You know, the kind you're having tomorrow."

Jenna nodded and wished she could have a glass of wine, a big one. And then a Sonata so she could sleep without thinking about swimming fetuses. "Yeah."

"You still want me to go with you?" Jolie asked, setting a plate full of spinach and onions and sautéed chicken in front of Jenna, and then returning to the range to serve herself. "Ralph's okay with my coming in then."

"Yes. Of course," Jenna said, knowing that suddenly she didn't want her cousin to go with her. She wanted her mother, really. Lois. Now that she was actually here in Pine Flat, her leave of absence approved, her classes taken care of, she wanted her mother. "And—I think I'll call my mom. I want her to be there at the appointment tomorrow."

Jolie sat down, her lips pinched between her teeth,

and then she nodded. "That sounds good. Aunt Lois will want to be in on this. You don't—you think you'll go live with her?"

Jenna thought of the girls buying the charms and the girl who wanted the lip gloss more than anything. All day the door had *ding-dong*ed, the outside air rushing in as someone entirely new showed up, wanting something that the store and she could provide. Then it was Jolie's shift, and Jenna could walk home and lie in bed and read a book. "No. I like it here. But only if it's okay with you."

Putting down her fork, Jolie took Jenna's hand. "Of course it's okay. For as long as you like. If you want to stay here with the baby, that's fine, too."

Jenna squeezed Jolie's hand and then looked down at her plate, all the healthy food and her cousin's help making her believe in some kind of luck.

IN BED, THE TALL, dark building next to the house blocking the moonlight that had finally broken free of storm clouds, Jenna sat up, her reading glasses on, the light a widening triangle of yellow in the bedroom. At home she would have turned on the news, stunned and silenced into a zombie-like, slack-jawed confusion by the thirty minutes of terrible events, the political machinations, the murders, the kidnappings. But Jolie only had one television, a small, ancient castoff Lois had apparently given her. Instead of cable, Jolie had strung up to the back of the set an antenna that looked more like an art project, the wires curved and twisted and tacked onto the ceiling. Jenna had only turned it on once, the cooking show on the screen a flicker of white.

"I get channels three and nine," Jolie had said. "That's it."

"Why have it at all?" Jenna asked, turning it off.

"In case of an emergency."

Jenna had almost laughed, but then she thought, *Yes*. You never knew. Everything comes on suddenly.

So she sat up in bed, the room quiet, an unread novel on her lap, something she'd bought at the store, a glossy paperback with embossed letters, a woman on the front cover running away from a man in the background. A good-looking man, though, Jenna could tell, and maybe that's why she had picked it, ringing herself up before closing down the register. She'd done that herself. Run away from Tim. And Mark, in a way. Just like this girl.

But she hadn't read a word. Instead, she pulled out the piece of paper she'd written the word *Hello* on at the store. The last thing she'd done before leaving work was pull it from under the register and tuck it into the novel. She didn't know why she needed that particular piece of paper. She'd had no problem throwing away the letter she'd begun to Mark, and obviously, she could have started this one over. But she'd liked the cream paper, the expressive feel under her hand and the way the *Hello* looked on it, sure and solid and firm, as if Jenna finally knew what she was doing when she wrote it. Evidence, then, of sanity.

But she'd also turned into a thief. Though she'd paid for the book, she'd stolen the Grand Canyon pen she'd

190

found in the drawer at work, tucking it in her pocket along with the store keys. Tilting the pen back and forth, she now watched the words float over the little canyon backdrop, the fluid in the pen viscous and slow, making the whole slide last longer than it would have in water. Clicking the pen top, she put the paper on the novel and then thought about what she should say. When she called her mother tomorrow, Lois would be mad. But her irritation would be pushed aside by forgiveness, and before Jenna knew it, Lois would be on her way up with a Crock-Pot full of split pea soup. Jenna wouldn't have to say much more than "I freaked."

She and Tim had talked again on the phone and even e-mailed a few times, Jenna using Jolie's computer. Mark wouldn't be so easy. He would be silent, and then his words would push against her ear, his tone low, his words rushed. "What were you thinking? That you could hide from me? That I'd never find out? Did you think you could do this all alone?"

"Yes," she'd say. "I did it before. I did it with Sofie."

He'd be still, a world of static air between them. He would pause, curve around, come back at her from another direction, and again, she'd be clear. *I've done this before. I've been a mother by myself. I am still a mother by myself, even without her.*

So who was she writing to, then? Who actually wanted to hear what she had to say? Jenna pushed the pen into her chin, feeling the plastic tip against the hard point of bone. What did she tell her students? Just write? You don't have anything to say? How do you know? Just write. Why? Because you will be filled with ideas. You will find out your topic as you drag that pen across paper. All will be revealed. You will know what you are thinking. Trust me. *Trust* me.

So she sat back, put the pen on the paper, let her brain follow her hand against the page.

How are you? Did it hurt? Were you in pain? You can tell me about the fire and the heat and the pressure of the metal. Maybe I can hear it all now, not like when Robert came to show me his hands, to tell me the story of your death. But now. How is it now? How have you been? Do you need anything? Is there anything I can do for you? I'm so far away, and I still want to help. Can I help? Will they let me? There's another now, one I may have hurt as much as I hurt you. But I can't talk to either of you. One is in, and you are out. So far away. So gone. I saw you. I saw you on the floor under a sheet. I saw your hair and your toe. The home toe. Remember that? Remember how I would sing that song? How will I sing that song to the one who is inside me? Is it a girl or a boy? You know, don't you? It doesn't matter. I will find out tomorrow. But you know. Or is it you? Are you coming back? Can you come back so soon? Is that permitted? If it is, please say yes. Please leave your grandpa and come to me. I'll do things better now. I'll change. I won't make you the center of everything. Do you want to be in this life with me again? I miss you. I want to see you. You, Sofie, not this other one, this other person. That's why I want you to ask if you can come back. But you'll have to make up your mind. Because tomorrow, I'll see the baby on the screen, close up, like a Kodak picture. But if it's you, your hair, your voice, your arms, I know I can do it. Oh, why can't you be there, inside, again? I miss you. I miss you all over.

Jenna stared at her words, and then put the paper and the pen on the table by her bed. Pushing away the covers, she got out of bed and crossed the room. Even though it was late, she wanted to call her mother now. Wake her up. Tell her the news. Stop missing a person she didn't have to miss at all.

DR. VELÁZQUEZ RAN the regular ultrasound transducer over Jenna's belly, the slick goo warming up from the friction. Jenna's bladder was ready to burst, and this was only the first test. After this was over, Dr. Velázquez would use the other machine, the one Jolie was certain would be as clear as could be. In the corner of the room, Jolie sat on a chair in the darkness, the only light the luminous blue from the screen. Lois sat next to the examination table, holding Jenna's hand, talking with the doctor about changes in technology and asking the doctor personal questions, such as "How many children do you have?" even as she squeezed Jenna tight, her warm, round fingers so strong.

Jenna didn't want to look at the screen, having awakened this morning with all her new optimism gone. Now she imagined all the deformities this child was bound to have, a one in fifty chance. Once when she had been at the bookstore at Virgin Records in San Francisco with Tim, she'd picked up a coffee-table book called *Monsters*. The cover had a wolfman on it, one of those people whose hair was thick where it should be thin and who looked exactly like Lon Cheney in those werewolf movies. Why had she opened that book? Tim was off reading music magazines, drinking coffee, and she just stood there, flipping through stills from the 1800s, terrible, pristine photographs of Victorian-era monsters, all wearing lace-up boots and high collars. People with no arms or too many arms. Enormously fat people, giants, dwarves, albinos. One girl had four legs, her conjoined twin somehow embedded inside her, nothing but her alive torso emerging from her sister's stomach. Somehow, the four-legged girl had survived childhood, gotten married, and had children, two from one vagina, three from the other. Jenna had read it all, almost screaming when Tim touched her shoulder. And for weeks, she'd seen in her mind's eye the terrible crab boy and the bearded fat woman and the girl with the four legs.

Now in the office, she was scared that if she looked at the monitor, she'd see something from the book, the horror real now, not sealed away in old photographs. Because late last night Jenna had scoured the Internet for answers, she knew Dr. Velázquez was looking for short thigh and upper arm bones, a thick neck, and something called an echogenic bowl. At this very moment, the doctor was tracing the baby's brain, heart, and kidneys, looking at the cord insertion, checking amniotic fluid and placental position, all of which could go terribly wrong.

Turning away from Dr. Velázquez as she squinted in the dim light and adjusted her glasses, Jenna remembered Lois talking about the summer she'd spent with her parents in Hampton, Iowa, when she was pregnant with Jenna. Lois arrived for an extended visit in June because Ted had been sent off for a month to Holland and then to Saudi Arabia for work. By July, Lois's father, the local GP, had found a collection of malformed fruits and vegetables, the beefsteak tomato with two full, red bodies, the Macintosh apple almost split in two like a rosy derriere, the summer squash, yellow, bulbous, doubled. With each discovery, he walked solemnly toward Lois, who sat in the screened porch drinking iced tea.

"Lookie at this one," he'd said. "Two bodies."

Lois had first told Jenna the story during the summer of their failed vegetable garden in Monte Veda, cucumbers and squash wilting on the vine. "For about a second, I was sure I was carrying a pumpkin. Everywhere I looked, nature was going haywire."

Closing her eyes, Jenna tried to think of all the wholeness around her, the flat Arizona desert, the wide-open world of the Grand Canyon, the way that Mark and she had even been able to conceive in the first place, a

195

daughter dead, a baby in the womb. Around and around and around.

"There's your baby."

Jenna turned slowly, opened her eyes, trying to make out the shape flickering before her. Blinking, her eyes watering, she saw its mouth opening and closing, an arm waving.

"Here's the heart. See? It's beating away just as it's supposed to," Dr. Velázquez said, putting a tiny X on the screen by the flutter inside the baby.

"Oh, my," Lois said, leaning forward, her bosom on Jenna's arm and chest. "Look at my grandbaby."

Jenna turned to her mother, who stared straight ahead. Jolie, too, was leaning toward the screen. Both were smiling.

"There's the spine. See?" Dr. Velázquez motioned with her finger, the baby's spine a perfect swirl of black. "And the skull."

"Does it look okay?" Jolie asked. "Is there any sign of spina bifida or hydrocephaly?"

Dr. Velázquez paused and adjusted her glasses on her thin nose. "Not at all, but I'm taking a digital record, and I will have my colleagues consult. Just for safe measure."

At the words *not at all,* Jenna felt heat pulse through her chest and she almost sat up, needing to clutch on to the doctor. But gradually as she relaxed, she realized her reaction—this intense feeling—was happiness. Joy.

Jenna focused on the *beat, beat* of the tiny heart muscle under the skin, wondering how she could have missed that for so long. All those sad days, this baby had been living inside her. "Is the heart—is it normal?"

"Again, I'll say yes for now, but I have to consult. I'm collecting the information right now." Dr. Velázquez pushed a couple buttons, and the machine hummed. "Let's do the next test, shall we?"

Jenna nodded and then closed her eyes, listening to the wheels of the carts sliding on the clean linoleum, the repositioning of chairs. And then there was more goo and another transducer. Lois still grasped her hand, squeezing slightly.

"This is going to blow you away," Dr. Velázquez said. "Wait until you see these images. It's a breakthrough."

Before she could think, she heard Jolie's and Lois's gasps, the light pulsing into the room like sunrise.

"Jenna! Look!"

Turning to the monitor, Jenna felt the air leaving her lungs. In a gold, glistening cavern sat a golden baby, tiny, eyes closed, huddled against her womb, the umbilical cord floating translucent in front of it. The baby seemed asleep or scared; she couldn't tell. But it was pressed back as far as it could go, its hands shielding its eyes. The image shifted, the light in her womb like fire.

"Stop!" Jenna cried out, not wanting to intrude on the baby's little world. "Leave it alone."

"Jenna, I can do some good checking here. Close your eyes. This isn't bad for the baby."

"Mom!" Jenna cried. "Why is it that color? Why is it so bright?"

"It's fine. It's okay. Let the doctor do what she needs

to. Everything will be all right."

Holding on to Lois's hand, Jenna shut her eyes and clenched her jaw. It was too soon to see it, because seeing it meant it was real. And already, she knew that the fetus could be hurt, as it was now, trying to sleep despite their spying. All it wanted was quiet, peace, the gentle rocking of fluid and flesh.

"With this test," Dr. Velázquez said, "your baby looks like— Do you want to know the sex?"

Jenna opened her eyes and grabbed her mother's shoulder, wanting to ask her a hundred questions. Her mother must know the answers. But like Lois, Jenna had only had one child, and she didn't know how to ask if it was possible to love another as much, or the same, or at all. And if this baby were a girl, would she be able to look at her without seeing Sofie? A boy would be better. Mark would finally have the boy he'd talked about. In fact, he could take the baby and then toddler and then son to his beloved A's games that Sofie had refused to go to, and play with him on the weekends at Heather Farms Park, throwing a ball back and forth. The boy would grow up and take Mark to games, helping his old father into the stands, making sure Mark woke up before the seventh-inning stretch. Jenna wouldn't have to see Sofie over and over again.

"Jenna? Sweetie?" Lois asked. "Do you want to know?"

"I— No. No. I don't."

"But Jenna, it would make things easier in terms of preparation," Jolie said. "You know. Clothes and stuff."

The transducer pressed on her belly, and Jenna turned to look at the ceiling. Preparation. Nothing prepared you for anything. They still didn't know if the baby was okay. The chromosome analysis was still forthcoming. What could prepare her for a Down's baby or . . . or worse, whatever worse could be. But she knew worse was out there. She'd seen Sofie under the sheet.

"No. No. Not yet. Maybe not until it's— No."

"Fine. That's quite all right," Dr. Velázquez said. "These tests are very positive. But I'll have the consult with my colleagues, and then there will be the CVS later. We'll have some clear results in a couple of weeks. But remember, we can never know everything."

Lois squeezed Jenna's hand, and Jolie patted the part of the pillow she could reach from the chair. Up on the ceiling, orange light from the ultrasound flickered and spun like a crazy sun. Jenna began to close her eyes and looked for the white space in the darkness, the figures of her father and daughter, a message from them about what would happen next.

Eight

Three SUVs just went by. And . . . one of those new Hum things. Giant." Jenna leaned on the counter, her belly against the glass back.

Dee sighed on the other end of the phone line, student voices in the background stopped suddenly by the sound of the sliding glass door slamming closed.

"Listen, tell me *again* why you're doing this, Jenna. I know you've explained it to me about once a week. But this time, do it for the record. Just so I can really get this straight."

"Oh, Dee. Not now, okay?"

"But is this car watching any better for you than being here, teaching? Or even just gardening at home. What have you sold today? A couple of mugs and a Grand Canyon banner?"

"I've sold three packs of gum, a set of commemorative spoons, and a visor."

Dee clicked a fingernail against the receiver, her habit when she was thinking. Jenna knew she should be serious. So much was. Dr. Velázquez hadn't called with the test results yet; Lois was making plans to all but move up to Flagstaff during Jenna's pregnancy; and Mark had phoned Lois five times, wanting to know what in the hell was going on. Back in Monte Veda, the house sat empty, even the cats gone. Susan and her husband, Kenneth, had finally cornered Bean and Peanut under Jenna's bed, lured them into cat carriers with fresh tuna fillets, and taken them to their house.

"Now I know where the word *caterwauling* comes from," Susan said. "My God, I could hear them going at it from inside my house. At first, I thought someone was murdering you in your bed."

All the perennials along the driveway needed to be cut back, and if it wasn't for Susan's son Julien, who mowed the lawn, the house would look like the Munsters' from TV, ramshakle and blowing with tumble-

200

weeds. Everything fell apart sooner or later. Even though Jenna knew that pipes could be leaking, causing wood rot, inviting in termites and ants, her windowsills damp and turning moldy, her furniture collecting dust, she had no answer for Dee, no way to explain why she was doing anything.

Dee exhaled and then cleared her throat. "Tim's kind of a mess, you know."

"He's okay. We've talked a few times."

"Maybe he's all right on the phone, but you don't see him in the halls. He looks at me like I have some kind of solution. I don't know what to say. I have no idea why being pregnant in the desert is better than being pregnant here. No matter what you say."

The baby fluttered. Jenna pressed her hand to the bowl of her pelvis.

"It wouldn't be good anywhere, not yet. I haven't gotten all the tests back."

"Are you flipped out?"

Shrugging, the phone rubbing up against her cheek, Jenna sighed. Of course she was flipped out. The Zoloft was eking out of her system, the tension with her even before she woke up in the morning, the shadow of Sofie like a blind she couldn't pull up. But all the anxiety seemed to coalesce into a stilted calm, a wink of time before the next terrible thing would happen. She was like a woman on a sinking raft, wearing a life preserver with a slow leak. She should scream and cry and pull out her hair, but not yet. There was time before she slipped under the dark water.

"Of course. But I'll know soon."

"Look," Dee said, "a student's here. You'd think they'd know I need my office hours for my phone calls. Call me when you find out. Love you."

Dee hung up, and Jenna put down the phone. In a couple of hours, it would be Jolie's shift, and Jenna could go home and go to bed, pull the big blanket over her shoulders, fall into sleep, as if it were the water that would never let her go.

WHEN SHE WOKE up from her nap, the sun was on the edge of the sky. Jenna had been asleep for hours, her cheeks flushed red and her eyes swollen with dreams. Rubbing her face, she sat up and leaned against the headboard, looking up at the flicks of dust slowly swirling in the room. In her last dream, she'd been back in Bali, and this time, she'd been able to go to the beach, running through the surf, the warm water at her thighs. She'd turned to face the hotel, and Sofie and Mark had been sitting on large yellow towels, waving at her.

"Don't you love the water?" Sofie had called out. "Don't you want to stay in there forever?"

Behind them, the hotel lobby rose like a Hindu temple against the sky. Jenna had waved back and then continued running through the water, fish at her ankles.

Jenna picked up the half-filled glass of water on the bedside table and drank it, the water lukewarm. Putting down the glass, she listened to the quiet house. Jolie would be back soon, and she would probably start cooking one of her healthy dinners, a thick piece of meat, dark green vegetable, fruit for dessert. Since Jenna had moved in, Jolie had taken over the Lois role, making sure Jenna took her prenatal vitamins and called Dr. Velázquez back and drank enough milk. It also seemed to Jenna that Jolie had been spending less and less time painting. In fact, she hadn't been out to her workshop this whole week, instead sitting at the dining room table and reading the thick pregnancy books she must have collected during her in vitro treatments.

"Calcium reduces leg cramps. . . . Sleep on your left side because you won't block the vena cava and the blood flow to the baby. . . . It's folic acid all the way," she'd said, looking up at Jenna, who had been rereading, again, *Sense and Sensibility* while Jenna lay sprawled on the living room couch. "So much to learn."

But, Jenna thought, she already knew all that from when she'd had Sofie. She'd slept on her left side even when—in her ninth month—her hip began to ache and burn, all her weight pinned on the joint. She wanted Jolie to put down the book and go out to her workshop and pick up her brush and paints—umber, slate, ruby, coal, pumpkin, titian—but then she knew she'd sound ungrateful, rude, selfish. She was staying in Jolie's house, after all, having arrived unannounced in the night, laying all her terrible story on her cousin's doorstep.

Throwing back the blankets, Jenna pulled her legs to the side of the bed. On the nightstand was the letter she'd begun. The letter to Sofie.

She saw the words *I miss you* scrawled toward the end of the page, and she returned her hand to her stomach. This baby should not be hers. This was Sofie's baby, the next woman in line, the mother handing off to the daughter the reproductive baton.

When Sofie had called her after the international water-rights conference, Jenna had heard something adult, something woman in her voice as she said, "Mom, the conference was great. There was this guy. This man."

At the sound of her daughter's real, true, adult longing and desire, Jenna had begun to imagine grand-children, all the bedrooms full at holidays, blond babies from Australia filling the living room at Christmas, Mark standing in the corner smiling, Renata some-where, anywhere but there. Jenna had actually gone into the attic and found the box labeled SOFIE'S CLOTHES, sneezing as she held up tiny dresses and ancient blankets. Her time, she'd thought, was past, Sofie's just beginning.

Jenna picked up the letter and a pen from the night-stand, setting the paper on a book—an art book of Jolie's. She leaned back, sticking the pen end gently into her cheek. What did she miss? The obvious things, mostly; Sofie's body, her voice, her calls from her dorm room in Berkeley. But what else?

I miss the curve of your cheekbones under your skin. I miss the way you picked up my hand when we'd go to the movies, holding me in that quiet way, in the dark, when no one could see and later tease you. I miss the way you crunched through Froot Loops and Coco Puffs, and then later how you would only eat steel-cut oatmeal with organic molasses and naturally dried raisins. I miss the late-night phone calls, how you began to tell me your secrets. You said that you loved your dad but hated the way he breathed through his nose while reading the paper. You loved men with big hands. You wanted to have children, but later, when you were thirty or thirty-two. I miss your knees and your elbows, so white, so pokey, so Celtic, freckled and pale. I miss when you'd get angry and sneer at me, slamming your bedroom door, the house echoing with your anger. I miss trick or treating, your skin electric with sugar until bedtime. I miss your presence, that you made me whole. I miss being a mother, Sofie's mother. I miss that I don't know what I'm supposed to do.

Putting down the pen and paper and resting against the headboard, Jenna felt disembodied, her head filled with dark air. The weight of the afternoon sank down onto Jenna's breastbone. Still, after all these months, she couldn't believe it had actually happened. That a life without Sofie had exploded into her own. She'd been carrying around all these memories, pressing them against her thoughts so hard that in ways, Sofie had never died. When she'd been home, she'd wandered the rooms, snatching recollections out of the corners and cabinets and closets. And then, when she wasn't searching for what remained, she'd been listening to something else, a book, a movie, Tim's beating heart. Or she'd been trying to lighten her thoughts with drugs, hoping that one wouldn't grab her and pull her down.

Her chest shook; her hands were still. All she could hear was *No, no* beating in her blood. And then, despite her sadness, despite the truth about Sofie, the baby swam a circle, traversing its uterine world. *No,* Jenna thought again, but she put her hand on her belly, felt the blip of, yes, life inside her.

"SO WHILE YOU were at work, I went to Target. The one off the interstate? Well, do they have a great selection of baby stuff." Jolie was pulling packages out of a shopping bag she'd set on the dining room table when she came home from work. "It's going to be a breeze getting ready for this baby."

Jenna had decided to cook, beating Jolie to the kitchen, and was preparing a lasagna, full of mozzarella and ricotta. She put down the hot pads and walked into the dining room, standing in front of Jolie.

"You know, I haven't heard back about the tests."

Jolie waved her hand. "The ultrasound was the key. Everything's going to be fine."

"No, Jolie. That's not true. This baby isn't officially a baby until the chromosomes check out."

Looking up from the shopping bag, Jolie stared at her. "You don't believe that. This is a baby already."

Jenna sighed, knowing what Jolie was going to say. A week ago, she'd told her cousin about the vision at the Grand Canyon.

"Jolie," Jenna began.

"You told me about what you saw. That couldn't be warning about trouble." Jolie looked at Jenna, nodded, and then went back to pulling out items. Jenna blinked against the sight: pacifiers, tiny white T-shirts in three-packs, soft towels with hoods, pastel sleepers with bears and kitties embroidered on the front. "And I talked with a friend of mine. From the infertility support group. She got pregnant right away, five years ago, and said you could borrow her crib. She doesn't need it anymore. And a bassinet. That can go in your room. Maybe you're going to do the 'family bed' though. It's easier. I would have. For nursing. But you'll have the crib and bassinet all the same."

"Jolie . . ." Jenna began, and then stopped. Her cousin didn't stop moving, unpacking the rest—baby booties, Desitin, lotions and shampoos in tiny pink bottles—her face flushed and shiny. Folding up the bag, she looked at Jenna, her eyes wide with excitement, the kind Jenna had seen in Sofie's eyes when she'd told Jenna about Robert. Jolie was in love with Jenna's baby, the baby that wasn't official yet, that could turn out as disappointing as the months of Jolie's failed pregnancies.

"So you made lasagna," Jolie said. "Did you put spinach in it?"

"No, I didn't. Cheese and meat. You don't— You've got to— Well, I can make a salad."

Jolie tucked the folded bag under her arm and picked up the packages of clothes. "Cooking releases the vitamins. I'm going to wash these and get them ready. I bought some Downy. It doesn't irritate the skin."

Jolie walked down the hall, and Jenna sat at the table, the air around her full of tomatoes and meat. With the smell, she was back in Lois's kitchen, sitting at the counter watching her mother make dinner. There it was, a spoon to her mother's appreciative lips, a sigh, a full "Wonderful." So wonderful indeed, the warm kitchen, her mother's energy, the safety Jenna felt in her whole body, not one thing wrong in the entire world. Picking up the pacifiers, Jenna tapped the cardboard against the tabletop. Steam rose from the pot of almost-boiling water. Soon, she'd layer the noodles and sauce and cheese. At least that would make sense, the white, the red, the white, the red. Nothing was like that anymore, no easy lasagna metaphor she could live by. She'd thought she was making a smart decision to stay in Arizona, a safe one, and now her cousin was being seduced by something neither of them might ever have.

The pot clacked; water hissed on the hot range. The gas oven pinged with heat. Jenna stood up and pushed back her hair. For now, she'd concentrate on food. Tomorrow, she would call Dr. Velázquez and ask for answers, learn what to do to try to save them all.

• • •

When I found out I was pregnant with you, I was not afraid. Not for a minute. I went to the main library near Lake Merritt and read everything. I knew what to eat and how to sleep and what to avoid. I stopped drinking coffee and had a headache for a month that was so bad, I thought maybe I had a brain tumor. But I would have done anything to make sure you were okay, and I thought I could control it all. And I did. Sofie, when you were born, you were perfect. You were always perfect. I remember when the nurse placed you in my arms, I said your name, "Sofie." And you turned right to me, looked at me with your almost-clear eyes. You'd remembered or already knew. You knew me.

I loved being pregnant. I hated labor, of course. I remember your father holding me up, his hands under my belly, and I thought, I'm getting the hell out of here. I guess I thought I could just get up and walk out, leaving the pain behind. But then came the pushing and that was so good, so productive, all sorts of people staring at my vagina, shouting out encouragement, like some kind of sporting event. I wasn't good, though. I screamed, "Get it out." And then, when you slipped out of me, it was over. The pain—instantaneously—was gone. I had you. Held you. You looked at me. It was everything the books promised.

But then your father left. Things were not as they were supposed to have been. You were pulled in two ways, but you remained whole. You dealt with us. Did you know we still slept together sometimes? Did you ever think we were going to get back together? Did you put your ear to the wall and listen closely, hoping that the sounds we made meant your life would go back to normal? I'm sorry. I should have explained to you what all the sneaking around meant. But I was ashamed at how I still needed him.

I've done nothing right with this baby. I don't know anything yet. I'm waiting, Sofie, for the words that will change my life. I'm down in Arizona, waiting. Do you know what will happen? Could you tell me? Or don't. I don't want to know. It also hurts too much to see you in dreams, even though every time you come to me in my mind, you are happy. I want to remember, but not that clearly. I think I will just not know for now. Is that okay? Can I do that?

After dinner, the dishes done, the house still full of steam and tomatoes, Jenna decided to go sit outside, putting on an Oxford shirt of Tim's she'd accidentally packed in her suitcase. Or maybe it wasn't an accident. She'd balled it into her suitcase while he was in the shower. When she'd unpacked at Jolie's, she'd laid it on the bed, smoothing it with her hands. Then she'd picked it up and smelled the collar, the underarms, the back. If she breathed in deep, she could still pick up his scent, the clean white hotel soap, his dark hair, the sweat in his underarm hair.

For the first night in over a week, Jolie was in her workshop, having jumped up after dinner and told Jenna to just leave the dishes. Of course, Jenna hadn't, hoping that Jolie would paint for a long time. Maybe the Target shopping had inspired her, made her remember where her true inspiration lay.

Sitting back on the wooden chair, Jenna looked into the sky. The night was clear, the stars a swirl of white. Putting her hands on her belly, she closed her eyes. Soft music slipped from under the workshop door, and Jenna could almost imagine the colors Jolie was using—magenta, vermilion, persimmon, and sunflower. Between her hands, Jenna felt the same colors, life colors, and she knew, as she had with Sofie, that all creation has the same sharpness, the same energy. She'd always wanted to write or to paint or to act, but all Jenna had been good at was being a mother and teaching.

"I don't have a creative bone in my body. I tried once, to find it. But there's nothing," Jenna complained to Dee now and again.

"Oh, stop it. Being a mother is your poem. Teaching these kids is your famous work, your raison d'etre!" Dee would say. "You don't have to write the great American novel or perform on Broadway or recite an original work at a presidential inauguration. You do what you do, and that's your poem. My poem is teaching. Mark's poem is being a doctor. We have different poems. We have different creations. You can't keep judging yourself by what you think you *should* do. Just do what you do."

But her project, Sofie, was over. That poem was finished. Teaching seemed finished for now, as well, this semester cruising along fine without her. This baby under her palms was her new creative work, but even though Jenna loved raising Sofie, she could never do it again, with the same focus and concentration and interest.

She needed something else. Maybe she would turn into that Diane woman she'd met at the Grand Canyon, her poem the conversion of others. Or even worse, she'd start accosting people at parks as that Buddhist woman had done to her years before. Jenna didn't want a poem that big, something that meant she had to change others. Politics, the law, spiritual movements— all of that seemed huge, a poem that absorbed everything around it, wanting everyone to speak with one voice. But what did she have? The letters she'd started writing? No one else could ever see them, of course. She couldn't exactly send them to her mother or Mark or, especially, Sofie. But other than conferences and class lectures, meeting minutes, and notes to students, they were the most writing she'd done in years, since her master's thesis. Maybe for now, they could be her work, along with this baby. And if she wrote about Sofie and the baby, she would have something. She would finally know her poem, and she would hold it tight.

I am waiting in mystery, just like I waited on that bench in Bali. It was so warm there, the air light as cotton, as if it knew it needed to hold us gently. But I couldn't feel the air or the water. Or anything.

Maybe I didn't touch anything in Bali, not really. I should have touched you more, let my fingers feel your hair and skin and fingernails that last time. Even though you were dead, I didn't really know it was the last time. I couldn't feel that. At that moment, no one could have told me that was really true.

But I felt your father. I touched your father. The baby's father. I pulled him to me as I had so many times before. He was the same. Just the same, even though we are older. You can't understand that. You never saw your flesh change from smooth to lined and rougher. Didn't we laugh once about how many quarts of Keri lotion I went through? All those loofahs and pumice stones. Remember how we went to Calistoga during your last spring break and you made me take a mud bath?

"It's so good for your skin, Mom," you told me. "You'll be so happy you did it."

And I was happy, not because of my skin, but because of the way I could turn to you in the mud tub and see you next to me, your hair wrapped in a towel, your arms and shoulders smeared with mud, your face green with the kelp mask. I was happy because you said, "Watch out, I'm the creature from the black lagoon."

I was happy because we were together.

You'd like it here in Arizona, Sofie. The air here— it's warm, even though it is winter. Not hot yet. Not really even warm, but a promise, a hint, a warning.

If you lived here, I'd have to make sure you had sunscreen. Remember how you told me in Australia the schoolchildren are made to wear hats to protect them from skin cancer? You'd have to wear a hat here, too. But now I'll never have to worry about all the melanomas you might develop. I blamed myself for every sunburn. But you lived, you felt the sun, ran in the waves, free and happy. You enjoyed it.

I'm going to bed. The window is open and I feel safe, even though downtown is only steps away, even though I have an untold story inside me. I'm waiting, Sofie. I'm waiting for answers.

Nine

Come back in two weeks. We'll start a regular course of prenatal. Take your vitamins. Exercise. Eat right."

Dr. Velázquez hung up, and Jenna pressed the TALK button, holding the phone in her hand like a dead blackbird. *Fine. Fine. F-ine.* The word she'd hated since childhood, knowing that under the push of air from between tooth and lip was criticism, the truth, something not quite good enough. When she was in college and learned the angry name of the *f* sound, she knew she'd been right all along: fricative. *Fric-a-tive.*

"Well, what?" Jolie scooted next to her, putting a hand on Jenna's knee. "What did she say? Is the baby okay?"

Jenna scratched her head with one hand, bounced the phone in her palm. "I've got to call my mom."

"Jenna? What? What is it?"

Looking up at Jolie, Jenna breathed in quickly. Jolie's face was pulled tight, her eyes watering. "No. No. Everything's fine. Nothing abnormal. I promise."

Jolie threw herself into Jenna's body, her arms cradling Jenna's head. "Oh, I'm so glad. I knew it. I knew that finally— I just knew everything would work out." Jolie's body shook, her ribs moving up and down with her sobs. Jenna patted her on the back, eventually pushing her cousin back a bit, watching as Jolie wiped her eyes and took in a couple of deep breaths.

"I start now with regular visits. The drill, once a month for a while, and then the last month—"

"Every week. I know, I know! How exciting! Aunt Lois is going to be so happy. Are you going to call? Right now? I can't wait!"

"Well, yeah. I was going—"

"We should tape the call. Or let me listen. I want to hear her voice." Jolie scooted to the edge of the couch, rubbing her palms on her thighs. Was she sweaty? Nervous. Jenna's stomach began to pulse with morning sickness déjà vu.

"Why don't you go into your room on that extension? Then you can listen in."

Jolie jumped up and almost ran into the bedroom, yelling out, "Okay. I'm here. You can start dialing."

The phone was still in her hand, the plastic warm and clammy from her grip. Nothing Dr. Velázquez had said felt real to her yet, her words still floating around in her brain. The baby was fine? Fine? Was it possible that she would be able to go through the entire pregnancy and actually give birth? And then what? Raise a child?

"Okay, Jenna. I'm ready!"

Jenna sighed and looked up at Jolie's paintings, the color less intense in the daylight, oranges and reds and greens flat and muted in the 11 A.M. light. She pressed the TALK button and dialed, ignoring Jolie's "Did you dial? Are you done?" Bringing the phone to her ear, she listened to the ringing, praying for her mother to pick up fast. In the background, Jolie yelled out again, "Have you dialed yet? What are you doing?"

Just as Jenna heard Jolie coming down the hallway, Lois answered.

"Mom, come get me," Jenna whispered. "Now."

"WHAT IS GOING on there?" Lois locked her arm in Jenna's as they walked down Jolie's street, away from downtown, passing cottages, a few with flamingos in the garden and boxes of early spring flowers in pots. A breeze pushed Jenna's hair away from her face, and she closed her eyes. At Contra Loma, early each semester the psychology teachers would do a trust lesson, sending out pairs of students to walk together, one blindfolded. As Jenna was teaching, she'd look out to the quad and see the slowly moving couples, one trying to trust, letting a stranger hold an arm, a hand, an elbow. Sometimes two boys would be paired, one refusing to let the other touch him, walking blindfolded alone, coached only by voice. But with Lois, Jenna knew she could trust her pregnant body and everything else. She could squeeze her eyes tight and never open them, her mother bringing her home safe.

"It's gotten strange."

"How, sweetie?"

Jenna turned to her mother. "You knew that Jolie was trying to have a baby."

Lois nodded and then stopped at the corner, looking both ways before continuing across the road. "Yes. It was a sad time. She did everything possible, but to no end. All she wanted was a baby."

"You never told me about it. You never said a thing."

Lois squeezed Jenna's forearm between hers and her body. "She didn't want me to. I guess she didn't want to worry about other people being disappointed. But you were busy. You had Sofie to take care of and your teaching, and I really didn't think you'd be interested," she said without blame, and Jenna knew it was true. Jolie's life experiences of seven, five, three years ago wouldn't have done more than make Jenna tune out Lois's voice on the phone, grade a paper while Lois went on about treatments and hormones and procedures, write down scores in her grade book as the story wound down.

"She's not over it, Mom. She's acting like my baby is what she's been waiting for all along."

"Jolie's excited. She wants to help you. You did show up unannounced and ask to stay, even though you knew you could come to my house. She let you in. She got you a job. I'm not sure why you'd think she'd do any less."

"She wants my baby."

"Oh, Jenna. No, she doesn't. Jolie's not like that. She's just happy for you."

Shrugging, Jenna pulled her arm free and tucked her hands in her sweater pockets. "Okay, she doesn't want my baby. She wants my pregnancy. I don't think it's good for her that I'm there. I think I want to come stay with you."

Lois nodded and kept walking, their strides matching. When Jenna was a teenager, she had complained once in a Macy's dressing room about the shape of her thighs. At the time, Lois didn't even seem to acknowledge Jenna's words, but later she pulled Jenna away from her homework and walked her up Las Vegas Road and El Gavilan, down to La Campana and around the long loop of La Espiral, and then home. Lois never panted or complained like Jenna, who wailed that her calves, her shins, her stomach hurt. But after a month of walks, everything stopped hurting, and she and Lois cruised all spring and summer and fall, only stopping when it rained. Jenna never complained about any body part again, worried that Lois would find another activity for them, something worse involving free weights or ocean swimming or scuba diving.

"Do you really want to come home with me?" Lois asked.

"Of course," Jenna began, and then stopped. She took

her mother's arm again and leaned close. "I don't know."

"Do you like Dr. Velázquez? She seemed to be on the ball, but do you want to go home and try to find another doctor? And are you ready to deal with Mark? I can't keep putting him off anymore, Jenna. I won't."

"You don't want me to leave. And you don't want me to go to your house, either, do you?" Jenna stopped walking and sat down on a step that led to a large white house where plastic sunflower windmills twirled slowly on the thick lawn. She felt her hip bones on the concrete, her belly between her legs, the sadness in her throat. She had nowhere, no one who really wanted her. Leaning her forehead on her knees, she began to cry, wanting some place, some time where it could all be better, fine, perfect, if that was allowed, or a space where she didn't know what she knew or hadn't felt all of this, this terrible realness of time since Sofie. Where had she last felt that? Not in the meditation. Even that was fake, her own mind, something she couldn't count on. It was an average day she wanted.

A single day five months ago. Sofie would have called in the morning to say hi, and Jenna would have talked to her until she had to leave for Contra Loma. She would have taught a grammar class, a lesson that was easy: prepositional phrases. No verb tenses. No subjunctive. No adjective clauses. Words that the students could identify: *over, under, around,* and *through.* After class, she would talk with Dee and then Tim, flirting in that way she'd never mastered, pushing her hair behind her ear, smiling so her whitened teeth would show. Through everything—talking, teaching, driving home—nothing tragic, nothing wrong, nothing weird would be happening. She wouldn't be pregnant or bereaved. She was who she'd thought she was supposed to be, the woman she'd imagined, one who would grow old and live in her house alone. Later, there'd be grandchildren and holidays. It was how it was supposed to have been. Not this Arizona street, her bones pressed on hard rock, her mother telling her that all that normalcy was not for her again.

Lois sat down on the step and patted her back. "All I want is for you to be happy. I can't tell you what that is. If I really thought it was going back to your house and teaching and having this baby there, I'd tell you, sweetie. I would. If it was living down in Phoenix with Stan and me, I'd pack you up now. If it was to live with Jolie, I'd insist that you get yourself together and walk back there and make nice to your cousin. This is your life. All I asked was a question. And all you have to do is answer it."

Lois chuckled and rubbed Jenna's spine up and down, the same way she had when Jenna was sick in bed with the flu, coughing at three in the morning, both of them waiting for the medicine to kick in. "That's all any of us have to do. Try to answer the hardest questions."

"That just sucks," Jenna said, wiping her nose and then sitting up. "How can I answer any of these questions? I keep trying. I keep thinking I have the answer. And then I don't know anything. I don't know what to

220

do or how to act or where to go. I'm a mess."

"Oh, sweetie. No, you're not. You've been through the worst of all. Something I've never had to go through. You are not a mess. You are a beautiful, wonderful woman, who has so much in front of her. You've lost everything, and now you can get some of it back."

A beautiful, wonderful woman? Lois had obviously not seen her with Tim in the car or at the Grand Canyon with Diane or in Bali with Robert or in the kitchen with Mark. Nowhere in the past four months had she been beautiful or wonderful. That's what Sofie had been, not Jenna. Not now, not ever. The fact there was a flighty wisp of life inside her didn't make her anything more than the crazy, selfish, stupid pathetic lump that she was right now, a ball of dough on a step in the middle of a town where she was a stranger.

Jenna bent back down and stared at an ant crawling into a crack in the sidewalk. Her tears splotched, one, two, on the dry concrete, spreading into uneven circles. "I don't know what to do. And I've never felt like this. I can't even turn my head without running into a question. And Jolie's there, pulling shit out of bags and acting so happy. And Sofie's dead, Mom. How can I be happy?"

Lois continued rubbing her back. A large sage thrasher flew onto a pine branch and chucked out its call. "When your father died, I swore I'd never be happy again. And then I walked down the hallway in my nightgown two days after the funeral, certain I should kill myself in the kitchen, and there you were.

You were holding out a cup of tea and a plate of buttered toast, telling me to eat. Making me eat. Just like that, I knew I had to live. I had to go on, drink the tea, eat the toast. Even with the pain that beat in my heart like a bad drummer. One bite, one sip, I was still alive. Soon, it wasn't about you anymore. I remembered that I liked living. The air outside. The stupid, funny shows on TV. The morning just before sunrise, the mockingbirds outside on the tips of sycamore trees. All that. One little thing at a time. Before I knew it, there was Stan. Life, it keeps happening. If you let it."

"It keeps going on, even though I wish it would stop." Jenna snuffled and rubbed her eyes. "I keep thinking that maybe something will slow it down. Like coming here. It seemed slower. Jolie's life seemed better. But it wasn't slower, and her life—it's no better than mine. She never had what I lost. And at home? Mark. And Tim. Work. There's no place to go."

Taking Jenna's hands from her face, Lois kissed her knuckles. At her mother's touch, Jenna closed her eyes, thinking about the letter she'd written to Lois on the way from Phoenix to Pine Flat.

Jenna put her hands on her mother's face, seeing how beautiful she was, how she was still the same woman striding up out of Park Pool in her swimming cap, adjusting the thick straps of her black swimsuit.

"Thank you," Jenna said. "For everything. For being there, here, even when I didn't know how to tell you the truth."

"Oh," Lois said, smiling, "you always kept secrets,

Jenna. Somehow, though, I always found them out."

"This secret is going to be hard to keep after a while," Jenna said, patting her stomach.

Lois rubbed her thighs with her palms and looked up as a car passed, a little girl staring out the window at them, one middle-aged and one older woman on a step, one blotchy from tears, one strong and sound and sure. "Why don't we just walk back to Jolie's? That's enough for now. We can all talk. We can hash out the whole story."

Closing her eyes, Jenna tried out her muscles, not sure that her legs could push her up. This was what she wanted, this stillness, like the white circle of light in her meditation, where everything was strung into sticky taffy time, nothing happening. "A Zen moment," Dee would call it. But how to get that all the time, where nothing was more important than the ant, the widening blotches of tears on the pavement, the thrasher in the pine tree, her mother's warm side pressed against her own, the girl in the speeding car? And could she reclaim all the other moments she'd let slip by because she was tired or correcting papers or watching television? The time Sofie sat eating Raisin Bran at the kitchen table while wearing headphones, her feet tapping out a beat? The sun on Jenna's face as she lay on the beach, listening to Sofie dig a hole to China? The slam of Sofie's angry teenaged door when Jenna refused to let her go to the unchaperoned keg party at Deena Smerling's parents' beach house? Those moments? Could she get them back and live in them instead of in the world that kept pushing past her, taking away everything?

"Jenna."

"Hmm."

"Let's go back to Jolie's."

Jenna blinked against the light blue sky. "Okay." She pushed up, and her muscles worked, her body straight, her sit bones aching. "Let's go."

Lois took her arm again, and they headed back to Jolie's. They didn't talk, and Jenna tried to imagine the seconds under her feet. *This piece of sand under my shoe,* she thought. *This crack in the sidewalk. My mother holding me tight. This day. This exact day.*

THERE WAS A big white car in front of Jolie's house when they returned, the same kind that Tim had rented at Christmas. As Jenna stared at the round metal curves of the hood, she felt the separate moments she'd collected on the walk home whisk away as her heart jumped strangely against her ribs. Tim could take her home. He could get her out of here. Letting go of Lois, she walked quickly up the path and opened the front door. But it wasn't Tim. Sitting cross-legged on the couch next to Jolie was Mark, holding a beer.

"Mark!" Lois said, moving forward past Jenna, her arms open. "How good to see you."

Mark hugged Lois back, looking at Jenna over Lois's shoulder, his eyes dark and wide, his forehead set with the three deep, horizontal lines he'd been working on since medical school. How she remembered that! His face over a book, the light reflecting white on his cheeks and lips and hair, his forehead pressed tight, as if that would help him understand the body, the way veins and blood and bone worked. "Stop it," Jenna would say, walking over to him, running her fingers over the puckers of tight skin. "Stop stressing out."

If she was lucky, he'd sit back, pull her onto his lap, and hold her with one hand as he continued to flip pages with the other. But if it were an average night, he'd look up and then quickly go back to the sentence he'd left behind, trying to catch up with it before the idea disappeared.

Now it was too late. The lines were set, a part of his face, just as stressing had become a part of his nature, the mechanism that got him through each day. For a second, she thought to move toward him and her mother, but before she could, he closed his eyes, relaxed, bent his face into Lois's sweater, letting Jenna see the hug she'd witnessed so many times before at holiday parties and in hospital rooms and family gatherings. Her tall ex-husband curled over and somehow into the body of her shorter, full mother. Always, Lois seemed bigger and stronger than Mark. Than anyone. Even now, all these years later, she still did. She pulled him in, stopped his forehead from creasing, let him close his eyes and forget.

"When did you get here?" she asked, looking at Jolie when the hug didn't stop, Mark's head still at rest. "Why are you here?"

"Jenna," Jolie began, but Jenna stopped her, holding up the palm she'd used on her students when they tried to turn in late papers.

"Mark?"

Sighing, he lifted his head away from Lois, holding Lois's shoulders in his hands. "It's good to see you, Lois. We didn't get to really talk. . . ."

"I know, sweetie. Listen, I'll make some tea. Or coffee—it's coffee, isn't it? Decaf for this time of day, right?"

"Right." He put his hands in his pockets and looked at Jenna. His eyes were red and slightly glistening, his face pale. "Why didn't you call me?"

Jenna dropped her arms to her sides and then brought them in front of her belly, imagining that the baby was pushing toward its father. Jolie moved closer, and Jenna clenched her jaw, the same feeling she used to have when Jolie wanted to play with her toys all those years ago. "Get out of my room," she wanted to yell back then, but didn't, not wanting Lois to stare at her with open, disapproving eyes. Now she needed to be alone, without her cousin watching her as she had been for weeks.

"Let's go to the patio, Mark. We can talk there."

Jolie flushed, and Jenna relaxed the muscles in her face, trying to find an expression that wasn't a grimace. "Tell Mom we're out there, okay?"

"Fine. Okay." Jolie crossed her arms and sat down on the couch.

Jenna walked past Mark, opening the door and moving out into the sunshine. She and Lois should have stayed on the curb and then just walked on by, headed straight out of town, back to the Grand Canyon, away from Jolie and Mark and his dark eyes.

But here she was, they were. Pulling two chairs together, Jenna sat and so did Mark. Above them a flock of white-throated swifts *jejejeje*ded in the air, and someone in the building next door slammed a window shut.

"What are you doing here, Jenna?"

She looked up, taking him in, allowing her eyes to see everything: his tired face, his new haircut, the curls tight against his head, his neat, button-down shirt, the first two buttons open, his smooth white hands, the soft dark hair on the first knuckles, the white band of flesh on his ring finger. Renata. Where was she? Why did she let him do this? What had been going on since Christmas? What had he wanted to tell her that afternoon he came over and then left without saying a word?

"I couldn't go home," she began quietly. "I realized—"

"Realized what? What could you possibly realize that you didn't realize before? And how could you just go?" He crossed and uncrossed his legs, running a hand over his hair. "God, you haven't changed at all. Always you. Never me. Never us."

"There isn't an us, Mark. There hasn't been for quite a while."

"There's always been an us, at least on your terms. You know that."

Jenna looked down at her feet, hitting the toes of her

shoes together, the sound a canvas *tap, tap, tap*. He was right. They'd let the thinnest bit of *us* survive through the divorce, Mark on the periphery of her life no matter what. And it hadn't been just about Sofie. Jenna was lying if she thought otherwise. "I know."

"So what is going on? What are you doing here?"

"What's going on with you? Where's Renata? Why are you here?"

"Jenna! Stop it. Could you face this? Could we actually talk without you spacing out?"

Rubbing her forehead with her fingers, she knew the answer to his question was no. She'd been spacing out for months, nothing real, everything feeling like she was floating in shallow water. And it was possible, probable, that she'd spaced out all the time since Mark had left her. What had she done but go on? Wasn't that what people did? Go on? Try not to die? Stay afloat even when there was loneliness and death and despair and so much fear everywhere? Wasn't this what all this worldwide clawing was about, nations trying to stay on top? Who was paying attention to anything? Nobody could walk around in a permanent state of meditation or grace. The Grand Canyon faded from view, as had her vision of Sofie and her father. Nothing was permanent but suffering. The Buddhist woman at Montclair Park must have known that. Jesus knew that. Every story in the world ended with that.

"Jenna!"

There was a rush in her ears, waves of sound from her own brain, everything empty, empty, an ache, a fire in her throat. "I'm pregnant. I'm having a baby. It's yours."

Through the rush of sound in her head and face, she looked at Mark, watching him change, his mouth opening, the creases in his forehead relaxing, his body softening, flexing, falling back to the chair, his hands opening and closing. The air thinned, the swifts stopped calling, the buildings next to Jolie's house became hollowed boxes. *This is what it must be like when you die,* Jenna thought, this stillness, this acute perception, this floating feeling, her body suspended on top of her words. If she stood and walked away, no one would know. Time would hold her form in the chair, but she could take off, escape Mark's questions, leave behind her aching stomach, her dry mouth. But she'd never been able to escape her body. Not in labor. Not when Sofie was a corpse in front of her.

"I'm sorry," she whispered.

"Are you— How did . . . ?" He put his face in his hands, mumbling into his fingers.

"You know, in Bali. The night after I found her. The night you showed up. We did it the way we did the first time."

He looked up, his face wet from quiet tears. "Really?"

"This is Sofie's brother or sister."

"Yes," he said, his voice an ache cracking open in the air between them.

"And the baby's healthy, as far as they can tell. I have a good doctor here."

"Why didn't you tell me? I deserved to know, Jenna."

She nodded. He was right. He'd deserved to know everything. But he'd also deserved to be there with the first baby, their first child. He'd gone, and Jenna was so used to holding the responsibility—or was it taking? Or was it needing? Having to have. Must have. Needs to have now. Hers. All of it. Everything. "There was nothing you could have done. I didn't know until today that the baby was all right. I couldn't even make a decision until I found out."

"You mean about abortion."

"Yes. No. I couldn't— I don't think I could have aborted. I couldn't lose . . . but I didn't really know what I was going to do, until I heard Dr. Velázquez's voice today."

"Were you going to tell me? Or were you just going to hide out here? Jesus, Jenna. I should have known from the beginning. It's mine, too." Mark lowered his face into his hands again, and she remembered the cracking pain of his tears in Bali. In them, she'd heard how much he'd lost long before Sofie had died.

"Where's Renata?"

He shook his head and didn't say anything. Jenna turned to the house and saw the dark shapes of her mother and Jolie on the couch. Everyone was waiting for an answer, and Jenna couldn't figure out the question; there were too many. When she was little and her father came home from work, he would pull her to his lap, jiggling his legs like a bucking bronco, and say, "What do you say, little girl? What does my little girl want?" Jenna would laugh and grab his shoulders, never answering because of the laughter in her throat.

Later, in high school, when she learned the word *rhetorical,* she knew that her father was repeating, night after night, a pleasing question that would remain unanswered, the point of the question a happy sound to go along with the ride. But what did she want? And Mark was as confused as Jenna.

"I want to come home," she said quietly.

Mark looked up, wiped his eyes, and then sat straight. "Okay."

"I don't want to work for a while. I might do something other than teaching, but whatever it is, I want time off from the college."

"Fine."

"I want to write something. I am writing something."

"Okay. But. Well—"

Jenna felt heat in her face. "You asked me what I was doing, Mark. Now the answer isn't good?"

He waved his hand. "No. It's not that."

"What is it, then?"

"I left Renata. A while ago. I haven't been—since Bali. I've been a mess. I've been living at the office. I tried to tell you that day before Christmas. She's going to stay in our house. I've got the payment on your house, too. And if you don't want to work for a year, it would be—I'd have to stay with you."

"I can make the payments for a year. I have some savings," Jenna said, but she really didn't. All her extra money had gone toward Sofie—camps and trips and lessons and vacations. Then there were books and half of the tuition at Cal and the trip to Bali that Jenna had almost said no to.

"Property taxes are due, Sof," she had said. "I don't think I can come up with much more than plane fare."

"That's great, Mom," Sofie had said, flinging her arms around her mother's shoulders. "Thanks so much. For everything."

Mark slapped his hand down on his thigh. "Jesus, Jenna, I know what you make at the college. And didn't they cut your salary by five percent last year? Budget cuts? The new governor trying to make a point? Maybe you can pay the mortgage on the house, but not much else."

When they bought the house when Sofie was a baby, Jenna had loved it because of the wide entry hall, big enough for a table and a coat rack and long family hugs. She'd loved the quarter-acre backyard and the huge chef's kitchen with the Viking stove and the double sink, all of it overwhelming after the small, dank apartments they'd rented.

"Look at the pantry!" she'd said, as if discovering gold. "A laundry room!"

Mark hadn't been able to say anything, and judging by the dazed, euphoric look on both their faces, their agent sat down at the kitchen table and started filling out the offer forms.

Most of all, she'd loved that there were four bedrooms, the master for her and Mark, and one each for the three children she'd imagined she'd have. But it had only been she and Mark and Sofie, and then she and

Sofie, and then her. One bedroom had become an office, and the other was full of broken, leftover, outgrown junk: pom-poms, broken chairs, Life and Monopoly games, Barbie dolls, Lois's sewing machine, essays and journals and tests Jenna couldn't throw away, and boxes of tax information from years and years. Sofie's room was empty, but now it would become a nursery again.

Since Sofie had gone to college, Jenna rarely prepared her own meals—picking up salads and sandwiches at the Monte Veda Grill—and the refrigerator was full of only condiments and Calistoga water, except when Tim came over and cooked, leaving leftover pastas, pestos, hunks of French bread, jars of Kalamata olives, pancetta, and tomatoes. The house probably wouldn't know how to hold a family anymore.

"Live there." Jenna brought her hands to her face, pressing her fingertips to her cheekbones. Even if Mark was already lost to her, how would she be able to tell Tim this news? No matter how she would say it—Mark and she would be living together as parents and friends, not lovers—it would sound absurd. And did this mean Mark wanted to go back to their old life, their old marriage? "What—you don't mean *together?*"

"No, not together. Not like that. In the spare bedroom. Like roommates. I was going to tell you that I needed you to buy me out or we had to sell it altogether, but I couldn't. I know we should have figured all of this out years ago. . . ."

He stopped, rubbing his cheek. "I could never deal

with buying you out or selling the house. Not then, and not now. And when we came back from Bali, it was like we'd lost Sofie again. That's where she still is for me. At the house. Not in Bali or at Cal. So it's all I could come up with. That or move back in with Renata, but she doesn't want me anymore."

Jenna closed her eyes and leaned back in the chair, the air alive again, moving across her face. "It's never going to be over."

"We'll always think about her, Jenna. How could it be over?"

Jenna opened her eyes. "No, I meant our marriage."

Mark started to say something, and then the words stilled on his tongue. He shrugged and sat back, folding his hands in his lap.

"Okay," she said. "For maybe, well, a year after the baby. Then we'll decide what to do. Sell the house. Whatever. I'll go back to work."

"Are you sure?" Mark's eyebrows were dark against his forehead, the three quizzical lines back.

"No. I'm not sure about anything."

• • •

All the things I didn't tell you about your father are still true. I didn't tell you how he looked when he left us, his face pinched and white, his eyes averted, his shoulders set back. I never mentioned how I held you in my arms as I followed him around the house, asking him questions, like, "Why are you really going? Is it really another woman? Or is it something else you can't say?"

I was crying; you were crying. Your diaper was wet, and you started to hiccup. But it felt like your heart was trying to come out of your tiny body. My heart felt dead, made still by your father's flat voice.

"I'm leaving because of you, Jenna. Because you can't share."

That happened. And it's also true that I had to call him two weeks, one week, one day before all your events and recitals and plays. It's true that he didn't show up, and not because of the reasons I gave you, Sofie. What did I say? "Oh, your father had an emergency at the hospital."

So many times, that wasn't it. The meanness in me wanted to lay it all out, throw the carpet of your father's weaknesses before you so you could step on it. But then you'd come home from an afternoon with him, smiling, sun on your nose and cheeks, a bag of new clothes Renata had picked out. You wanted to talk about his brand-new VCR and the restaurant he'd taken you to that gave every child free ice-cream cones.

I held all the bad things about your father inside me, but then what did I do? I held him to me, too, for years. So I'm going to say these things, Sofie. I'm going to tell you about your father, good things.

He wants the best. The right thing. Our marriage didn't work out, but he wanted it to, even if he didn't know how to fix it. He had no language that I could understand, and I don't know if I could have heard him. He wanted to be a better father; I could hear it in his voice over the phone when he canceled a date with you. I could see it when he dropped you off early because there really was an emergency at the hospital. He loved me and he loved you, maybe not in the way I wanted him to, but he loved the best he could.

He's smart. You know that. He can look at a situation and see through it, as if it were a puzzle. Maybe he can't put the pieces back together, but he can see where the spaces are, the breaks, the connections.

Your father always supported us. I never had to worry that his check wouldn't show up or that your tuition wouldn't be paid. He didn't take his anger out on us through withholding, not once.

He's good in bed. Are you shocked? I would have told you that one day, maybe after you and Robert had been together longer. But I was always happy being next to your father's skin. Maybe not the last time. I don't think I was feeling anything but your death. But all those times he snuck into my bed, it was nice. He's a generous man with his mouth and body. There I had nothing to hold back from you except for the topic itself.

He doesn't know how wonderful he could be. Maybe no one does. Your grandma and Dee always tell me nice things about myself, but I can't see them. Your dad can't, either. He's always just about ready to take off, and then something pulls him down. When your father was a boy, he was outside with his sister, your aunt Miranda. It was hot, and they were in their swimsuits, playing with the hose. At some point, your father felt himself lift off the concrete patio and hover in the air, over Miranda. He moved his arms, he kicked, but he stayed in the air, until very slowly, he came back down to earth. When he touched ground, he ran inside to tell Grandma Rose. He said, "Mommy, I flew. I flew in the backyard. Randi saw me."

Grandma Rose kept her back to the kitchen sink and said, "You just fell asleep, Markie. It was a dream. That's all."

To this day, your father believes he's flown, hovered in the backyard of his childhood home, and Miranda remembers it, too. Or at least she thinks she does. It might be that your father told the story so often, she remembers his words rather than the actual flight. But here's what I think. I think his soul left for one brief moment, the air too hot, the day too long, and then came back, pulling your father off the ground, and then settled back into his body, bringing him down to earth and keeping him there.

Ten

The house was dark and stale with unbreathed air. In the 2.5 months Jenna had been gone, the cats had settled in at Susan's, and now they turned away with flickering tails when Jenna walked into her neighbor's house with a can of opened Meat Treat.

"They're angry. It might take them awhile," Susan said apologetically, as Bean hugged her around the neck, his claws clinging to her shirt. "I'll carry him. Peanut's over there behind the curtain."

So they carried the cats back into the house, Susan recommending a good three days inside, no outside trips. "It'll remind them this is where they live."

Jenna thought that maybe she should do the same thing herself: close the door and wander the rooms. But this time, she wasn't simply walking through the house with grief. She would see the house as an expectant mother; she would look at the rooms as a roommate. Before Mark came over later in the evening, she had to figure a way to get rid of the mess in the spare bedroom.

"But don't do it all yourself," Mark had said. "Call Dee. Ask Susan. Or wait for me to get there. I can sleep on the couch for a night or two." Mark had dropped her off and gone to his office and to Renata's, to tell everyone the weird news that they were moving back in together.

Bean and Peanut had run into her bedroom and under her bed, and Jenna sat on the edge of the mattress, looking into the mirror she'd looked into for years. She didn't appear any different than she had in December. There wasn't anything that showed yet, save for her fuller belly, and she was hiding that under a loose blouse.

Jenna watched herself. Really, in this soft afternoon

light, she was the same pregnant mother she'd been with Sofie. Sure, up close everything was different, her skin, her hair, her body, but inside, she was exactly the same. Her heart beat in the same slow, easy rhythm, her blood pumped, her body made a placenta, nourished the baby in her womb. She worked. She functioned. She was alive and reproducing, growing not just the baby, but herself, too. Her cells, her skin, her blood.

Letting herself fall back to the mattress, Jenna brought her hands to her face. It wasn't fair that she had all this and Sofie had none of it, but that was how it was. And instead of feeling guilty about all the life inside of her, she should take it up and crack open the future, let it all happen. Let all the bad and good and miserable and joyous happen.

She sat up again, blinking into her own reflection. There she was. Jenna. Mother, twice over.

The phone rang, and she turned to the nightstand, looking at the phone. *Here it starts,* she thought, *life.* Leaning over, she answered it.

"Hello?"

"You're there," Lois said. "Thank goodness."

"I was going to call. I was looking around here. It feels like I've been gone for years, not weeks. The cats won't even speak to me."

"If they did, I'd be flying up right now to put you in a different kind of hospital." Lois laughed, and Jenna could imagine her walking around her kitchen, watering the poinsettias she was trying to nurture through the year into the next holiday season. "So how's it going? Is Mark at the house with you?"

"No, after we flew in, he dropped me off. He's taking care of some stuff at his office. And then Renata's. It's so awkward, Mom. I can't believe I agreed to this."

"It makes sense for now. Gives you both some time to forget and forgive."

Jenna nodded. "Maybe. For now . . . how's Jolie?"

In the pause of her mother's thought, Jenna thought of how her cousin had looked when she and Mark walked back into the house and announced their plan. Jenna hadn't been thinking, still full of the mystery of Mark's rental car out front, his idea of moving in together, her own actual acceptance of it. But as Mark spoke, she saw Jolie's color fade, her body slump, her fingers clutch the arm of the couch. "No! No!" Jenna wanted to say, waving her hands, hoping that the motion would startle Jolie back into color.

Mark didn't notice anything wrong, talking about his work and the office, vaguely mentioning Renata, the separation. But Jenna knew what was really happening. Jolie was losing another baby—the same way she lost all those embryos in the years before. She'd seen this baby floating in the sonogram, bought it clothes, secretly knew the sex, as did Lois, both of them keeping the details in whispers behind their hands.

And then when Jenna thought Jolie would burst out crying, she stood up. "That's great," she said. "I think it will help you both. Look, I've got to go to work. Call me, Jenna. Let me know how it goes. Don't forget all the baby stuff."

Most anyone would have thought she'd recovered amazingly well, but Jenna later noticed that Jolie didn't take her purse or the keys to the store. She wasn't going to go sell postcards and Grand Canyon mugs to tourists. She was going to cry somewhere.

Now on the phone, Lois cleared her throat. "She says she's okay. I'm going up later in the week. But, sweetie, it's better that you left sooner rather than later. What if you had the baby and then Mark came up with this plan? How do you think Jolie would have felt if you moved out then? It's for the best. Jolie needs to keep painting. To find someone. It's time for her to let this baby thing go."

"I still feel bad. I just plopped down there and then got all weirded out when she became involved. I probably would have left even if Mark hadn't shown up."

"Well, it's water under the bridge. Write her a letter. Let her know how thankful you are. And then she can figure her life out for herself. Or not. It's not everyone who can, believe you me."

Jenna smoothed the comforter with her hand. "Mom?"

"What, sweetie?"

"Thanks."

"It's nothing. Call me when Mark settles in. Love you."

"Love you, too." Jenna hung up. The air was filled with stillness and a million dust motes. Standing up, she walked to the window and opened it wide, rubbing her arms against the chill. If her bedroom was this musty, then she could only imagine what her study was like. She thought of Lois's words: *Write her a letter.* She had come home for her writing—at least in part—and she could start with a letter. So she needed to clear up her office first, before Mark's room. She would organize the stacks of papers and folders and books, write Jolie a thank-you letter, and then get to her project, whatever it was going to be. Mark could clean up most of the mess himself. She wasn't his mother. She wasn't his wife. Not this time. Not anymore.

• • •

Dear Jolie,

I don't know if I have the words to thank you for taking me in on the spot, providing me with a wonderful place to live, finding me a job, and caring for me. All you did for me was too much to ask, and I didn't even have to ask. You were there and welcoming and amazing.

And even though I know you understand why I had to leave, I feel like I abandoned you. Your life without me and the baby is so full. That's why I made Tim drive me to your house. All that color, all that life in your hands—well, it inspired me. As we were driving, all I could imagine was living a life where art was possible. Where I could be pregnant for a while and absorb what you seemed to have. Did have. Do have.

Then you told me about how you wanted a baby. There we were, two women, cousins, one having what the other didn't. Is that true, though? You are a mother, Jolie, in the way you took care of me, the way you treat people at the store, the life you are living. You nurture yourself. I may have had Sofie and I may have this baby, but I haven't known how to nurture myself for years. That I am here—that I just managed to clear off my desk for writing—is a testament to your care. You don't need to have a baby for that. It's something you carry inside you. You also have the gift of saying what you feel, of saying the truth, and I know I have that somewhere inside of me. I'm going to find it. I have to. I need it.

If I could do it over again, I wouldn't have left so abruptly, would have given you more than a day's notice. I wouldn't have flown away so quickly with Mark. But of course, you can't do it all over again, even if you want to. Life comes at you in a straight line with a strong current, pushing you forward. I'm trying to swim, Jolie. I'm trying to stay afloat.

All my thanks for your kindness. And thank you for the time you spend with Lois. She loves having you close.

Love, Jenna

•   •   •

"JENNA?" MARK knocked on her study and pushed open the door. "There you are."

Nodding, she looked up, wiping her eyes. She was on the carpet, surrounded by boxes of photos, the past all around her. "Hi."

"What are you doing?"

"I uncovered these boxes when I was cleaning up earlier. I hadn't wanted to open them before. I thought I was ready to see her, but I was wrong."

She leaned against the bookcase. "She was so amazing, Mark. She was a miracle."

Mark held the door and looked at her. "I can't do that now."

"Okay."

"I just can't see her."

"All right."

He pushed the door open a bit and stepped into the room. "Didn't you used to put them in albums?"

"I did for years. But then I snapped away, got them developed, and stashed them in these boxes. There were so many pictures. Soccer matches. Dance recitals. Field trips. Birthday parties. Graduations. Trips to Phoenix. Maybe I knew that I had to keep a record. And maybe I knew that I wouldn't want to make them easy to look at."

"You couldn't have known." Mark sat in the chair at her desk, crossing his legs.

"Are you sure? I sometimes think that Sofie knew. Last Thanksgiving in Phoenix, she asked us to all hold hands, and she told us how much she loved us. Individually. It was like she was saying good-bye."

Turning the chair so he could look out the window, Mark was silent, tapping his fingers on the desk. "I never got to say good-bye to her."

There were so many ways to reply to that statement. Jenna had to bite her mean tongue, almost ready to remind Mark of all he'd missed, and because of what?

A woman he would leave, anyway. But with Sofie surrounding her in a colorful time line, she couldn't. What would it serve? Who would it serve? Instead, she held up one of the last photos, a picture of Sofie at San Francisco International Airport, on her way to Bali.

"Look at this one. Just this one."

Mark sighed and held out his hand. "Okay."

She leaned over and placed it on his palm, feeling the slip of the photos under her legs as she settled back on the rug. Closing her eyes, she put out her own palms and felt them under her skin, the evidence of a life she used to have. Sofie's evidence. This year, she was going to put the photos in albums, if not for herself, then for this baby who would never know his or her sister. And the sister would loom large in mythology, the one who died in the flames, the one whose death created the new baby's own life. A Phoenix. Jenna knew that such a heavy burden of story would be too much for any child, so she had to make it possible to understand.

"Oh," Mark said. "Oh."

"Yes," Jenna said, her eyes still closed. *Oh, indeed.*

"She was so beautiful."

Jenna nodded, not knowing if he saw her do so. She let her hands touch the photos again, and knew that Sofie would always be beautiful in the photos, in Mark's mind, in the minds of everyone who knew her. Even under the sheet in the auditorium, burns and all, she'd been beautiful. "She was."

"She looked like you, Jenna. When I met you. Just like you."

245

Her throat tightened, and she opened her eyes. Mark was staring at the photo, his glasses in one hand. He was somewhere else, maybe back in college, at Moffitt Library. He was a tall, gangly young man, leaning over to whisper in her ear, "Do you have another pen?"

She'd pushed her Farrah Fawcett hair (the style possible even with red hair) away from her face and stared at him, his pale skin, his curls, his thick science textbooks. "Yeah," she said, handing him a Bic. "Here."

That was his come-on line. "Do you have another pen?" And it had worked, everything starting from that moment. Jenna could still feel the hushed warmth and the wooden table under her elbows, smell the books and magazines and his soap, something clean and white and strong.

Here they were, almost twenty-five years later, in a study surrounded by books, the pictures of their dead daughter spread around them. A pain hitched in her chest, but then it flowed away, and she felt something else rise. Her cheeks pulled up, her eyes crinkled, the tears that had become laughter moved to her throat, on her tongue, in the air.

"What?" He put on his glasses. "What's so funny?"

Jenna leaned back. "So what are you saying? I'm not beautiful now? What a nice thing to say on our first night together."

Mark put on his glasses and let the photos fall gently to the desk. "That's not what I meant."

But she couldn't stop, his comments to her so Mark, the pen, the lost beauty, all of it exactly what was on his mind, and she convulsed, lying down on the ground, her family under her arms and cheek and waist. The laughter felt so good, brought her so much air and pain, her stomach tight.

"Stop," Mark said, standing up and walking to her. "Don't."

But she couldn't stop. Didn't want to, something so big trying to come out. "I . . . I . . . ." And then she was caught again, the waves of feeling everywhere, her eyes watering, her mouth pulled back on her teeth.

"Jenna." He swished some photos away and sat down, rubbing her waist. "What's so funny?"

At his question, she felt the laughter turn deeper, darker, a blue color inside her, and she was crying, weeping, her hands over her eyes. "Everything," she cried.

"No. No," he murmured, lying down next to her, fitting his body against hers, holding her tight. "It's not funny. None of it."

She could no longer speak. So she cried, holding her ex-husband, embracing on top of the record of their entire life together.

MARK WAS IN the spare room, making a space for himself, the walls thumping as he lifted and moved furniture and packed up years of castoff hobbies: boxes of yarn and crochet needles, a child's loom Lois had bought for Sofie, stacks of puzzles Jenna had started doing when Sofie began high school. Jenna was in bed, trying to read *Mansfield Park*, but the words were blurring, the sentences bleeding into smudged paragraphs, words drifting entirely off the page. For a second, she imagined she was going into a pregnancy-induced diabetic coma or suffering from a preeclamptic stroke, but when the tears hit the page, she realized she was crying still, hours after her strange behavior in her study. She wiped her eyes, focused on the story, wiped her eyes, and then closed the book and leaned back against the headboard.

When the phone rang, her heart thumped like the walls in Mark's room. Even though she and Mark hadn't lived together for years, she was convinced it was the hospital, just as she had been back when he was a resident. Nothing was more important than those calls and the people who made them, especially in those technologically stunted times before call-waiting and e-mail and voice mail. She picked it up, her voice tight and small, imagining she would hand the receiver over to him, his life already more important than hers.

"Hello?"

"Jenna," Tim said, his voice surprised and angry. "You *are* home."

"Tim. Hi. Hello. I just got back today."

In the pause, Jenna heard the stillness in his apartment. No music, no television, no radio. She could see him sitting at his kitchen table, leaning back in a chair, his dark hair shiny in the overhead light. He was wearing jeans and a white T-shirt. Tevas. No, running shoes. He was pushing his hair back with one hand. His neck was salty from working in the kitchen. He smelled like tomatoes and red wine.

"Why didn't you call right away? I couldn't believe it when Jolie told me you'd flown home."

"How is Jolie?"

"Sad. She misses you."

"Did she tell you what happened?"

"The baby's okay, isn't it?" Tim's voice deepened. "You're okay?"

"I'm fine. We're both fine. It's just that some things have . . . changed. Or they haven't really changed. I need to tell you something. It's kind of weird."

In this next pause, she heard his body, the way his muscles flexed and his blood beat. His hair fell over his eyes. He rubbed his palm on the table, wanting to slap it. A tiny trickle of sweat ran along his sternum and onto his belly. "What?"

"Mark flew down. I told him about the baby. I was going to, anyway, because the baby's fine. Healthy."

In Tim's apartment, relief flew in the window. He sat back, the sweat dried. The light over the table grew yellow, sunflower, warm. "How'd he take it? About the baby, I mean. Now that the baby's okay. And that's good, Jenna. I'm so glad."

"Okay. He was mad at first. But he had some things to tell me, too."

"Like what . . . Jenna?"

"Oh, um, Mark left his wife. Or she asked him to leave. A mutual thing, I think. And now that I don't want to work for a year—"

"You're not coming back to work?"

"I can't. Not now. I wasn't doing a good job, Tim. I'd started hating the students, resenting them for being alive, Tim. I don't think that's a great way to teach."

What was she hearing now in his apartment? Gusts of wind? Electricity surging in his walls? The tin of anger from his throat *ting, ting, ting*ing?

"So what is Mark going to do?"

"This is the weird part. And it doesn't mean what you might think it does. He's—he's moving into the spare bedroom," she said, feeling all the breath in her voice. "You see, he was living in his office."

Now she knew it was anger that she heard, the roar of red coming from his body. Or was it purple? She pulled the phone away from her ear, letting the energy escape. When she pressed her ear back, all she heard was breathing.

"Tim?"

"When were you going to tell me?"

Jenna closed her eyes and tried to swallow down a lump of feeling in the back of her throat. It was so thick, she could hardly breathe, but she remembered it from somewhere. Where? And then she saw it, the night that Mark left her, his still, impassive expression, Sofie crying in the nursery, the circle of light that surrounded him as he turned to face her and then closed the door. That's what she felt now; the truth of this relationship with Tim ending. It would end, and she'd be left with this feeling again. How it hurt her throat, and now her face and her eyes. The world began to smudge and smear, her tears coming again. No wonder she never stayed with anyone longer than a few months. It was this pain. She hated it.

"I don't know. I didn't want you to get the wrong idea. It's not like we're together again."

Tim laughed, a cracked leather whip lashing the phone line. "You may as well be. What's the difference? You slept with him when he was married to someone else. Why not now, when he's separated? What's a spare bedroom and a hallway to people who never gave up on each other?"

"That's not fair!" Jenna pushed past the pain in her throat. "How can you . . . ?" But she knew how he could say it. He was right. What was the difference?

"How can I what?"

She sighed. "I know I don't even deserve to say this, but I don't want to lose you. I know I probably already did, back in Pine Flat when I decided to stay at Jolie's. But I keep thinking that maybe later, maybe some-time—"

"Look," Tim said, "I don't want to talk about this any-more. I'm hanging up." And he did, the phone dead in her hand. He was gone, not even a flash of his apart-ment light, not a whiff of his sauce on the stove. There wasn't anything left of him in her ear or mouth or eyes. It was just her, like always, in bed with a book.

• • •

You were going to save the world. Do you remember telling me that? You were sixteen and we were reading the paper at the kitchen table. You threw the paper down and snorted.

251

"They're killing everything!" you said. "By the time I have kids, there won't be any ocean left. No redwoods. No tigers or elephants. Barely a condor. The air will be brown. Maybe we'll have to live underground."

I didn't laugh. What I wanted to do was just stare at you, your eyes so full of anger and outrage, your face flushed. But then I said, "What should we do?"

"Vote them all out of office. Protest. Get arrested."

"What about go to school, study, find a job where you can really make a difference?" I said. I couldn't see you in jail at that point, not when you were in a habit of taking hour-long soaking baths at night and polishing your toenails a different color every week.

"What good would thinking do? We need action," you said, moving your hand through the air. "I'm going to change the world."

I believed you. And it astounded me. How did I raise a girl like you? How did you come from my body? When I was young, I didn't imagine that I would be anything but a wife and mother. I never thought that I could stand in front of a classroom and teach anyone anything. My mother was the strong one, the one who argued with the man behind the meat counter or my teachers or the Monte Veda police officer who pulled her over for a true, sliding California stop. But what was she? A homemaker. A housewife. That's what we called them. She didn't blink when over on the other side of the hills, Berkeley students gathered and cried out for freedoms. She didn't march or burn her bra. She didn't tell my father to stop opening doors for her at restaurants or bringing her flowers.

So if she did the dishes in the sink, not asking for a dishwasher like all the other moms, why should I have aspired to Congress or business or creativity? Instead, I worried about my body, how large my thighs were, how many split ends I had in my long hair, how to smooth my rough elbows with lemons. I followed my friends into college because that's what we were doing, and I met Mark. He sat at a table in the library. All he had to do was ask me for a pen. Later, I saw him leaning against a brick wall with a pencil between his teeth. He reminded me that I loved to read and think and write and draw, pulling me along with him as he read everything in the medical library. Before I knew it, I fell in love with late nights and dim lamps, books piled high on the library table, the still, loud hush of a hundred brains thinking at once. We went to coffee shops and talked about ideas. He was going to save children in Third World countries, and I was going to teach them how to read. We made love all night, and didn't comb our hair before leaving for school in the morning. Nothing mattered but us and ideas and a future that didn't yet include you. We didn't even imagine you. You would have held us down, made us break the promise we made to the world. We were going to change it all. And we were wrong. About everything.

Eleven

Mark cleaned out the spare room and moved in so completely that Jenna forgot to think of it as a spare room at all. All the things she remembered about living with Mark came back, the calls—as she'd anticipated—from the hospital and his office; the smell of his soap in the shower, musky and clean; the rings of coffee on the counter in the morning because he'd always read the newspaper as he poured, slopping liquid everywhere. He came home late, turning the television on low and reading a *Scientific American* until he was sleepy, his steps slow on the stairs. But now, in this new life, Jenna didn't care. She wasn't waiting for him to warm her bed or talk with her or take over a nighttime feeding. She didn't wake at 5 A.M. with a crying baby, knowing she had to slap down some sort of breakfast in front of him and then consider how to grade her ESL students' narrative essays, stories of such pain—swimming from angry Vietnamese shores to boats filled with desolate, sodden refugees, leaving a weeping mother behind in North Korea, calling night after night at the Berlin Wall—that she didn't care about articles or possessive pronouns or diction.

In this new version of their living together, Mark was often gone before she even got out of bed, the house hers for hours and hours, just as it had been since Sofie went to school.

One morning, Jenna got in her car and drove into West Contra Costa County to the Bay View Library, and sat through the Reading Readiness tutoring orientation. Valerie DuLaney stood in front of the mostly retired people and talked about the importance of literacy and early intervention.

"Don't laugh," she said. "I know you think it's obvious. I know you think no one is illiterate anymore. But look at me. I worked for twelve years in a dentist's office without knowing how to read. I recognized symbols and diagrams, and listened closely to every word coming out of anyone's mouth. By the time I got home at night, I was exhausted. Let's not let another generation of kids live like I did."

So after the orientation and training sessions, Jenna found herself sitting with Hazel, an eight-year-old from Rodeo with a chipped front tooth and dry, electric-blond hair.

"This is so *th*tupid," Hazel said, her *stupid* slippery from the space in her mouth. "I don't need to come here. My *th*tupid foster mother made me. Anyway, are you, like, fat?"

Jenna put a hand on her belly and nodded. "Yes, I am fat. And it's because I'm having a baby."

"Oh. Okay. Don't you have a job or something?"

"My job is to help you read," Jenna said, her words exactly the same as they had been when Sofie was five and looking at a Henry and Mudge book.

"I can read," Hazel said, rolling her eyes and sitting back in her chair.

"That's great. So why don't you show me?"

Jenna pulled out the book Valerie DuLaney had given all the elementary tutors. "It's funny and well written," Valerie had said. "That's important."

"Here," Jenna said, laying the book out flat in front of Hazel. "It's called *Wilbur Eats Everything*."

"*Th*tupid," said Hazel. "Don't you have any comic books?"

The next session—after *Wilbur Eats Everything* turned out to be a bust—Jenna brought in three books that Susan's son Julien had lent her.

"I loved these," he'd said. "This little kid, Calvin? He thinks his toy tiger Hobbes can, like, talk!" Julien had handed them to her. "You'll bring them back, right?"

Jenna had promised to return them on pain of replacement, and now Hazel stared at the big tiger on the front of the first book.

"Who's that?"

"That's Hobbes. He's real but not real. Only Calvin can see him."

"He's pretend?" Hazel's eyes widened. "No one else knows about him?"

"Something like that."

Turning to the first page, Jenna pointed at the first box, where Calvin and Hobbes looked out a bedroom window. "What is he saying, Hazel?"

Hazel put her finger on the first letter. "Ta."

"Right. What next?"

"Is this about them? Look, they're sliding down a hill!"

"Right. They are. So what's this next letter? An i, right?"

"Ta-*i*-g . . ."

"Taig what?"

"Taig-rs. Tigers."

Jenna smiled and almost put a hand on Hazel's shoulder, but then simply rested her hand on the back of the chair. "Right. Tigers. And then what?"

Hazel smiled. "They're going to crash the sled. I bet they're going to be bad together. Like me. I like to be bad." She looked up at Jenna, her brown eyes almost gold. "I'm grounded all the time at my foster home."

Jenna looked at Hazel, knowing that if she were Hazel's mother, she'd slow down, ask how Hazel felt about being grounded. How she felt about being in a foster home. But this little girl with the straw hair and pumpkin face wasn't her child, so Jenna laughed.

Hazel put her hand on the book and glanced up at Jenna. "What?"

"I've always wanted to be bad, Hazel. Real bad. But I couldn't. Now I'm just mean sometimes."

The girl nodded. "Mean's good, too. Mean hurts."

After her second session with Hazel, Jenna drove into Walnut Creek for an appointment with her OB-GYN, Dr. Zahri, who'd sent away for Dr. Velázquez's reports and agreed with them all. But Dr. Zahri wanted her to come in every two weeks.

"Just a precaution. I want to monitor you for a while. I don't usually take patients so far along in their pregnancies, not even old favorites." She looked at Jenna over her glasses. "Mark was very persuasive. But you already *know* that." Dr. Zahri laughed, her cheeks reddening.

"Oh, you've made a funny," Lois would have said, wagging her finger, her eyebrows raised.

But Jenna had simply nodded, staying still on the examination table, her body cold under the gown. Mark had arranged everything, making sure that "the damn best OB in the state" would keep her as a patient. And so far, Jenna agreed with Mark, because Dr. Zahri thought her baby would be fine, and she wanted to believe her.

She wore loose tops, her pants unbuttoned, one, then two, then all of the buttons wide open. Finally, she'd driven to Walnut Creek and slipped into A Pea in the Pod. Before she'd left the house, she'd pulled her hair into a short ponytail and covered her wrinkles with her "age-defying cover-up." The last thing she wanted was a helpful salesperson sidling up to her and saying, "Oh, that's a perfect present for a new grandchild." But maybe, Jenna thought as she pushed through the racks of surprisingly attractive clothing, these salespeople were used to older, richer, more prepared mothers, in vitro and drugs making miracles happen, giving women older than she the opportunity to shop here and buy maternity shirts that clung to their rounded bellies. Gone were the bows and apronlike dresses she'd worn with Sofie, every new outfit making her look like some kind of Humpty Dumpty schoolgirl. This time when she returned home with three bags of new clothes, she tried everything on again, and was surprised at how her larger breasts and full stomach looked—like a perfect, sensuous landscape, hills against a dusky sky.

In the next weeks, the weather shifted, the cool middle of March turning to a warm spring. The grass was green on the hills of Monte Veda, the oak trees shooting out their yellow-green leaf buds, the acacias a poof of yellow mist along the highways. A swarm of cedar waxwings had found the pyracantha and privet bushes in the backyard, raucously stripping them clean before buzzing off to breed. Jenna had decided to do some planting, pulling up the woody lamb's ears and dusty miller, and was in the front yard laying on mulch when Dee pulled up in her new Toyota Prius, the long-awaited environment saver Dee had convinced her husband, Rick, to buy.

"I bet you never thought he'd agree to the car," Dee said, closing the door behind her. "But here it is. The current answer to all our woes."

Jenna began to push herself up, but Dee shook her head, waving her hands. "Stay there. I'm coming down to you. It's a picnic in the grass."

"It's a really cute car," Jenna said. "I know that's the real reason you wanted it. And it's blue."

Dee pretended to look around for eavesdroppers, whispering, "You're right, of course. I just told Rick the purchase was because of all the war talk. Stop the fuel madness."

"Likely reason. Sit down. What do you have for me? I've been starving for hours. Days, maybe."

Dee arranged herself on the grass and began to open the bag. "You better eat when you're hungry, for god's sake."

"Oh, I have," Jenna said, taking the wrapped sandwich Dee held out to her. "Every hour on the hour. Nothing seems to do the trick."

"This will. Your fave. Salami, tomatoes, and mayo on whole wheat. Nothing healthy but the tomatoes."

"Perfect." Jenna unwrapped the sandwich, and the smell of the slightly warm bread and the tang of the wine in the salami made her eyes water and made her think of Tim and his Italian kitchen. She kept her head down and took a bite, letting the smooth mayo coat her tongue.

"So enough of this picture-postcard stuff. What's going on around here? How's the tutoring going?"

"Hazel has been a bad influence on me," Jenna said, wiping her mouth. "She's teaching me how to be bad."

"Oh, no," Dee said, laughing. "Just a few weeks on the job, and you're going to be fired. From a volunteer position, no less. What are you reading to her? Camus? Sartre? Nietzsche?"

"No. We're reading comic books instead of *Wilbur Eats Everything*."

"Oh, you wild woman," Dee said. "But I like the part about being bad. A shame Hazel can't influence you more."

"In what other way do I need to be bad?" Jenna sipped her sparkling water.

"Maybe with what's-his-name. You know, this man

you let move in and can't get rid of. You can't tell me it's working out."

"It's fine," Jenna mumbled through her mouthful.

Shaking her head, Dee bit into her turkey and Swiss on rye. They chewed together, cars slowly passing by the house, the air a swirl of plum blossoms and car exhaust. "I just don't get it."

"What's to get?" Jenna picked up a chip. "It makes sense. I'm going to be out of savings soon, and he can't pay the bills on three places. And really, we've known each other forever. He's the baby's father, anyway."

Dee opened a plastic container of olives and popped one in her mouth, searching in the bag for the napkins. "I know, I know. It just seemed to me that you had moved on. I know when Sofie— I know that you were brought together, but after that, while you were in Arizona, you seemed to be happier. Like you didn't care about all the things that'd been bothering you."

Jenna thought of Ralph and his store, Jolie, Dr. Velázquez and trips to Flagstaff, Lois driving up for lunch, shopping excursions at Target off the highway. The letters to Sofie she'd written, was still writing. "Maybe I needed to care about those things. Maybe I was fooling myself into thinking I could just disappear. You said the very same thing, Dee. You didn't get it."

"Well, maybe I do now. So have you told Dr. Kovacic about the new arrangements here with Mark? Did you tell him about Tim?"

"No. I'm not going to him anymore. We've talked on the phone a couple of times, and he's got me off the drugs and he's got me writing."

"Well, we all know the curative powers of the written sentence."

Jenna looked at Dee to see if she was kidding, to see if she was being bad, but Dee's face wasn't full of tease.

Finishing her sandwich, Jenna crunched the white paper into a ball and put it in the bag. She ate some more chips and took a sip of water. "So how is Tim? Does he have another girlfriend already?" she asked.

Dee shrugged, wiping her mouth. "I don't know. I never see him, except at meetings. He doesn't seem to want to talk about anything, at least to me. Have you spoken to him?"

"Just that once. When I got home. I didn't know what else to say after that. He was upset."

"Can you blame him? One minute he has a girlfriend, the next she's forcing him to pull over on the highway and dump her at her cousin's house. Then, just when he thinks she's come home, he finds out she's living with her ex, the father of her baby. I think that would put me over the edge."

"What should I have done?" Jenna felt her eyes fill and her face tighten into tears.

"Oh, hon, I don't know. I'm sorry. It's just that you've had so much change. I guess no one would figure it all out at once. I just want you to be happy."

Jenna looked at her friend and took a deep breath, her face letting go of sadness. That's what Dee wanted, had always wanted. She'd fixed Jenna up with every viable single man for years (once even a married man—

though his wife was in Bangladesh) before giving up; she'd invited Jenna and Sofie to holiday dinners and family events, wanting to include them, especially after Lois moved to Phoenix. "I know you do."

"Come on. Let's go inside to eat these cookies with milk. Just to seal the caloric assault."

They stood up, and Jenna put her arms around Dee, pulling her close. "Thanks," she whispered, and they turned and walked into the house.

"Chocolate," Dee said, as Jenna closed the front door. "Cures everything."

"Do you got anything I could have?" Hazel asked at the next session. They were halfway through the first Calvin and Hobbes book, and both of them were learning more about being bad. Calvin peed out of his bedroom window, crashed his sled into everything, and invented stories that boggled his parents' minds.

At Hazel's question, Jenna stopped reading and thought for a second. Then she reached down for her purse. Unzipping it, she rummaged at the bottom and found the Thunderbird key chain Tim had forgotten to turn in at the El Tovar Hotel.

"Here's something," Jenna said, holding it up, the totem pole bird wild-eyed and painted red and white and blue. "It's called a Thunderbird."

"Where did you get it?"

"It's a hotel key. My friend forgot to turn it in."

Hazel reached out and took it from her, dangling it in front of her face. "He stole it!"

Jenna almost argued, and then nodded. "Kind of."

Staring at the key chain, Hazel smiled. "Its face is mean."

"Maybe," Jenna said. "It's a good spirit, though. It will protect you. Keep you safe."

As she said the words, Jenna wanted to take them back. How could she give this little girl in foster care any hope at all? Nothing had protected Sofie, and she'd had all the care in the world.

But Hazel nodded. "Can I keep it forever?"

Jenna couldn't breathe. This year, she'd learned that forever was short. Forever didn't last, no matter how hard you tried.

"Of course," Jenna said. "It's a gift."

"Whoever gave you this musta really wanted you safe," Hazel said. "To steal it for you and everything."

Hazel tucked the key chain into her pocket and then looked back at the book, sounding out the world *balloon,* the one Calvin and Hobbes were going to fly away in.

JENNA KNEW SHE would find him at the Starbucks around the corner from his apartment. In the short months they'd been seeing each other, she had learned his Saturday-morning routine: sleep as long as possible, get dressed, pick up the paper on the way out of the building, and head to Starbucks for an espresso and a cranberry scone. How many times had she accompanied him, her hair puffy and slightly oily from their night in bed, her yesterday clothes not quite wrinkled but certainly not pressed. Jenna hadn't moved a hair dryer to his place, but before they'd gone to Arizona, she'd thought about it, knowing she wanted to ask him to add a step to the Saturday routine. A quick shower and a blow dry before walking down Main Street, both of them seconds from caffeine withdrawal.

He was sitting at his usual table, the back of his hair sticking straight up, the paper open in front of him. As she watched him flip the pages, she realized that he could have been here with someone else, a new woman, and right then, as she stared at his hair, the perfect shape of his head, his long fingers, she could feel how that tableau of new love would have knocked the wind out of her body.

Jenna could have walked right into the situation and would have had to walk slowly backwards out of the café, trying to avoid his gaze. There would have been no way to explain her presence in Walnut Creek at 9 A.M. *How stupid,* she thought. But she was here and he was alone, so she moved toward him, clutching her purse against her side.

"Hi." Her voice sounded strange, as if she were a high school freshman, only squeaky air moving from her lungs to lips. "I was hoping I'd find you."

Tim tried not to react, but his pupils dilated and a slight flush spread across his cheeks. He started to stand up, changed his mind, and then did stand up, his thigh knocking the tabletop, his espresso slopping in the cup. "Jenna. How are you?" He motioned to the table. "Sit?"

"Is it okay?"

And then he was familiar Tim again, cocking his head, shaking it slightly. "No. But sit anyway."

She shrugged out of her sweater and hung it and her purse on the chair back. As she turned to sit down, she saw he was looking at her belly, round in one of her tight new maternity shirts. "Yeah, it's out of control," she said.

He pushed his hair back. "It looks— You look great."

Sitting, she pushed her chair in, crossed her arms over her chest, then uncrossed them, leaning an elbow on the table. "I wanted to see you. You didn't call me back. I left a couple of messages."

Tim looked up, his eyes dark. Why would she think he wanted or needed to see her? This wasn't about him. Just like before, it was about her and what she needed. Jenna closed her eyes. "Oh, Tim."

"Jenna—" he began.

"I know. I know. It's too weird, hard, crazy—whatever—to see each other. I miss you, though. I tried to tell you. It's not like Mark and I are together."

He shook his head again. "You are exactly that, Jenna. You're living in the same house and having a baby. I'm not sure that sex or a deeper relationship would make you any more together. What more is there than living together and creating a new life? I mean, come on!" Brushing his hair back once, twice, he lowered his eyes and grabbed his coffee cup. "There's no room for me there. Just like there wasn't room for me at Jolie's. I'm expendable."

"That's not true!"

"Of course it is. Do you see me living at your house?

Do you see me helping you make the big decisions? No. It's you and it's Mark, and probably Dee and your mom and your neighbor, who have more to do with you than I do. So why pretend otherwise?"

The espresso machine hissed, and people passed by their table, holding rolled *New York Times* copies and coffee cups. Outside, the sycamores were sending out fine, pale green leaves, the sky a rich March blue. She shouldn't have come; she knew that now. She should have taken her trowel and pruning shears and gone into the backyard, digging out the dead lavender and salvia, planting monarda and golden sage, plants no deer would touch. Or better yet, she should have stayed in bed with *Fried Green Tomatoes*, a sad book at times, but mostly full of love and characters of cartoon quality. She would have laughed, waking up Mark, who would have made her coffee, bringing it to her in bed.

Looking up, though, Tim's face flat and sad, she knew she'd had to come here. She owed him that. She owed herself.

"You're right. I didn't think about you like I should have. It was wrong of me, and I'm sorry. It was stupid, and it was cruel."

Tim looked up, his eyes wide and clear. He rubbed his cheek, and Jenna remembered how he tasted after sleep, sweat and linen and her own smells clinging to his skin. He didn't say anything.

"If I hadn't gotten pregnant— If Sofie—"

He waved his hand. "We can't do the *if*s, Jenna. Let's not, okay?"

"You're right."

"It's really hard to see you, you know? These past three months have sucked."

Jenna smiled. "You sound like our students."

"I've learned so much from them." He was smiling, but she knew he meant it. He was still new enough to teaching to be hopeful, not like her, with all the students' excuses and unrelated questions and sad sonnets stuck in a repeating loop in her head. She must have felt the way he did back when she was teaching ESL, sounding out lines from poetry to teach them English: "My mistress's eyes are nothing like the sun. . . ." How proud she'd been when her Japanese students found the letter *L*, the tips of their tongues planted against their palates, spitting out the sound. She'd come home and told Mark, who was reading a chart on the couch.

"Lovely. Literally lovely and luscious, my little lollipop," he'd said, hugging her but continuing to read his chart.

Reaching out her hand, she grabbed Tim's wrist, holding his long, solid bones in her palm. "You are lovely." She felt her tongue against her palate, her teeth. "Truly lovely."

He shook his head and blushed, but he let her hold his wrist.

"I need time, Tim."

"For what? To decide between us?"

"No. It's not about deciding between you. It's for . . . well, for this." Jenna touched her belly where it rubbed against the table.

"I don't know," Tim said, his dark eyes on her. "I don't really know what you're asking me."

"Neither do I." Jenna sat watching him, seeing the flush of red growing on his cheeks.

For a long moment, he didn't say a word. The noise of the coffee shop dimmed, the machines silenced, the customers' voices muffled in her thoughts. Her breath caught on her ribs. Her mouth felt dry.

Finally Tim shrugged. "Maybe," he said. "All right."

Jenna relaxed. Tim pushed back his hair. They sat without talking, even as his coffee grew cold, even as the morning crowd thinned, the sky outside warming into spring.

• • •

Dear Tim,

Out of all the letters I've written during these months, this will be the first one I send. I have the envelope here. A stamp. And I'm out in front of the post office, just down the street from Starbucks. The last mail goes out at twelve, and this letter will be in the pile.

So here are all my apologies, for all the things I did and might do in the next few months. Here is a sorry for how I will focus on myself and my baby. Here I beg forgiveness for living with Mark. Now I apologize for thinking that you and I, we, were not a couple, but something else, something temporary and transient and less than.

I thank you in advance for waiting. I thank you for not making me state what you are waiting for.

269

And finally, here is where I say what I couldn't. I love you.
Jenna

• • •

"WHERE DID YOU go today?" Mark stood at the kitchen counter, stirring parsley butter into steamed green beans. He carried the bowl to the table. "You must have left before I got up."

"I—" she began, and then stopped, a lie like an *L* on her tongue. Shopping. Dee. Susan. A walk. A colleague. Any colleague. Lunch with Sofie's best friend, Rachel. The library. Two novels in one day. The Monte Veda Book Shop. "I went to see Tim."

Mark sat down, scooting his chair close to the table, lifting his fork. He raised an eyebrow. "Oh. How did that go?"

Invisible bugs swarmed in her stomach, and she sat back, trying to keep Mark's gaze. How could she tell him what she said to Tim?

Mark didn't eat, kept looking at her, a pierced bean on his fork. "Well?"

She felt the truth slip behind her and press its head against her shirt. "Fine. Awkward. We hadn't really had a good talk since December. Not really."

"He knows, of course. About the baby."

Jenna poked at the beans and the chicken on her plate. "Of course. He was the first to know. He always knew."

Mark was silent then, his fork clicking on the plate as he speared beans. Outside, Susan's husband, Kenneth, started up a Weedwhacker, and Jenna stood and walked to the window. "What could he be doing at this late hour?" She wished she was in the yard, a machine in her hands, cutting down problems she could see. Everything decisive, clear, obvious.

"Are you going to see him again?" Mark asked finally. Jenna turned from the window and sat back down. The piece of chicken on her plate looked like Illinois. Or Indiana. She couldn't remember which.

"We were colleagues and friends before—"

"Before you were lovers."

"Yes. He was really there for me after Sofie. And we . . . we became really close."

Leaning back, Mark almost threw down his fork. "You let him be there for you. You wouldn't return my calls."

"Mark." She leaned forward, but he made no move toward her. "We've already talked about this."

"Right." He shoved his chair back, stood up, and picked up his plate. "Like I feel any better that you were in Arizona, pregnant, and didn't call me. Like I feel better about anything. It's just going to all go away."

Kenneth was getting closer to the strip of lawn that separated the two houses, the motor whirring loud, echoing up over the roofline. Jenna tucked her hair behind her ears, looking at Mark as he leaned up against the sink, his back to her. "What are we doing?" she asked.

"Eating dinner." Mark's plate clattered in the sink. "Or finishing it."

"No. I mean us. What are we doing here together?"

He turned on the faucet and ran the garbage disposal, drowning the outside sounds for a moment. Jenna stood up and walked to him, leaning a hip against the counter. He wouldn't meet her gaze.

"I'm scared to do this. I'm scared to have another baby."

He nodded, swirling water in the sink.

"I can't lose anyone else."

Mark turned off the water and looked at her, his eyes full of questions. "Like Tim?"

"Like anyone. Like you."

"How do you want me, Jenna?"

Who do I want and how? How do I want anything? she wondered. The days were still confusing to her. Hazel needed her, but tutoring was only once a week. Tim needed her, and Mark seemed to need her in a way he hadn't since they were first married, before he was too busy with his practice or Renata.

"I don't know."

Mark sighed. "Fine."

"Here, though. I want you here for this. For the baby."

As he opened the dishwasher, he turned to her, looking at her with the same expression he'd had that day in December when he'd come over. She knew at this moment that when he looked at her, he saw her, but he also saw Sofie. He saw himself. He saw all three of them together in one look. The past. An old life, one pretty and mellowed with time, one that seemed far better than the future.

Nodding, he filled the soap dish, closed the washer,

and turned it on. "Okay."

As she held out her hand, he moved away, reaching for a baking pan, and she let her hand drop, her palm cool on the counter tile. The neighborhood was suddenly quiet, still, as if nothing had been out there at all.

• • •

When I was in eighth grade, my friend Elissa Roche walked up to where El Toyonal Road ends and hiked up the hill, straight to the stand of eucalyptus, the ones you can see from the freeway—the ones you told me weren't good for the environment. I told Elissa, "I want to run along the ridge." For years, I'd pictured myself running downhill along the slope, the sky arcing blue above us, Contra Costa just out of reach from my left hand, the Bay from the right.

What I hadn't imagined was trudging up that steep hill, our feet stuck in mud, the foggy sky against our cheeks, the lone enormous white bull behind a boulder, steam blowing out his nose.

"Don't run. Walk backwards," Elissa suggested, holding my hand. We stepped back, the ring under the bull's nose shaking with his breath. One step, two, three, ten, twenty, and then we ran, up, up, all the way to the top, far away from the bull, just in front of the trees.

Now, of course, everything is fenced up there, patrolled, only people with a pass from the East Bay Water District able to walk the hills. But back then, it was perfect. I know you'd roll your eyes, hearing me, a middle-aged woman, slipping into nostalgia. But you should have seen me! I was tired, but I ran to the top of a knoll, and then let myself pound down, my feet against the soft earth, my head full of air I'd never breathed before, my hands and arms wings I almost believed would fly me away.

Now I see that ridge every day as I drive home. I wonder that I never told you about it, Sofie. I never took you up there because I knew we'd need wire cutters and binoculars. Part of me thinks I should have let you feel that air and the ground under your feet, just once, but then I know that you flew all the way to Bali and held the body of your beloved. You turned and faced the fire, the blast that took you higher than I've ever gone, ever will go.

Twelve

Nothing much seemed to have changed since the last time Jenna had sat on a carpeted floor, Mark holding her against his chest, other pregnant couples around them. As before, the instructor— Joanne Gere—sat in the middle of the lumpy circle they made, talking about emotional support, positive energy, and comforting massage. The only difference Jenna could discern was that there had been a lecture the week before on epidurals. When she'd been pregnant with Sofie—Jenna couldn't bear the pronoun *we* in front of that phrase, all the younger couples saying, "When we got pregnant"—there was no talk of anesthesia of any kind. No pain medications. She and her friends expected their births to be completely natural, the baby sliding out exactly as it did in the movies the prenatal classes showed. Somehow, in twenty years, people had become much more rational, and Jenna knew she'd want what she could get, enough to help her and not harm the baby.

"So, Dads," Joanne Gere was saying, "the worst part of labor is transition. Mom is going to need you to be there, especially if she doesn't have the epidural. Let's go over what you can do to make it better for her."

"What about a good C-section?" Mark whispered.

Jenna nudged him, keeping her eyes on Joanne, but she whispered back, "My skin's too old to recover from that. Between an incision and stretch marks, I'll have to keep my clothes on forever."

Mark stilled, and Jenna winced. Why had she said that? He probably thought she meant she wouldn't be able to take her clothes off for Tim or some other man. And not him. But he knew she wouldn't say that, Mark having seen her in every stage her body had gone through. He knew she'd let him see her new stretch marks and puckered C-section scar if he asked, if he wanted to.

"No more itsy-bitsy bathing suits," she added. "No string bikinis. No thong underwear!" Jenna tried to chuckle softly, and pressed her back into his chest. *There,* she thought. *There.*

"So, Dads, let's try that massage. Up the back with

smooth hands, and down the arms. Up. That's right. And down. Talk into her ear. Say something encouraging."

"You can have a big glass of whiskey when this is over," Mark said. "A cigar. A huge cup of coffee, full strength."

"But will I get a full night's sleep?"

Mark rubbed her back and brought his hands down her arms. "I'm going to take time off. I've been talking with Glenn Ogilvy. He can take some of my patients, and most I'll be able to reschedule. Two weeks, maybe three."

With Sofie, Mark had gone back to the hospital the night he brought them both home, on call for the next twenty-four hours, coming home to find Jenna weeping at the kitchen table.

"She cried every twenty minutes. I didn't sleep. My breasts hurt!" she had wailed, her nightgown stiff with dried breast milk, her vagina—her entire body—sore, her underwear stuffed with two supersized Kotex pads. The kitchen counter was awash with bowls and towels and wadded baby sleepers Jenna had brought down from the nursery. "I can't do this. I can't."

Exhausted himself, his eyes watery, Mark had first slammed down his briefcase on the table, throwing himself into a chair. Jenna had closed her eyes, ready for his anger, but he'd said, "Go to bed. I'll take care of this mess."

Her breasts aching as she hugged him, she'd gone into the living room, pulling the afghan around her, not wanting to be upstairs, near the baby. She knew that with each sound, she'd flinch awake, listen, take care, her eyes and ears and breasts alert for each whimper, cry, turn. If she was anywhere near Sofie, she'd have to be next to the crib, wondering what to do, trying desperately to do it.

"Jenna," Mark said, "roll on your left side. It's sacrum massage time. This is compassionate, comforting massage."

"Hmm," Jenna said, and she turned, resting her head on her arm, closing her eyes. How different it was this time; how she would have done anything to have Mark so attentive when she was pregnant with Sofie. He'd just been so busy with being a doctor, coming home distracted, tired, putting his hands on Jenna's belly in bed and then falling asleep before the baby moved. Before Sofie moved.

Sofie. Jenna's throat thickened, and she felt Mark's hands on her lower back. She let herself feel his firm strokes, and she thought of nothing, letting memory float away until there was just her body, his hands, her breath, the pulse of life within her.

After class, Mark first dropped her off and then went to the grocery store, having composed a mental list on the drive home.

"Salmon," he said. "Deep, leafy greens. Fruits and veggies. Joanne's making me nervous. I'll probably end up buying you prune juice to prevent hemorrhoids."

"Chocolate ice cream," Jenna said as she stepped out of the car. "Oreos. Froot Loops. Hostess Sno Balls."

"Maybe one Twinkie," he said. "But that's it."

Walking up to the front door, Jenna heard the phone ringing. In something like slow motion, she opened the door and grabbed the receiver off the entryway table, feeling a strange pulse of adrenaline as she punched the button, hearing the echo of emergency calls, the kind she'd had too many of. How had it been when the government man called about Sofie? She'd answered the phone normally, expecting any old call, but from then on, the second after she hung up with him, her heart beat to imagined calls. More danger, more damage. Jenna tried to relax as she said hello.

"Jenna? It's me. Jolie."

"Oh, Jolie!" Jenna smiled and walked into the living room, sitting down on the couch. "Oh, it's you! Thank god."

"Who were you thinking it was?"

"No one really. I just— Well, how are you?"

"I'm good. Ralph says hello."

Closing her eyes, Jenna brought back the big window of the stationery store, the girls who had bought the Italian bracelet. The way she pressed her stomach against the glass counter, feeling the baby jolt to life. That period seemed two lifetimes ago, thousands of miles away, a vacation story belonging to another person.

"Say hi for me. So, how's it going?"

"I got your letter."

"Oh."

"Thank you."

278

"For what, Jolie? I should be thanking you over and over again. You saved me. I don't know what I was thinking, but I needed to stop. I needed to rest. You gave me that." Jenna spoke without taking a breath, her chest empty when she finally stopped. But she wanted to give all her energy to her cousin, let her know that she had done so much with so little in return.

"No, it's you who helped me. I didn't realize how way out there I was about the baby. I really thought I'd gotten over it. Put it behind me. But watching you—I knew I still had that desire. I kind of went nuts. So I wanted to let you know."

There was a pause, and Jenna asked, "Know what?"

"I've made a decision. I'm going to adopt."

"You are? From where? China?" Jenna had a colleague who had traveled to China with her husband, picking up her new daughter from an orphanage packed with girls, most waiting for their American parents to come and get them. Now little Mei Mei was four, precocious, a brat, really, the shiny apple of her parents' eyes. "She'll never know how close she came to living in poverty and horror," Dee had said once. "And look at her now. Lace socks and patent leather." Mei Mei was the center of attention at all the Contra Loma parties, singing songs, climbing over people sitting in chairs, swirling in her fluffy dresses in the middle of every room.

"No. Not China," said Jolie. "There's a place locally that works with children and families. I probably won't get a baby. More likely a toddler. But like you said in the letter, you don't have to have a baby to create. There are other ways to give birth."

Jenna blushed, hating the slightly condescending tinge she heard in her words now. But she had really meant it. Jolie was already bringing images to life through her painting, and this child would give her more of that feeling.

"That is so wonderful, Jolie. When will it happen?"

"Not for a while. Tons of paperwork, of course. Social workers and such. But probably by the end of the year."

"Does my mom know what you're up to?"

Jolie paused and then said, "She helped me, Jenna. She's the one who really talked with me after you left. I was—I was angry. And then I was so depressed. It was like my whole life had been denied once again. I had so many questions. . . ."

As Jolie talked, Jenna knew exactly what she was saying. Even though it had lessened, Jenna still had so much anger—in her dreams, when she looked at Mark sometimes, when she thought of losing Tim, when she went through the box of photos in her study. Her life— the one she'd grown accustomed to and had liked—had been denied, just as Jolie said. So had Sofie's. And how to find it? How to go on? That's what she'd been asking herself, and what Jolie had to ask herself, too.

But after a flare of this hot anger, she would see that the loss was really part of the story. That not knowing what to do next was exactly what was supposed to happen.

"Maybe that's what we need to do," Jenna broke in. "Maybe we need to have questions. We shouldn't expect the downtime, the quiet time. When I was younger, I imagined that there was all the struggle earlier, and then you could coast along. But I was wrong. I've figured that out, at least. There's not a perfect flat line of existence. It's supposed to be rough and terrifying and beautiful all at once."

"I'm sorry. You've been through—"

"I've been through life, Jolie. So have you. All of it, even Sofie's death, was life. For me, the questions have been a way to keep going. How to figure out how to open up and take it in. Like you're doing. With this child."

The cousins were silent. In that pause, Jenna could feel the time of all the years before, both of them with their dolls, playing as a way to figure out who they were. Jenna wasn't sure either of them had done such a good job at that, but they were trying. Wasn't that all anyone could do?

"You'll come up, won't you?" Jenna asked.

"Of course! I'll really want to see the baby."

"No, I mean to be with me in the delivery room."

"Um, well, will there be time?"

"What is it? Two hours plus by air from Phoenix? I want my mom to come, too. And if the past is any indication, I'll be in labor for days."

"Okay. Sure. Of course. I'd love to, Jenna. Thanks. I'm honored."

"Don't thank me. I owe you. So much."

Jenna said good-bye and hung up the phone, looking around her house with relief. Almost everything was smoothed over, kind of fixed, set in an uneven but clear path. In moments, Mark would come home with groceries, and they would make dinner together. A healthy dinner, one with green and orange vegetables and protein and little salt. Together, they were taking care of their child, who at this single moment was safe. That was all Jenna knew she could count on.

"I'M MOVING," HAZEL said, her lips flat, her eyes dull. "Again."

Valerie from Reading Readiness had called Jenna the week before to warn her. "She's really upset," Valerie had said. "Don't expect much from her during the session."

"But why is this happening?" Jenna had asked. "Why does she have to switch homes?"

Valerie had been silent on the other end of the phone for a second, and then she sighed. "Jenna, I used to try to fight all of this when I first started. But I don't anymore. They don't have enough case workers to answer half of what I want to know. But from what I understand, Hazel will be happier. She'll be the only child in the house, and the foster mother has said she will continue the tutoring."

"So I can see her, then? Maybe in the fall after I have my baby?"

"The new home is in Lodi."

Jenna thought of all the things she should say. "It

doesn't matter," she should cry out. "I'll do it. I'll work with her." But she knew that even if she wanted to, with a new baby, driving out to Lodi and back once a week wasn't going to work.

Now Hazel picked at the table, running her finger along the deeply grooved wood. Jenna nodded, and then she pulled a wrapped package from her lap.

"I brought you something to do at your new home," she said, handing the package to the girl.

Hazel sat up. Jenna saw that the Thunderbird key chain was attached to one of her belt loops.

"What is it?"

"You have to open it to know," Jenna said. As Hazel smiled and pulled at the ribbon, Jenna saw Sofie at eight and ten and twelve, ripping open birthday presents with the same happy, satisfied smile that Hazel wore now.

"It's them all!" Hazel said, holding up five Calvin and Hobbes books. "I can read forever!"

Jenna nodded, unable to speak, watching as Hazel touched each cover and then opened a book, her eyes catching the words, her mouth whispering them out into the room.

She wanted to promise the girl a world of happiness, but that wasn't in Jenna's power to do. She couldn't save her—she couldn't save anyone. But as Hazel thanked her, Jenna knew that in ten years, Hazel might be like the students in her classes at Contra Loma College, hopefully one who paid attention. In ten years, Hazel would still be Hazel—rough and angry but ready to learn. Jenna had never saved anyone, couldn't, but teaching was where she could help, one Hazel at a time.

"And here." Jenna pulled a piece of paper from her purse. "When you get more practice with your writing, send me a note. Let me know how you are doing."

Hazel took the paper and put it inside the book, and then closed it tight. "I will. I will write everything."

• • •

Things I Never Told You:

I wanted to talk with you about sex. Yes, we did have that funny little talk when you were in fifth grade and you brought home the pamphlets from sex education class. And yes, we had the AIDS talk in eighth grade. You knew about condoms and all the diseases we pass along to each other. But I always thought I'd be able to talk to you about enjoying it. About liking to be in your own body and relaxing into the arousal. About not worrying constantly about what the man was feeling or enjoying or thinking. I didn't want you to worry about how flat your stomach was or what the guy thought about your hips or thighs or breasts. Now I really believe that if you are able to enjoy, that enjoyment comes out of your skin in a pleasure drift your partner can breathe in. I didn't really enjoy sex until I met your father, and I learned to enjoy sex with him. I even enjoyed it more after we were divorced. Maybe because I didn't need him anymore and could be myself completely. Horrible, isn't it? Sad, isn't it? So I wanted it to be different for you. But

284

maybe you already knew. Probably, you did. You were into your body, Sofie. All your bones and muscles seemed to be entirely yours, so it wouldn't surprise me now to hear you say, "Mom, of course. Of course I enjoyed it. What else would I do?"

I wanted to talk with you about getting older, but I was waiting until I had figured that one out myself. I should have been able to look at Grandma Lois and see how to age well, but I'm not there yet. I'm pregnant and worried about wrinkles and gray hair and gravity. My hope was that I could sit you down and tell you, "You only grow more beautiful. Everything that happens to you is natural." But I can't say it and believe it completely. Maybe if you'd lived, by the time I was fifty-five or sixty, I could have taken you out to lunch and let you know. With this new baby, I'll be sixty-seven when it's twenty-two, and perhaps I'll know by then.

I wanted to tell you that there is no answer. I looked for it myself. For some reason, I expected some human on earth to be able to explain to me why we are here. With every therapist and teacher and new friend, I imagined the answer was only a conversation away. But no one knows anything. No religion holds the key, despite the way people carry on, killing each other over their perceived "true" answers. I've taught mythology for too long, Sofie, to imagine that any one people has the knowledge sewn up tight. You can't travel to find it, unless, of course, it's the kind of travel you've done, away *from this plane, somewhere heavenly, astral, spiritual. You could tell me more now than I could have ever told you here. But I wanted that conversation after a time of you trying to find it on your own.*

I wanted to tell you that laundry isn't that important. Separating colors is useful, but you don't need the most expensive detergent or all that ridiculous fabric softener. A good hour-and-a-half massage is worth a month of therapy. You don't need a lot of friends, only two or three really good ones. Your family is important, even if you don't see them often. Look at Jolie and me, all these years later. Taking care of yourself—making sure you have socks without holes and a good lunch on a long day and a couple of bottles of water wherever you go—is necessary, even if it seems to take too much time to organize. And this last thing: You can't plan anything. You can try. You can help. You can make things the best they can be for small, liquid amounts of time. But nothing worth having is under our control.

Thirteen

Jenna had never given up a baby easily to the world. Sofie had taken forever to arrive, Jenna's cervix like a sticky door. All her laboring and pushing moved it only slight fractions at a time. So this time, she knew that the first pangs of labor meant nothing, were just a small knock on the door that wouldn't open for hours.

All night, she'd been reading *The Mists of Avalon*. She'd read it years ago when it first came out, but as she had paced the floors, trying to ignore the small contractions that were coming every fifteen to twenty minutes, she'd found the book in a box in the attic, stacked with others she'd packed away after Sofie's death: *Crime and Punishment*, *Beloved*, *Anna Karenina* (everything Russian, really), *The Mill on the Floss*.

Walking as her uterus contracted, she went downstairs, turned on the living room lamp, and cracked open the book, feeling the familiarity of the sad story. Jenna knew the ending—as everyone did. The peaceful reign falls, the king is felled, feminism dies for nine hundred years, mists encompass compassion and magic and warmth. No one gets the one she loves. Everyone dies. The same old story.

In the wee hours—two, three, four—her body pulling and widening in the silent house, the old story lulled her, the ache of her uterus the same as the ache of everything, the world pulling and twisting, countries battling for power, friends turning on each other, mothers and sisters and fathers and husbands and wives all at odds. Strangely, though, as she read in the yellow light, she was almost an observer to her body tugging at itself, looking away from the words as another contraction began, feeling the hardness of her muscles, the ache deep inside as she rounded open in order to set this baby free. Then it would stop, and she'd go back to the novel, falling into the darkness and light, the same darkness and light of every story she'd ever read.

"What's going on?" Mark clomped into the living room.

She looked up and there he was, just as he had been twenty years before, blinking against the light, his hair curled wild with sleep. He patted his robe pockets for his glasses.

"You really should have that surgery," Jenna said, putting the book in her lap. "What is it? Radial kerato-tomy? It would be a lot easier in an emergency than searching around for your glasses."

"Jenna? What are you doing?" He sat down next to her on the couch. "It's four in the morning. Have you slept?"

"No. Not yet. I've been having contractions every twenty minutes or so. This happened with—with Sofie. Remember? They kept sending me back home." She picked up the book and found her spot, Arthur and Guinevere so sadly infertile. What could they do now? Go for treatments? Find a surrogate? If they'd only had a baby, Jenna knew, the Round Table would never have crumbled.

A wave of muscles tightened inside her and she closed her eyes. *Guinevere never had this,* she thought, and then she felt Mark sitting down next to her, his palm on her shoulder. "Take a breath. That looks like a big one."

Jenna nodded, keeping her eyes closed. The last three or four had been harder, longer, slightly closer together.

Even though she was certain this baby would take days to be born, Jenna was glad that at midnight, she'd phoned her mother, who'd promised to alert Jolie and get them both to the airport. Then the hand inside her unclenched, and she opened her eyes, exhaling breath she knew she shouldn't have held.

"Yeah, the last few have been like that."

"Should we go in? Or call? Let's call Dr. Zahri."

"It's too early."

Mark laughed. "That's what she's paid for."

"No, I mean too early to go in. I don't want to just lie there with the monitor around my belly. Remember how we did that with Sofie? I felt like I was there for days before anything happened. I'll just read for a while."

"Your water hasn't broken?" Mark looked at her, wide awake now.

"No, but then I don't remember it breaking with Sofie. I always wanted that big gush. A clear sign that something was happening." She picked up the book, trying to find her place. Mark pulled it down, watching her face.

"I can't believe this," he said.

She knew what he meant. The baby. Having the chance to do it again, their lives in some horrible, amazing rewind. And after all of that time and disaster, their marriage and their child dead, here they sat on the same couch, doing the same things they'd done before. How was that possible? And was it real? Jenna nodded. "Neither can I."

Mark leaned over and kissed her, first on the right cheek, the left, and then on the lips, softly, then again and again. She kissed him back, letting the book fall away, holding his shoulders, the moving bulge of their baby between them. Here he was, her husband. Had she ever really stopped thinking about him that way? Maybe in her mind he'd never been Renata's husband at all. Maybe in his mind, he hadn't been either.

Mark kissed her a last time and then pulled away. "I'm going to make some herb tea. And then I'm going to call Dr. Zahri's service. To let her know what's going on. Just in case. You know what she said about older mothers."

Nodding, Jenna picked up the book and watched him walk toward the kitchen. During the night, the world had shrunk down into this house and then into this room and now into the form of this couch, her body and its landscape the only thing that mattered. She couldn't read; she knew that now. No words would help. Nothing would keep her from what was happening in her womb, so she leaned back on the pillows and waited for the next contraction.

AS SHE HAD known it would, Jenna's labor went on for hours, the herb tea turning into dry morning toast and then early luncheon soda crackers. Her mother and Jolie arrived, Dee picking them up at the airport and coming in with them. Jenna had taken another shower and was lying on her left side on the couch, holding a hand on her belly.

"Why aren't you at the hospital?" Dee asked. "It's time for the epidural. The drugs. Mark, this is what modern science is supposed to avoid."

"She wanted to wait for everyone to get here."

Jenna closed her eyes, unable to listen to them. When it had been only Mark asking her questions, she'd given him quick, one-word answers, pretending to read her book. But with everyone here, she couldn't concentrate on what was happening inside, life in motion in her uterus, the baby pushing against her cervix. She knew she should go to the hospital. Her water hadn't broken yet, but she was sure there was some moisture down there, something leaking. Dr. Zahri had been right all along. She was old and needed all the medical intervention available, but when she thought about getting in the car and driving to the hospital, she wanted to weep. The darkness from the old story had covered her overnight, wiping out the light. She felt as insignificant as Hazel had that last day of tutoring, small and sad and clear that the world had taken over again.

"Sweetie," Lois said, sitting down on the couch in the small curve below Jenna's belly, "let's go. We're all here now."

Shaking her head, Jenna gripped her mother's hand and whispered, "Mom."

"Don't be scared. It's going to be okay. The baby is fine. We'll be able to watch, okay?"

Jenna's legs started to shake, and she tightened her grip on her mother. Her eyes still closed, she heard whispers and heard footsteps, doors closing, the roar of the car outside. Dee muttered, "Jesus," and then there was the clinking of glasses and footsteps moving toward the kitchen.

Breathing into a contraction and then falling into the pull and pain, she wished she could tell her mother that it was better here, at the house, where nothing had happened yet. The baby was fine, alive. She could feel its movements, its very heartbeat inside her. At the hospital, and then later when the baby was brought into the wide world, Jenna wouldn't be able to offer it much more than hope. And where did hope get you? So Jenna was going to stay here, at home, with the pain and the possibility that nothing wrong would happen to this child.

"Okay," Jolie said as she got hold of Jenna's other arm. "It's going to be fine."

"I think that one's over," Lois said. "Come on, let's go. Let's go to the hospital so I can hold my grand-baby."

At her mother's voice, Jenna calmed. Maybe it would work out all right.

Jenna couldn't open her eyes, but she knew she was moving up and off the couch, her body in the hands of her mother and Jolie and Dee. They were holding her, and she was walking, and she was full of life. Life. It couldn't be stopped. Look at this—she was floating between them, out the door, Mark waiting behind the wheel. She heard them all, felt the cold metal of the car's body, the smoothness of the leather seats. She slid in and then leaned her head back, her mother pushing the hair away from her face. Mark pulled out into traffic, ignoring Dee's driving suggestions, the motor humming. Jenna sat silent next to her mother, letting her body do what it had to, going along for the ride.

"PUSH, JENNA," MARK said, gripping her shoulders. "That's it. That's right. Push, push!"

Ragged from labor and an hour of pushing, Jenna strained, feeling her head fill with swirling light. *Push,* she thought. Where had she heard that? When had she heard that? Where was she? She thought she opened her eyes, but she must not have, because she was suddenly in a delivery room of twenty years ago, no thought to pleasure or comfort, monitors everywhere, the nurses in white uniforms and caps. Everything was green and gray, but there was Mark behind her, gripping her arms, saying, "Push, Jenna."

Looking down, she saw her younger pregnant body, her long red hair lank and sweaty against her gown. But why were Dr. Zahri's eyes smiling from between the V of her legs?

"No," Jenna said, blinking. There were her mother, Jolie, Dee, everyone in gowns, Mark's breath on her cheek.

"Come on, sweetie," her mother said, holding one of her legs back. "You're doing so great!"

Jolie was crying, holding on to Dee's arm. Jenna closed her eyes, and there was Sofie's head in the mirror, her red hair matted and soaked in fluid and blood. *Oh, she is coming,* Jenna thought, bearing down again. *She's being born again.*

"Great. You're doing great. Okay, stop. It's only one more," Mark said in his older man's voice, his older man's body against her. She panted, breathing against the circle of pain from her vagina, ignoring all the pressure, knowing that Sofie was on her way again, coming back. A daughter! Her girl.

"Okay. Okay," said Dr. Zahri. "Push. Yes. Yes. Now stop."

She could hear them sucking fluid from the baby's nose and mouth, and then a slight sound, a tiny whimper.

"Look! Oh, Jenna. Look at that little face!" Jolie said.

Jenna kept her eyes closed, knowing she didn't need to look. She'd watched Sofie grow up. She'd recognize her daughter anywhere. She could find her in any life.

"One more good push and we'll have the shoulders," Dr. Zahri said. Jenna felt the tug, and then a whoosh of fluid and blood, tiny limbs against her stretched-out flesh. She imagined the gold light from the ultrasound filling the room, the air itself welcoming Sofie back to life.

"That's it! That's wonderful. There. You have a beautiful boy," Dr. Zahri said.

Jenna looked up over her still-large stomach as the nurse handed Mark the scissors to cut the cord. The baby was crying, a wobbly, angry sound.

"He is beautiful," Jolie said. "What a big baby."

"Honey, this is one fabulous boy!" Dee said, crowding in to look at the baby. "He's so cute. He's going to keep everyone running."

"You did it, Jenna. You did it!" Mark kissed her, and she let her head fall back to the pillow.

Then Dr. Zahri was holding out her baby, his little red face in hers. "Here he is. So wonderful. Good job, Jenna."

The baby's weight on her chest felt like boulders. She was tired, so tired. She wanted to lift her arms to press the baby to her, but she couldn't move them. Everything was so heavy, so big, the room growing and folding out into the universe.

"Jenna?" Mark said. "Jenna?"

"Nurse?" Dr. Zahri said, and then there was nothing but gray with pinpoints of light, and then nothing but darkness.

"Don't say anything. Go back to sleep."

Fine, she thought. *I'll do that.* But she didn't know if she was asleep in this new hospital room in front of her. She could see Dee, Jolie, and Mark. Where was her mother? Oh yes. Her mother was the voice. The voice beside her. Who was missing? Sofie? Where was Sofie? Then there was a cry, and Jenna saw that Mark was holding Sofie. No, not Sofie. A boy.

"You lost a lot of blood. Go back to sleep. Everything's fine."

No it's not, she thought, but then the room disappeared.

"You scared us," Mark said.

Jenna stared at him. He looked pale, tired, his eyes red. "I wasn't scared. At least about myself."

"Maybe you knew more than we did."

Jenna thought of the circle of light holding Sofie and her father, both of them so wise and silent, the secrets of the universe trapped in their mouths. "I don't know anything."

"That's good. Who needs to know? It's all right now. You and our son are fine."

Jenna turned her head and winced. She was so sore. Muscles she didn't know she had hurt, everything from her jaw to her thighs. "Where is he?"

"In the nursery. He's so beautiful, Jenna. You won't believe it."

"Is he okay?"

"He's fine. He's so big. Nine pounds, eleven ounces. You grew him just right. And Jenna?"

She closed her eyes, nodding instead of answering because she was so tired.

"There's nothing the matter," Mark said, his hand on her forehead. "He's perfect. He's completely fine."

So was Sofie, she tried to say, but then couldn't, her mouth too heavy to move, her eyes too weighty to open. So she listened to them talk about the baby, about her, the noise of family talk lulling her into sleep.

SITTING UP IN her hospital bed, the pillows fluffed behind her back, Jenna held her boy. He was big, a giant, meaty creature compared to how delicate Sofie had been as an infant. He slept almost all day, except for squalls that only stopped when she nursed awkwardly, her breasts hard and aching. He was hairless, ruddy skinned, and full of fat rolls. Jenna didn't know what to do with him.

"What a big boy! What a beautiful big boy," Lois had cooed over his plastic bassinet. Even though he was full term and healthy, tested fine, and was eating well, Jenna needed to stay in the hospital one more night for observation.

"That's what we say when we're hedging our bets," Mark had said after Dr. Zahri left the room. "You lost some blood, but you're going to snap right back."

But as she watched her baby sleep, Jenna wasn't sure she would snap back. Nothing seemed right, not even after all her planning and organizing these last months. Not after all her decisions about leaving Arizona and coming home to live with Mark. She felt almost disconnected, attached to the earth and this baby by a balloon string. Jenna had lost something besides blood in the delivery room, and she wondered if she'd ever find it.

"So, Mom," a nurse said, bustling into the room with a pitcher of water and Jenna's chart. "How are we feeling? Baby eating okay?"

"He's eating great," Jenna said. "My breasts are killing me, but he seems to be getting enough."

Holding out her hands, the nurse asked, "Let me see the baby."

Jenna lifted him up and into the nurse's waiting arms. He didn't stir, still in womb time, quiet and waiting.

"What a cutie pie." The nurse put him on the bed and took off his blanket onesie and diaper, checking his skin and the contents of the diaper. "Meconium poop?"

"Excuse me?"

"Has he had the black poop yet?"

Nodding, Jenna turned to look out the window, a cherry tree tapping its green leaves against the glass.

"Everything looks tip-top," the nurse said, wrapping up the baby and handing him back to Jenna. "Do you have a name for him yet?"

If Mark were in the room, Jenna would have lied, said something like, "Oh, we're thinking about it. Very soon. It just has to come to us." But Mark wasn't in the room; he was down in the cafeteria with Lois and Jolie. Looking into the nurse's face, she wondered how to tell her that she hadn't been able to join in when Mark brought up the name question. How could she name someone? How could she pick a name that would last?

"No," she said, trying to smile.

"Oh, that's normal," the nurse said. "I can't tell you the number of parents who leave here with little nameless ones. They all get named eventually."

The nurse picked up a soiled blanket and tucked the chart under her arm, nodding as she left. Jenna looked down at her boy. With Sofie, there had been an instant rush of feeling, as full as the milk in her breasts. She'd wondered how women could possibly have postpartum depression when there was this pulse of adrenaline, endorphins, love, all at once. She wasn't depressed now. She was—what was she?

The baby slept, and Jenna was glad. If he cried, she'd have to nurse him again. She'd have to comfort him, show him that being alive wasn't so bad. Of course, that was a lie. Life was brutal. Look what had happened to her trying to birth him. And it would only get worse. Dangers were everywhere.

Turning away from the baby's face, she studied the ugly wall, trying to keep herself from crying. But liquid seemed to pour out of her. Without feeling, she was crying and sweating and leaking onto a pad between her legs. Water, water everywhere.

"How are you doing?" Lois said, coming abruptly into the room. She reached out for the baby, and Jenna handed him to her, able to breathe once her mother took him into her arms.

Lois made *coo-coo*ing sounds, touching his face with an index finger. "Such a pretty baby. Such a good baby." She smiled at Jenna. "He's really something."

Leaning back on the pillow, Jenna winced as unknown, overused muscles pulled and throbbed. "Where's Mark?"

"He left to drop off Jolie at the house and then go in to the office. It's amazing, Jenna. He's getting everything ready to take some time off. He wants to spend all the time he can with little Mr. Baby here."

"That's nice," Jenna said flatly, wiping her eyes. A fist of heat began to beat under her sternum. Sweat ran down her temple, and she hit her palms on her thighs. "What about Sofie? Why wasn't he there when she was a baby and while she was growing up? Why did he have to leave us alone? Because he didn't feel loved enough? Who feels loved enough? Who can ever get enough love?"

"Sweetie," Lois said. "I thought— Mark and you have talked about all this, right?"

"For years." Jenna was crying heavily now. At the exertion, her letdown began, her breasts throbbing. "Could you give me the baby? My milk's coming in."

Lois set the baby in her arms, and Jenna touched his cheek, watched him sucking before she even put the nipple in his mouth. Totally asleep, he pulled long and hard on her breast. "God," Jenna said, feeling the pins and needles of milk flowing through her ducts. "I'd forgotten what this feels like." But she hadn't. Not really. Sofie's imprint was still on her skin and in her body, the tug of old feelings like a dream she could just remember.

"Have you thought about talking with him some more about how you feel? This is probably pretty important now that you're living together again."

Jenna shrugged, her mouth full of words, but then found herself unable to look at or think about anything but the baby. *Look at him,* she thought. *Look at him live.* He was so alive. Even asleep, he knew how to take in what would sustain him. She began to cry again, tears dropping onto his cheek.

"Oh, Mom," she sobbed. "I don't know what to do with him. I don't know how to do this. I'm no good at it."

Lois got off her chair and sat on the bed, holding

Jenna's arm. "Don't you say that. That's not true."

"But look what happened to Sofie. Look how I killed her."

The baby awoke, squalled, and then found the nipple again. Lois patted his bottom, her teeth on her lower lip.

"Don't say that," Lois said. "That is not true. You lived for that girl."

"I lived, but she didn't. I want to take her place. I want her to have this." Jenna motioned to the baby. "This shouldn't be me. It's Sofie's turn."

A nurse poked her head in the room and Lois waved her off, letting Jenna nurse him in silence. When the baby was done, Lois put him on her shoulder, patting his back.

"No, it's not. It's not Sofie's turn. Whatever turn Sofie was supposed to have ended. She lived, and then she died. You're still alive, and you are getting another chance at being a mother. It's just how it all turned out. And it's not your fault. Not one bit."

"But what if I make the same mistakes?" Jenna said, wiping her eyes on the sheet. "What if it all turns out the same way and he dies, too? I can't go through that again. I can't love him so much because it hurts too much."

With the baby still on her shoulder, Lois moved next to Jenna, holding Jenna's arm with her free hand. "You have no choice. You can't say that you won't love this beautiful child because he might die. It's the same as saying you are going to stop loving me because I'm going to die. And I am. And so are you. Should I give up on you? Should I have turned away from you yesterday in the delivery room because it looked bad there for a while? This is how it goes, sweetie. So you take today for what it is, and you go on. If you have problems, you ask for help. If you need me or Mark, you let us know. If you don't need us, you let us know. You won't make the same mistakes because even if you did, this little boy is not Sofie. He's another person altogether. They're siblings, but he's an individual. Do you understand?"

Jenna's heart beat so hard she wondered if her mother was prescient, a heart attack ready to knock her out at this moment. She fought for breath. Jenna did understand, and she hated it all. She hated that she could only see Sofie in visions or when she wrote her dead daughter letters. She hated that Mark was back at home now that she really didn't need him. She hated that she had lost Tim altogether, giving him up for this other life that refused to stop. She hated that she was scared to love her own baby, this warm creature squirming on her mother's shoulder.

"I hate it, Mom. I hate it."

"That's good," Lois said, her arm so strong on Jenna's. "That means you're alive."

"It hurts."

"I know, sweetie. I know."

Finding her breath, her heart slowing to a regular beat, Jenna leaned back into the pillow and her mother's warm side. She was supposed to hate it. She didn't have to be happy. She didn't have to find some kind of mystical meaning in the universe to explain it all. Sofie was dead. And Jenna hated that. She hated it because she was alive, and it all hurt. The air hurt to breathe in; this baby's body hurt because he was not Sofie. Okay. That's how it was.

She took the baby from her mother and gave him her other nipple. Half asleep, he took it, pulled as if the other breast and all its milk were already a faraway memory. This baby wanted to be here. He wanted to live so badly that he would burp while his mother and grandmother cried and talked, eat while asleep, drink the bitter milk from his mother's breast and turn it into flesh.

In the middle of the night, the hospital room silent for a rare moment, no nurse, no monitor, no television noise from down the hall, Jenna awoke. She sat up looking at the baby who slept quietly wrapped tight in his white bundle in the plastic bassinet. In a dream, she'd figured it out. What had she seen in her sleep that had led her to consciousness? What she remembered now was blue, palm fronds, striped chaises on the white beach. Sailboats like white tents in the aqua ocean. The fire burst of a red sun sinking below the horizon. Then there was fire, and she knew that she'd been scared, her heart beating fast. But in her dream, there was her baby, a boy already, a young man somehow, unconcerned, walking along a sidewalk, looking back at the explosion, the mayhem, the noise and dust and screams, and nodding, as if he understood. As if he knew. In her dream view, she followed him, but he didn't stop, kept walking alone, strong.

In the quiet room, Jenna realized she had the answer. What she wanted for him was the will to go on— exactly what she needed now. Though the sound of the name ringing in her head was similar to the word that meant a "wail of mourning," it meant something completely opposite. Because she wanted her son to be strong and healthy and prosperous, the name would be perfect. It would fit in this world, where he would have to fight. Maybe not physically, but with his head, adjusting as Jenna had barely managed to do. He would have to be a person who would walk down the sidewalk despite everything.

She would have to convince Mark. He liked classic, simple names that were easy to spell, so clear they were impossible to twist into childhood taunts. Thus, Sofia Elizabeth Thomas. But in the darkness, she said the baby's name under her breath. Keane. His name was Keane Thomas.

Dear Sofie,

Your brother was born yesterday. Keane. He is huge, enormous, full of spirit, eating up everything. I look at him now and wonder if you are whispering in his ear, telling him the secrets of how to live with me and your father. What are your words of wisdom? Or maybe you have things to say to us. What would you tell us about being better parents? I know I have so much to learn, and I'm sorry I had to practice being a mom with you.

Keane is so big, so solid, not like you were, fine and fragile. I was scared to hold you sometimes. When you were first in my arms, I imagined that there should be a class for clumsy mothers who bore delicate daughters—lovely daughters. But I learned that you were strong despite your tiny, thin fingers and almost transparent skin. I learned you were braver than I ever was.

I will write to you more often, I think. I want to let you know how your brother is growing. I wish I could send you a picture, but maybe you can see him without my help. Are you looking down on us? Is it true that the dead can make themselves visible? Can you come in with a wisp of light or become a glimmer in a mirror? One day, might I turn around and see your face reflected in the shine of the dining room table? If it's true, please come see me. I can take it. I promise, Sofie. I won't be scared.

He's stirring again, so I'll stop now. Say hello to whoever is taking care of you now, whoever you are close to. Love, Mom.

Fourteen

In the middle of August, something happened inside of Jenna, and at first, she had no idea what it was. It was a feeling and then a flavor and then a texture. She could hear it crackle under her shoes and taste the deep, smooth orange on her tongue. She imagined it was something to do with her body coming back into its own, the hormones adjusting, her internal meter set back to middle-aged woman. Her heart beat fast, even as she sat outside on a chaise longue feeding Keane, or in bed as she dropped into a heavy, short sleep, destined to be cut in two by Keane's cries at 1 A.M.

But it wasn't her hormones. Her hair, which had darkened to auburn during her pregnancy, began to thin and lighten. One night, she'd even stared at her temples, sure that she'd gone completely gray overnight. But it was merely her hair color returning to its lighter shade. Her period came back suddenly, even though she was breast-feeding, and the sheen of oil that had covered her forehead and cheeks, especially during the last few weeks of pregnancy, had dried up.

No. It wasn't hormones or the baby or some kind of strange dream or vision that kept her thinking about plaid skirts and starched white blouses and pencils and dried sycamore leaves and new binders and pumpkin pie. It was fall and school. Going back to school. Jenna hadn't *not* gone back to school since she was four years old. She remembered standing in front of the picture window at home, watching the children walk down El Verano Road toward the bus stop. They had carried red lunch boxes and thermoses full of Campbell's tomato soup. Girls held wicker baskets full of notepads and binder paper and sharpened number two pencils. Boys had front pockets stuffed with jacks, rubber bands, and playing cards, and rode by on Sting-Ray bikes with banana seats, baseball gloves shoved in the back pockets of their pants.

"Mommy," she'd cried, her small hands beige starfish on the glass. "I want to go, too."

"Next year," Lois said. "I promise. Let's make some cinnamon rolls for now."

Later, Lois told Jenna she'd wanted to say, "And one day you'll beg me to let you quit school." She'd been sure that Jenna would, just as she herself had. But Jenna loved school, the books, the words that formed into stories, the idea that there was a secret about life she would stumble across on every page and understand. At some point in her thirties, Jenna realized she actually believed that there was a single answer that a book would impart, truth rising up off the page. With a few words, she'd finally understand everything: why we were here, who the big boss was, what life was for. Maybe she'd stayed in school because she'd had that hope, imagining that a particular novel on a syllabus would finally be the key.

That's not why she still felt nostalgic for fall. Now it was more the promise that life could become new again, even as the leaves turned red and brown and yellow and floated to the streets, even as large, leafy pumpkin vines withered, leaving the orange roundness full of the future. To Jenna, this fall meant that life would go on despite Sofie and because of Keane.

"Are you coming back?" Dee asked as she held the baby on her shoulder. The mid-August heat spread yellow across the patio outside, the sky a pale, exhausted blue. "There are still classes left to be staffed. Arnold's hiring part-time teachers like there's no tomorrow. That's right, isn't it?" She brought Keane in front of her face, and he seemed to smile, his eyes searching for Jenna. "That's right! You can come to school and sleep in my office," Dee said, singsong. "Then your mommy can go teach. Right, Keane?"

"He's too little." Jenna said. "He's not even two months old!"

"I know how old you are, Keane, my man," Dee said, ignoring Jenna's eyes. "You want to come to school with your mommy? All the pretty girls!"

"Can you even hear yourself?" Jenna smiled. "I think you've lost about thirty IQ points."

"They say babies respond to silly voices and exaggerated facial movements. It's so clear you never taught anything but college English." Dee shifted Keane to her other shoulder.

"What about Hazel? She's only eight," Jenna said. The week before, Hazel had sent her a valentine she must have gotten at school earlier in the year. The girl had scratched out *To Hazel* and *From Jaden* and had written *Thank you* in the middle of the little card. Someone else—the foster mother, Jenna imagined— had addressed the large envelope.

Jenna had written back to Hazel, sending a picture of Keane. She could almost hear Hazel say, "Babies don't look like that! Scrunched up and red and stuff."

Dee smiled. "Of course we can't forget Hazel. But seriously, about school—"

"He's too little, Dee."

"Is that it?"

Sighing, Jenna smoothed her shirt over her breasts. She was more voluptuous than she'd been with Sofie, and more leaky, too. The thought of teaching with nursing pads stuffed in her bra didn't sound appealing. And she was so tired, how would she ever put up with late papers and student questions? If Mark was going to stay here and help her pay the bills, she really didn't have to go back to work at all.

"Probably not. I can't even think about this semester. I've got to call personnel this week about what I'm doing. I do have six weeks of maternity leave. Between that and sick leave, I wouldn't have to go back until winter term." Jenna stood up. She didn't want to talk any more about school. What she really wanted was for Dee to go home so she could put Keane down for his nap. Then she could sleep for at least an hour.

"It's not Tim, is it?"

Jenna ran the faucet, rinsing away remnants of their herbal tea and cookies. It was Tim, and it wasn't. She'd asked him for time, but she'd forgotten to figure out what time meant. Seeing him every day would force her to remember.

"So what's going on with Mark?"

"Nothing."

"You're staying in the same house and nothing is going on?"

Jenna nodded and turned off the water. As strange as Dee's words sounded, they were true. Even though they'd slept together during their divorce—Keane the obvious result—she'd never wanted him to come to her, as he had in Bali. In fact, she closed her door each night, turned up the baby monitor on her nightstand, and fell as quickly asleep as she could. One night, she heard Mark standing outside her door, but he'd not knocked or whispered to her or asked her for anything.

"That part is over. It was long before Sofie died. What happened in Bali wasn't about attraction or desire, it was about loneliness and grief and sadness," Jenna said. She put a mug in the dishwasher and turned back to Dee. "We're parents to this baby. We're attracted to his life, not to each other."

Staring at Jenna, Dee sighed. "It's just so weird, Jenna. All those years of you two sort of being together, and now you have this baby and a whole house and no other wife somewhere."

Jenna flushed, and patted her sides, irritable and tired. She didn't understand her relationship with Mark, and she didn't know how to talk about it, not before she talked about it with Mark. And she would have to do that soon.

"I don't know. I have too much going on to really think about it, anyway. Who cares, even? It's working out, isn't it?"

"Okay," Dee said, standing up and gently handing Keane to Jenna. "I just think that it says something. About you and Mark. And just you."

Relaxing under the slight, lovely weight of Keane, Jenna let go of the tense prickles of irritation. "If I knew, Dee, I'd tell you. I promise. All I think about lately, though, is sleep and diaper changes and developmental stages."

Dee hugged her, pressing against both bodies. "You know I have no reference point on this, Jen. Just don't forget what you love. Don't let that disappear."

Later, after putting Keane down in his crib, Jenna thought about Dee's words. *What you love.* She'd always loved phrases and sentences and poems and stories and novels. A year ago, she'd loved teaching. Something used to come alive in her when she stood before students, talking. It hadn't mattered what she'd been teaching—a complex sentence or the bipolar stance in Hamlet's "To be or not to be" soliloquy. She'd loved watching their faces change from bored or apathetic to somewhat interested to totally engaged. That had been exciting. Was exciting.

Now she was focused on taking care of Keane and not thinking about Sofie. Yet neither was possible without the other. Keane's movements and cries and gassy smiles always brought forth Sofie. In his baby movements were the expressions of an older child—a toddler, a preschooler, a ten-year-old, a teenager—and in his older faces were Sofie's older faces. And when she closed her eyes against ideas about Sofie, she thought of Keane, knowing she should wash the crib sheets or go to Long's Drugs for more baby lotion.

Closing Keane's door softly, she went by Mark's room and peeked in. In the years since the divorce and with Renata's prodding, he'd become tidy, his bed made, his dirty clothes nowhere to be seen, books stacked neatly on the bedside table. Jenna stepped into the room, looking around as if she hadn't seen it before. And she hadn't, not like this. For years it was only full of assorted junk, the detritus of lives gone by. At some point, he'd actually painted the walls a lovely butternut color, the afternoon light shining off the latex, the room glowing like a lit-up squash. It was a room she could live in, much nicer than the flat oyster-shell color of her own bedroom, the same color it had been when Mark lived here before. Reaching out a hand, she touched the new color, the wall warm under her hand. *The house is alive,* she thought, *full of us, all the past and the sounds and the energy we've expended.* But then she dropped her hand, shaking her head. She was so tired. She needed to sleep.

As she turned to leave the room, something in the corner stopped her. She flashed to one night she awakened—or imagined she'd awakened—to the vision of a man in a trench coat and a top hat standing at the foot of her bed like Jack the Ripper. How she'd squeezed Mark's shoulder, her heart bouncing in her chest, her breath catching on her ribs. But as she slowly fell out of her dream, the man and his coat and hat turned into her desk and typewriter and stacks of novels. Nothing frightening there at all.

Now, her heat beating that same way, she tried to close her eyes, but when she opened them, it was still there, a lump of material and pain. Sofie's duffel bag from Bali.

Closing her eyes again, the warmth from the sun on her shoulders, she wondered if she could take her nap just like this. Cows fell asleep standing, didn't they? And she was something of a cow right now, lactating on a strict schedule. Horses never lay down unless they had to, didn't they? Jenna could stay here and never have to see the duffel bag again. When she awoke, she would have forgotten how it sat there on the floor. She would walk out the door, closing it behind her. Keane would be crying, and she'd have to change and feed him, and by nightfall, it would all have disappeared.

But with her heart beating so fast, her skin full of prickles and heat, she'd never fall asleep, even though fatigue stung her eyes. Her hand on her chest, Jenna turned to the bag and stared at it. In December, Mark had asked her if she wanted to know what was in the duffel. Had he opened it and searched through for clues and memories? Or had it been zipped shut since Robert packed up Sofie's belongings? Or maybe Robert hadn't had to pack anything, and it was Sofie's hands who touched the metal tabs last. Needing that delayed touch of her daughter, Jenna staggered forward, kneeling down to the bag, dropping the baby monitor on the floor. She rubbed a finger along the bumpy ride of the zipper. Sofie had been here, her scent on this bag, her life still inside it.

Sitting down and crossing her legs, Jenna leaned back against Mark's mattress, her hand still on the zipper. She moved her fingers along until she found the tab, and she slowly began opening it, one plastic tooth at a time. The zipper *click, click, click*ed like a beetle. As the bag opened, Jenna closed her eyes, not wanting to see right away, but she kept tugging slowly, and then it was fully open. For a second, she imagined that a wisp of trapped Balinese air swirled up and past her. What was that? Ocean? Salt? Hibiscus flowers? A shock of sunset? And then it was gone, the room still and full of heat.

Jenna opened her eyes and cried out as she recognized a T-shirt on the top of the pile of clothes. There it was, full of holes, faded, and thinning, the Cal T-shirt Jenna had bought for Sofie when they visited the campus Sofie's junior year of high school.

"I'm going here," Sofie had said, standing in front of Jenna, the T-shirt almost to her knees. "That's final."

"Maybe by then that shirt will have shrunk to normal size," Jenna had said, laughing. But she'd been so proud. Sofie had known what she'd wanted and earned the grades to get accepted right away—no waiting list for her.

She picked up the shirt and held it in her hands. The fabric was so worn, she could see through it, but when she brought it to her face, Sofie was still inside the shirt. How could that be? It was so thin and old and had been sitting in this bag for almost a year, yet Jenna could see her, taste her, breathe in her sweet, freckled skin. In the corner of her eye, she imagined Sofie sitting cross-legged next to her, looking into the bag, waiting for what might come out next. "Come on, Mom," she'd say, slightly irritated. "Stop wasting time. Just unpack it."

Wiping her face on the shirt and then placing it carefully in her lap, Jenna put her hand in the bag and pulled out a bathing suit top. Holding it by its tiny strings, Jenna shook her head, amazed to feel a smile on her face. This was Sofie's suit? It looked like two tiny triangles connected by thread. Sofie had taken after Jenna in the breast department, so this suit would have fit her just right. And looked good on her. Perfect.

Next were the bottoms, just as small and as stringy, and then a pair of shorts Jenna didn't recognize. A bra. A pair of panties. These didn't hurt. She'd cleared out drawerfuls from Sofie's room after the funeral, packing up boxes of clothes, so few with memories in the fabric. Then she felt something hard and flat with a wire on one edge, and she pulled it out. Holding it up before her and staring at it, Jenna felt her bones jam into the floor, her body heavy as earth and stone, cold as moon rock, solid as a Shiva statue in a Balinese temple. A journal.

The cover was a beautiful sand-colored paper, rough-hewn out of raw silk or linen. Sofie had written her name on the bottom in black pen, and as Jenna looked at the edges of the pages, she could see flicks of pen— the tails of words. Touching the closed pages, the paper a soft slice against her fingertips, Jenna thought to mail this to Lois or even Jolie. They could read it, and then call her to tell her what it said, leaving out all the parts that would hurt her. Tim would also know how to read it to Jenna, his voice used to reading long, moving sentences to students, his voice pitched just right to elicit the proper response. She could sit with him in the living room, and he would find the sections she needed to hear.

Mark could never read this to her. He would tackle every word, and they would both cry. It would be like that day they sobbed together on the floor as they lay atop the photos. Dee would cry the moment she saw the journal, saying, "That's our girl. A writer. Just like we always told her."

The journal flat on her thighs, Jenna opened the cover. Inside were cutout photos squeezed onto one page, all of Sofie and her college friends, nights out at local bars, visits to Stinson Beach and the Golden Gate Bridge. Sofie was smiling, hanging on to girls and boys Jenna recognized from visits to the campus. And on the next page, there was Sofie, her words in wide blue loops.

Hello! (I'm saying this to myself. How stupid!) This is my college journal. I'm going to record all sorts of stuff in here. I want to remember all of this because being at Cal is my dream. I'm, like, here!!!!! I know it kills my mom that I'm not at home anymore, but I'm just ten miles away. She let me live in the dorm, so she must be okay. Oh, my dorm mate just got here. So exciting! More later.

Jenna put the journal down because she didn't know how to hold it up anymore, all her muscles weak. Staring at the wall, she remembered Sofie's face that first day at Cal, the way she'd cried when Jenna drove off. For all these years, Jenna imagined that she was nervous and scared, but those had been tears of joy. Of excitement.

The air in the room pressed warm around her, and then there was a brief cry. Jenna jerked, looking around, and then remembered the baby monitor. She looked at it, willing Keane to stay asleep. How would she be able to pick him up and comfort him if her hands wouldn't work, if her legs collapsed, keeping her in this room forever? But there were no more cries, and Jenna breathed out, looking down at the journal. Swallowing, she opened it again, flipping a page or two.

We, like, bounced out of the dorm and kicked it on Telegraph. I've been here a million times during high school, but Rita, my roommate, is from St. Louis, so we had to go. I bought the coolest necklace. Leather and beads. We bought some CDs and then came home to listen to them. I met the cutest guy. He reminds me, sort of, of my dad. Not that I've seen him all that much lately. And he lives so close. But we talk at night sometimes. I call him before I go to bed, just to check in. And he sends me little e-mails, reminding me to do things I'll do anyway. He seems so sad when I see him, like he's lost a really important piece of himself. My mom never says anything about him, but I can tell he makes her totally pissed. Sometimes I think she still loves him. And then there were those nights he stayed late after dropping me off, and then slipped out of the house.

I pretended I didn't notice. Like, they thought I didn't know what was going on? I mean, get real! But wait! This isn't about them. This journal is about Cal. I love it here! It is so totally cool. Rita just came in with some beer. Gotta go.

There were more school adventure photos, Sofie decorating the pages with a glitter pen, fluorescent pink and green swirling on the pages. Jenna read more.

Came back from Grandma Lois's house in Phoenix. She is so amazing. I hope I can be just like her when I'm older. She never stops. She's so active and alive. In my Women in History class this quarter, we've talked about how active women have been throughout time, and Grandma Lois is like a warrior. She didn't let Grandpa Ted's death stop her. She kept moving. I think I'm going to ask her if I can do my oral history project on her. She's an inspiration.

The summer lasted forever. I worked at the rec center in Monte Veda with the kids, running the camps. It was hard to be with Mom. She doesn't seem to do much. I never really noticed before how lonely her life is. She goes to work and comes home. She talks with Dee and our neighbor Susan, but what does she do besides grade papers and read and go to teaching conferences? Why doesn't she have a boyfriend or go out more often? Maybe even a woman would be good for her! (I don't think she'd go there!) It really makes me sad. It's like she's wasted her whole life on me, and now I'm gone. All I want is for her to be happy. But it's her life, you know. I can't live it for her.

Rita and I moved into an apartment with two other girls from last year. It's like so great. We are going to have a blast.

Jenna felt hot, her neck and cheeks flushed. *My life wasn't lonely. I— I had my career and I had . . . you.* Jenna reread the sentences, wanting to fling the journal aside. *She doesn't seem to do much. . . . How lonely her life is.*

So Mark had been right all along. She'd loved Sofie too much, too hard, too long.

But no! Jenna slapped her hand on the journal. She wouldn't change it. Not a bit. She'd been right to love Sofie that much, because there hadn't been enough time. In a way, she'd condensed a lifetime of loving into twenty years. She wouldn't change a thing, give up an evening or an hour or a phone call, even if it meant she'd still be home alone, waiting. Now each second was precious, perfect, all she had left.

Tired now, Jenna knew that Keane would be up in minutes. Her nap wouldn't happen. She flipped to the end, wanting to get as close to Sofie as she could. Sand flaked white off the page and onto her skirt.

So even though this isn't school, I brought my journal with me. To Bali! With Robert. Oh, I've

319

written about him enough in here, but my God, he is amazing. So beautiful. So smart. I don't know how else to say it but to keep saying it. I know I've met the man I will be with for the rest of my life. . . .

At this, Jenna pulled away from the sentence, not wanting to feel how true Sofie's words were. As she waited, rubbing the page with her hand, she saw a swirl of smudged ink. Ocean water? Tears? Had Robert read the journal before packing it? Had Mark? And then she realized she was crying, too.

When I get home, I'm going to tell my mom he's the one. I'm going to thank her. It's because of her. It's because she taught me how to love. I swear it sounds stupid, but I can see her sometimes in the way Robert looks at me. It's like I can recognize when someone really loves me because of her. That sounds so corny and weird, but it's true. He'll be explaining something to me and I'll look into his eyes, and I can see that he really cares if I understand. And he listens to me. Like my stories are important, too. My mom was like that with me. All along I thought she was too much in my life, but I have my life. Here I am in the most beautiful place in the world with the most amazing guy I've ever met. She showed me how to find him. Oh, he just called from the lobby. We're going out tonight. This is such a perfect place. I want to stay here forever. Got to go!

Pushing the journal off her lap, weeping, hugging herself, Jenna tried to find the part of her body to squeeze in order to feel better. But she couldn't feel anything but the rip in her lungs and her throat, the pain of all the pain, the hurt of the worst hurt. Oh, it was so hot, so awful. These were the tears she'd left inside all along, the ones that hadn't made it out before. Where had she hidden them? How had there been room with Keane growing in her womb? Oh, these sobs hurt, each like a small child she had to expel. Oh, oh.

And she lay on the floor, her cheek rubbed raw on the hardwood, her head close to the baby monitor, letting all the terrible noise escape her, loudly, so loudly that when Keane finally did begin to cry, she thought the accompanying wails were the sound of the world mourning with her, the sound of the universe finally admitting that Sofie was gone.

"JENNA?" MARK POPPED his head into her room when he came back late from the hospital. She'd put Keane down later than usual because once he'd awakened from his nap, she hadn't wanted to put him to sleep, carrying him on her shoulder as she prepared her meal, needing his heft to keep her attached to the earth. Finally, after a bath and a few songs, he'd fallen asleep in her arms, and she'd stared at him, seeing for the first time how much he wasn't like Sofie, more like Mark, with his dark hair and eyes.

She put down her book. "Yeah?"

"How are you?"

That question. "Fine."

"The baby?"

"Great. He's great."

Mark stepped in and walked toward the bed. Jenna breathed in, seeing in his slow walk some kind of permission she knew she hadn't given him. This was what he had done a couple of times during the divorce, walking into her room and sitting on the edge of the bed they once shared, slowly making his way to her body.

"That's good. What did you two do today?"

She opened her mouth, feeling the duffel bag under her hands and the journal in her lap. He must know what was inside, and they could talk about how it felt to read their child's words. She needed to share this with someone, and who better than Sofie's father? But as Jenna looked at him, she did what she always had with Mark. She took what was hers and Sofie's and kept it to herself. Jenna couldn't share this with him. Clutching the blanket with her hand, she wondered if she could share Keane with him. There was something wrong with her. Something selfish and awful and wrong. She closed her mouth and then shook her head.

"Not much. Same old. Dee came over for a while."

Scooting closer to her, he put a hand on top of her blanketed shin. "Did she talk to you about work?"

"How did you know?"

"No reason. I just know she thinks you should go back."

"What do you think?" Jenna shifted her legs away from his touch. "Do you think I should go back?"

He looked down at his hand flat on the bedspread, and Jenna saw clearly what her going back to work could mean. Mark wouldn't have to live in her house anymore. She could pay her own mortgage and bills. There wasn't any more college tuition to pay, though now there would be day care expenses. Mark could find himself a really nice apartment in Walnut Creek, or he could go back to Renata. Unless there was another reason for them to go on living together. Her stomach ached and she closed her eyes, waiting for his words.

"What do you want?" he asked.

Jenna looked up and stared at him, her eyes watering and burning, a sliver of sobs still in her throat. What did she want? She wanted Sofie to be alive and happy and well, in love with her Robert, dashing through beautiful Balinese waves. She wanted to be back at work teaching, loving her work and the students, no matter what bizarre and ridiculous questions they asked her. She wanted warm, small, amazing Keane in her arms. She wanted lovely days in the garden and lunches with Dee and Susan. Maybe when Keane was a little older, she'd want another student, a girl like Hazel. Maybe Hazel herself. In this perfect world of wants, there were lots of good books, ones she'd read a hundred times and new ones she'd never cracked open. There were her own words, her own writing in sheaves on her desk. She wanted Jolie to get her toddler, and Lois and Stan to live for twenty, twenty-five more good years. There was something else she needed, that feeling she'd found in herself, the way her body could open and take in something essential, only for her, what she had to have for the first time in years. She wanted what she'd somehow been able to teach Sofie to look for.

"Jenna?"

"I think I'll—I'll think about it some more. I have maternity leave. And then I can make a decision."

She almost winced as Mark's face softened, his worry erased by her answer. *He's thinking he can stay,* she thought. He's thinking that he'll move in and stay forever. She wanted to tell him to stop, to think about what he wanted, and then he began to cry.

"Mark?" she said, touching his arm. "What's wrong?"

He took off his glasses and shook his head. "Nothing. Well—I'm so relieved. I don't know how I'd feel if I couldn't be here with you and Keane. I like this, Jenna. I like being here with both of you."

Patting him, she turned to look out the dark window, mayflies and oak moths batting against the screen. One lone cricket began to sing, the first to scratch out the mating ritual, the first to alert everyone to the coming fall. In some ways, it had always been fall. *That's a stupid idea,* she thought, listening to Mark blow his nose. But even though the thought seemed ridiculous, she knew what she meant. Everything since before she could remember was almost about to happen.

"I know. It's nice. It is."

"Jenna?"

"Yes," she said, closing her eyes.

"Can I stay here with you tonight?"

Not wanting to but unable to stay fixed on the window, Jenna turned, finding his dark eyes, his pale face staring at her. Here was the question like a wishbone between them. One snap, and it was only hope, someone left holding the dead wish. To say yes would make everything so much easier. He would burrow in, hold her tight, not let go until Keane was in college. Or would he? Would Mark leave as he had done before, finding Jenna too much of everything? Or would she push him away again, putting Keane first?

Tilting her head and watching him, Jenna wondered what Sofie would say. What was the lesson from all of this? Quite clearly, Sofie had known for quite a while about Mark and Jenna's curious divorce, the late-night lovemaking, Mark's quick escape back to Renata. Never once had she said, "Mom, just ask him back," or "Mom, you two belong together." And the Sofie from heaven, the one in Jenna's meditation and letters, could have sent a message, leaving clues in the wind and leaves and pat of rain on the windows.

As she sat looking at her former husband, at her former life as his wife, she realized that how things start is how they end. When she thought about Mark during their marriage, he was looking away, past her, at a book or a hospital or a patient. The Jenna from back then first tried to wave him down, and then turned inward and then toward their baby, their Sofie.

When Jenna thought about Tim, she saw him looking directly at her. And Jenna knew she saw him, could see him, finally.

"Oh, shit," Jenna said.

"What's wrong?" Mark leaned in closer.

Jenna didn't move, but she could feel Sofie sitting down on the side of the bed. "We can't do this."

"Do what?" He reached a hand to her face. "It's already done, Jenna. Look at us. We have a son."

Shaking him away gently, she bit her lip and then breathed out heavily. "No, this thing." She lifted up her hands and swept one to indicate the bed. "The old thing. The way we used to."

"I don't want to do it the way we used to. I want to stay. I want us to be together. Married."

She felt herself lift the knife of her words on her tongue. "We weren't good married, Mark. We didn't do it well then."

"We're older. We know more. We have a reason. We have the baby."

"We have Keane," she said. "But mostly we have sorrow. We share it. We have joint custody of it."

Mark put his hands between his knees, slumping on the edge of the bed. *Sorrow,* Jenna thought, *is supposed to teach us, just as it does in novels.* Even Sethe, the mother in Toni Morrison's novel *Beloved,* the one who killed her daughter, learned to live with murder, the deepest, reddest sorrow. She'd found a way to live her life. Why couldn't Jenna? It would be so easy for Jenna to slide right back to that mother-child life she'd had with Sofie. And then alone, she would be just as Sofie had written about, focusing only on her child, only on Keane. Would she find Keane's journal someday in his bag, saying, *She's wasted her whole life on me?*

"Sorrow isn't going to bring us together," he said. It was neither a statement nor a question. He pushed his hands through his hair.

"We'll always be together, Mark. You've said that yourself. We've never been able to really be apart. But all of those times—they were for the wrong reason. We weren't coming together like we did—"

"Before kids."

There was that time, she knew. Oh yes. When all she'd wanted was him, forgetting about a part of herself that wanted something else, too. And now, maybe, because of Sofie, she'd learn to love and learn to change all at the same time. She'd make the hay into gold, and she'd keep the child, just like the princess in "Rumpelstiltskin."

"What will you do?" she asked.

"I don't know."

"Renata?"

He shook his head and waved her off. And then, surprising her, he leaned down and kissed her, his lips slightly off her own. All those years, how simple it had been to cup his cheeks and pull him to the bed. This very thing had happened so many times, Jenna could already feel his stubble in her palms, smell his long day on his neck. Like always, they would come together and she could forget everything, just as she needed to. But Jenna didn't want that now, and she could feel her response to him in her bones and muscles. Mark could, too. Before Jenna could even think to do anything but kiss him back, he pulled away.

"It will be different this time," Mark said, avoiding her eyes.

She nodded, knowing he meant Sofie and all the time he'd been gone. "I know."

"I'll see you in the morning. We can talk more then."

He stood up and walked out of the room, leaving Jenna with an unspoken *oh* still in her mouth. Then she was alone, nothing but the noise from the baby monitor scratching the air, the moths and bugs silent against the screen.

Throwing back the blankets and standing up, Jenna turned off the light and walked to the window. Porch and walkway lights lit up the neighborhood night, and she could imagine watching Sofie riding her bike, as she had so often done, up and down the sidewalk. "Look at me, Mom! Look what I can do," she'd cry, holding on tight to the handlebars. "Look how fast I'm going."

How fast indeed. Sofie was gone, light-years ahead of Jenna. Gone into flame and smoke and sky, a star, a planet, a comet, a child of air.

As Jenna watched the night shimmer and settle into blackness, the neighbors turning off lights and going to bed, she looked up at the stars and thought, *Look at me, Sofie! Look what I did! Look how fast I'm going!*

• • •

Dear Robert,

This is probably the last thing you want to read, a letter from me. If you've been lucky, you don't think every single day about the past year, like I do. I keep hoping that being young helps, but that's probably my imagination. I think about Sofie and what happened every day, and I'm sure you do, too. You think of her, remember her, miss her. So do I.

A couple of days ago, I found Sofie's journal. My ex-husband had kept her duffel bag, and I hadn't wanted to know what was in it. Until now. As I was reading through it, I saw how much she loved you. If she had to spend her last days with anyone, I'm glad they were with you, Robert. She was lucky to have had you. I wish I'd said that to you that day in the bar. But I was so angry. I still am, in some ways, but that day, I was angry at you because you were tangible, visible, someone I could blame. I should have hugged you and thanked you and told you it wasn't your fault. It wasn't your fault. The world, of course, is all our fault. All the terrible things that happen come from particles of all of us—our choices, our actions—but to find the tiny bit of blame that belonged to you or to me or even to Sofie would be like hunting for a particular grain of sand.

You were there with her and wanted her safe. You hunted for her. You did your best. For Sofie, you did better than anyone else. Please know that. Please let me tell you that. I wish I had before.

She wrote that you were the most amazing guy she'd ever met. She wrote that you listened to her. Thank you. Thank you for being with my girl.

Have a wonderful life, Robert. I am going to say

to you what I hope for myself: Let her go. Don't press her memory to you so tightly that you can't see the present or the future. Live. Love. Be happy.

All my best,
Jenna Thomas

• • •

THE MORNING MARK left—packing up in the evening and leaving before Jenna awoke—Jenna found a postcard on the kitchen table. She'd come downstairs with Keane on her shoulder, and she thought she was hallucinating the bright, glossy beach on her table. *Here I go again,* she thought, knowing that between her visions and dreams, any sight was possible. But as she walked closer, she saw it was a postcard, a photograph of a Balinese beach on the front, yellow umbrellas on the beach, white-sailed boats in the water.

Setting Keane in his infant seat on the table, Jenna sat down and lightly brushed her fingers across the card. She wasn't sure if Mark had put it on the table—and if it wasn't a hallucination, perhaps it was a gift from Sofie. Her girl hadn't really left this plane, Jenna thought, showing up in journals and dreams and visions. But when she picked up the card and turned it over in her hands, she saw that it was addressed to Mark, dated the day before the bombing in Bali, and it was from Sofie.

Hi, Dad! Thanks so much for helping me get here—
Jenna looked up. Sofie had asked him for money? Mark had helped her? Jenna hadn't known that. Or

simply, she hadn't asked Sofie where she'd come up with the rest of the money she'd needed for the trip.

Bali is gorgeous. I wish you could see it. When I get home, I'll come over and show you my photos. I have a ton! I love you. Can't wait to talk when I get back. Say hi to Renata. Love, Sofie

"Aaaaa," Keane burbled. Jenna rocked his infant seat and stared at Sofie's words. All along they had been a family. Here was the evidence of more of a relationship than Jenna had known about. What else had they done together? Whatever it was, Jenna hadn't wanted to see because she was holding on to . . . what? Anger? Resentment? Her own loneliness? Her daughter?

Keane was waving his hands in front of his face, and Jenna kept rocking his seat with one hand, rubbing her forehead with the other.

She wouldn't do this with Keane. Or maybe she would because she knew evolution took a long time. Ice ages had to come and go, plates had to shift in the earth, creatures had to die out, civilizations would thrive and disappear, just like that. Whole canyons could be carved out of miles of hard rock and soil and ice, but it took time. She would try. She would try to do what she said in her letter to Robert. *Live. Love. Be happy*.

"Ooooo." Keane blew out the sound with a bubble of translucent spit, and Jenna stood and picked him up, breathing in his sweet baby scent.

Dear Tim,
It's time.
Love, Jenna

Fifteen

Iₜ t's a choice. He had a choice. And he chose wrong,"
Yau Sing said, as the class discussed the essay
about a boy who dressed as a girl and imagined that
one day, he would wake up with all the right girl parts.
"Why did he do that?"

"God," Shelley said, almost shouting, "you can't just
choose. It's like saying you chose to be straight. No one
chooses that. You just are."

"I think," Zan said, "he was born into the wrong body.
That's all."

"That's all," Yau Sing murmured. "Can't help it."

"So what can we choose in our lives? What are the
things we can pick?" Jenna asked. "Let's brainstorm."
She grabbed a dry-erase pen and wrote down their
answers as they flew toward her, turning to comment,
the class rapt. At moments like this, she forgot her own
body. It was there all right, moving perfectly in front of
them, her arms expressive, her walk encouraging,
cajoling them into answers. But that's not what she felt.
Jenna was somewhere in her head or over her head,
floating in the air that was crackling with ideas and
laughter, all eyes on her and all her eyes on them. It was

like she had more than two, could see them thinking, could watch herself as she wrote on the board and brought forth answers. Her head was filled with the buzz of all their thoughts.

The board was covered with the things that the class thought people could choose: clothes, food, movies, friends, books, places to live, jobs, shoes, weight, style, attitude, mood, reactions, success, feelings, children. She put down the pen.

"So if I'm depressed, have I chosen that?"

"Of course," said Arthur. "You chose not to be happy."

"Does that mean I would have chosen the situations that may or may not have made me unhappy in the first place? To get fired? To lose . . . someone?"

"Your reaction," Arthur said. "You chose that, right? That's what the one essay talked about. Making choices."

"That's crap," Shelley said. "It's totally biological. It's in your body. It's about chemicals. Who would choose to be depressed?"

"In this culture," Jenna asked, "who would choose to be gay? It's hard. Some people will reject you, hurt you, even kill you, like in the movie we watched last week."

"Ex-actly," Shelley said slowly. "My point. It's in the body!"

The class whispered and nodded, and Jenna looked at the clock. "Okay. We're done. But think about those rough drafts. And for goodness sake, read your hand-book about the correct essay format. And get to the

llebrook essay. It goes wonderfully with what
_ _ _ .e studied so far."

The students filed out, saying good-bye, even Arthur, who was still miffed by Shelley's response. He smiled shyly at Jenna and then made a quick, almost imperceptible bow with his head. Jenna packed up her books and walked out of the room into the corridor, the February light glinting gray off the rooftops, a thick mist hanging in the air. Students milled slowly, not wanting to walk down the open concrete stairs, water dripping from the overhang. Cigarette smoke circled and then hung over students as they lit up between classes; Jenna tried not to breathe as she passed by.

As she neared her office, she looked into Dee's, but of course her friend had already gone to her class. When they'd made out their schedules for the winter term, Dee had made an executive decision.

"We need to be available if something comes up with Keane. I know he's just at the day care center on campus, but if he needs you and you're in class, I can go get him." Dee filled in the scheduling form with her classes and then passed it to Jenna. "Work around this. It just makes sense."

So far, there had been no crises or emergencies, Keane happily rolling around on the floor with toys or sitting up on blankets, clapping his hands and watching other babies do the same. He was only at the center three or four hours a day, and then Jenna took him home. Mark came over on the weekends and took Keane out for daylong adventures in the stroller or

BabyBjörn, but until he was weaned, they'd bo decided Keane should stay overnight with Jenna.

"He'll know me, though. He won't be scared of my apartment or me," Mark had said as he'd unfolded the stroller and then hooked the diaper bag—full of small bottles of pumped breast milk and hand-ground carrots and chicken in a small cooler—over his shoulder. "He'll know I'm his dad."

Keane would know who his dad was, Jenna knew. Sofie had known, too, even though there were holes and spaces in her and Mark's relationship. And those holes weren't as big as Jenna had imagined, because, she knew now, she didn't orchestrate everything. She never had.

Arriving at her office doorway and glancing inside, she smiled. Tim was waiting for her, as he always did on Thursdays. They would grab a sandwich and then go up to the center to get Keane, drive home, and put Keane and themselves down for a nap. Later, when the baby awoke, they would take turns grading papers or writing, later setting Keane in the Johnny Jump-Up as they fixed dinner.

"Hi," Jenna said, putting her books and papers down on her desk and leaning over to kiss Tim on the cheek. "Let's go."

Center Point Publishing
600 Brooks Road • PO Box 1
Thorndike ME 04986-0001 USA

(207) 568-3717

US & Canada:
1 800 929-9108